AUNT DIMITY
AND THE VILLAGE WITCH

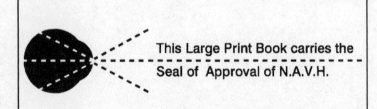

This Large Print Book carries the
Seal of Approval of N.A.V.H.

AUNT DIMITY
AND THE VILLAGE WITCH

NANCY ATHERTON

THORNDIKE PRESS
A part of Gale, Cengage Learning

GALE
CENGAGE Learning·

Detroit • New York • San Francisco • New Haven, Conn • Waterville, Maine • London

GALE
CENGAGE Learning·

LIBRARY OF CONGRESS CATALOGING-IN-PUBLICATION DATA

Atherton, Nancy.
  Aunt Dimity and the village witch / by Nancy Atherton.
    pages ; cm. — (Thorndike Press large print mystery)
  ISBN-13: 978-1-4104-4854-5 (hardcover)
  ISBN-10: 1-4104-4854-1 (hardcover)
  1. Dimity, Aunt (Fictitious character)—Fiction. 2. Women detectives—England—Cotswold Hills—Fiction. 3. Genealogy—Fiction. 4. Cotswold Hills (England)—Fiction. 5. Large type books. I. Title.
PS3551.T426A934425 2012b
813'.54—dc23   2012003346

Published in 2012 by arrangement with Viking, a member of Penguin Group (USA) Inc.

Printed in the United States of America
1 2 3 4 5 6 7 16 15 14 13 12

For
R. Patrick Atherton,
a good brother

One

The small village of Finch nestled sleepily in a bend of the Little Deeping River, a minor tributary that wound its way through the patchwork fields and rolling hills of the Cotswolds, a rural region in England's West Midlands.

Finch was in no way remarkable. Nothing of historical importance had happened there and no one born there had achieved the slightest degree of fame. Tour buses by-passed it, day-trippers ignored it, and scholars never mentioned it. The only people who cared about Finch were the people who lived there, and they thought it the most splendid place on earth.

A humpbacked stone bridge of medieval origin crossed the river at one end of the village and St. George's Church stood at the other, planted piously in the center of a walled churchyard filled with modest tombs, sorrowing angels, and carved headstones that had settled comfortably over the centuries into a variety of picturesque postures.

A village green stretched between the bridge and the church. The irregular oval of tufted grass was encircled by a cobbled lane lined with golden-hued stone cottages and small business establishments, all of which overlooked the green. The pub, the general store, and the greengrocer's shop sat with their backs to a rising landscape of dark woods and sheep-dotted pastures, while the tearoom, the vicarage, and the old village school, which had for many years served as the village hall, backed upon the willow-draped reaches of the Little Deeping. Similarly, each private home faced inward, toward the green.

Some might consider such an arrangement a shameful waste of good scenery, but the villagers would beg to disagree. They were perfectly content with the views from their front windows because, while they enjoyed watching lambs gambol as much as the next man, they preferred to watch each other. Every glance through a lace-curtained pane afforded them an opportunity to observe the ever-changing, utterly absorbing drama of village life — and to report on the details later. The river's murmur was indisputably melodious, but as far as Finch's residents were concerned, it couldn't hold a candle to the deeply satisfying hum of gossip.

When Sally Pyne opened the tearoom's front door first thing in the morning to admit her fiancé and assistant manager, Henry Cook, she could be sure that many, if not all, of her neighbors would be peering breathlessly through their curtains, awaiting a public display of affection that would be described and discussed relentlessly for the rest of the day. If the local vicar paid a call on Opal Taylor, he would inadvertently but unavoidably trigger speculations about Opal's fragile health, her troubled soul, and/ or the type of cake she would donate to the next church-sponsored bake sale. Chocolate gateau? Deathbed confession? It was all grist for Finch's rumor mill.

Finch's merry band of busybodies could also be relied upon to serve a useful purpose from time to time. If a child fell and scraped his knees, he would be nursed back to health by a flock of sympathetic grown-ups who would shower him with disinfectant, bandages, and as many cookies as he could hold in both hands. If a careless teenager sullied the village green with a discarded gum wrapper or a crushed soda can, eyewitness accounts of his misdeed would be telephoned directly to his parents, who would order him to retrieve the litter or risk forfeiting his car keys, his cell phone, and his dinner.

Perhaps the most useful task performed by Finch's keen-eyed residents was to render locked doors unnecessary. The villagers knew who belonged where and were only too happy to report suspicious activities to each other, to the police, and to anyone else who would listen. Privacy might be a rare commodity in Finch, but so, too, was crime.

For better and for worse, I avoided round-the-clock surveillance by living two miles south of Finch with my husband, Bill, and our sons, Will and Rob, a lively pair of identical twins who closely resembled their dark-eyed, dark-haired, and fractionally less lively father. Will and Rob were seven years old, unnervingly observant, and hopelessly horse crazy. They would gladly have slept in the stables with their gray ponies, Thunder and Storm, if their flint-hearted parents hadn't insisted on tucking them up in their own beds at night.

The other member of our family was Stanley, a sleek black cat with a long, curling tail and dandelion-yellow eyes. Stanley adored Bill and regarded the rest of us as second-best sources of food and affection. Bill, for his part, professed complete indifference to Stanley, without seeming to notice that his laptop computer invariably gave way to his laptop cat.

Although we all were American citizens — except for Stanley, who was English by birth and breeding — my husband and I had lived in England for nearly a decade and our sons had never lived anywhere else. Bill ran the international branch of his family's venerable Boston law firm from a high-tech office on Finch's village green, Will and Rob attended primary school in the nearby market town of Upper Deeping, and I scrambled to keep up with the demanding roles of wife, mother, neighbor, friend, community volunteer, gossipmonger-in-training, and head of the Westwood Trust, a philanthropic organization that funded worthy causes.

We lived in a honey-colored stone cottage with roses round the front door, a lichen-dappled slate roof, and a full complement of modern amenities. Our back garden opened onto a wildflower meadow that sloped down to a sparkling brook and we were sheltered from winter gales by a phalanx of tall hawthorne hedges and an oak forest carpeted with bluebells. Bill and

11

I could think of no finer place to raise our children, and when Bill's widowed father, William Arthur Willis, Sr., retired from the family firm and made a home for himself in nearby Fairworth House, our happiness was complete.

Oddly enough, my well-dressed, well-spoken, and extremely well-heeled father-in-law drew the attention and, in many cases, the adulation of Finch's coterie of ever-hopeful widows and spinsters. Bill had dubbed the most determined of these "Father's Handmaidens" because of their efforts to win Willis, Sr.'s, heart by catering to his every whim.

It was generally acknowledged that the Handmaidens would do anything, up to and including committing ruthless acts of social sabotage, to get ahead in the race to become the next Mrs. Willis. Had my father-in-law lived in the village, he would have been besieged by genteel ladies offering to mend his clothes, polish his silver, sweep his floors, clean his windows, cook his meals, and reveal to him the awful truth about their rivals.

Fortunately, Willis, Sr., did not live in Finch. The entrance to his property could be seen from the humpbacked bridge, but his house sat at the end of a private drive,

12

hidden from prying eyes by a dense shelter-belt of trees. A pair of tall, wrought-iron gates helped to keep the Handmaidens at bay, but Fairworth's main line of defense was human. Declan Donovan patrolled the grounds while carrying out his dual role of gardener-cum-handyman, and nothing short of an armed attack force could get past his wife, Deirdre, a tactful but resolute young woman who served as Willis, Sr.'s, housekeeper. My father-in-law was an affable gentleman who enjoyed his neighbors' company, but he recognized the value of good fences.

Mrs. Amelia Thistle, by contrast, had nowhere to hide. Finch's newest resident had elected to live in Pussywillows, the cottage next door to the tearoom, in full view of the entire village. Early reports — gleaned from her delightfully indiscreet real estate agent — pegged her as a mild-mannered, middle-aged widow of independent means who intended to make Pussywillows her principal residence. The previous owner, a Londoner who'd used the cottage for week-end getaways, hadn't made the slightest effort to blend into the community, but it was hoped that Mrs. Thistle, as a year-round resident, would.

Common courtesy obliged the villagers to

13

allow their new neighbor a decent interval of peace and quiet after she took possession of her property, but eventually they would descend on her with sign-up sheets for whist drives, flower shows, bring-and-buy sales, and a host of other village activities that were the breath of life to Finch. Would Mrs. Thistle join in the fun or would she live as a stranger among us? Only time would tell.

Though none of us would admit it, most of us believed that moving day would provide useful clues to Mrs. Thistle's character. A close inspection of her personal belongings as they were transferred from moving truck to cottage was bound to reveal a great deal about her, and the obvious place from which to conduct such an inspection was Sally Pyne's strategically located tearoom.

As luck would have it, I happened to be in Finch on the big day. After purchasing a few staples at Taxman's Emporium — Finch's well-stocked general store — and stowing them in my Range Rover, I nipped smartly across the green and darted into the tearoom, narrowly avoiding a collision with Henry Cook, who'd just turned up for work. I waved off Henry's gallant apologies, staked my claim to a table near the front windows, and ordered a stack of Sally's delectable apple fritters to go along with a large pot of Lapsang souchong tea. The fritters hadn't cooled before every available table had been taken.

I shared mine with Charles Bellingham and Grant Tavistock, a pair of middle-aged men who ran an art appraisal and restoration business from the cozy confines of their home, Crabtree Cottage. The Handmaidens, more commonly known as Millicent Scroggins, Opal Taylor, Elspeth Binney, and Selena Buxton, hogged four separate tables, but Mrs. Sciaparelli and Annie Hodge, a mother and daughter who lived on outlying farms, shared one, as did Mr. Barlow, a retired mechanic, and George Wetherhead, the most bashful man in the village. Christine Peacock had left her husband Dick to run their pub single-handedly in order to snag the last remaining table. She sat with a self-satisfied smirk on her face, savoring her triumph as well as her tea.

Those denied a prime vantage point inside Sally's tearoom stationed themselves before crates of freshly harvested apples, plums, and pears at the greengrocer's shop or surveyed the Emporium's window displays or paused to chat with whomever they met while strolling sedately on the green.

It was a good day to be out and about.

Autumn leaves swirled in a crisp breeze and curls of blue smoke rose from garden bonfires, reminding all and sundry that October had arrived, but the sun shone brightly and the blue sky held no threat of rain. It seemed unlikely that a sudden downpour would dampen Mrs. Thistle's spirits or her belongings.

In the tearoom, the occasional clink of cup on saucer could scarcely be heard above the lively flow of conversation. Since no one knew for certain when the newcomer would arrive, it was imperative to make each pot of tea last as long as possible.

Grant Tavistock smiled to himself as he surveyed his neighbors over the rim of his willow-patterned teacup. He was a well-dressed, good-looking man, short and lean, with a full head of neatly combed salt-and-pepper hair.

"Tell me, Lori," he said. "Did Charles and I attract the same amount of attention when we moved to Finch?"

"Of course," I said. "But, in your case, the green was less crowded. Almost everyone was driven indoors by the nasty weather."

"It was atrocious," Charles Bellingham agreed. Tall, bald, and portly, Charles could usually be found in bed at ten o'clock in the morning, but he'd abandoned the habits of a lifetime in order to witness Mrs. Thistle's arrival. "Wind, rain, sleet — I've never been more miserable in my life."

"The movers took the brunt of it," Grant reminded him. "As I recall, you spent most of the day in the kitchen, huddled over the Aga."

As the Aga cooker was a cast-iron range that emitted a constant supply of radiant heat, Charles's stratagem seemed perfectly reasonable to me, though I might have thought differently had I wanted his help to unload a moving truck.

"It was a beast of a day for all concerned," Charles declared. He gazed enviously at the clear sky. "It looks as though Mrs. Thistle will be more fortunate."

"And her furniture less wet," said Grant.

"I have a confession to make," Charles said suddenly. "The Thistle woman could stand three feet away from me and I wouldn't know who she was. It pains me to say it, Lori, but Grant and I have been in London every time she's come to Finch. We've never set eyes on her."

"I have," I said smugly. I patted the table with my hand. "I was sitting right here when she and the decorators came to spruce up the cottage last week."

17

"Description, please," said Charles, brightening.

"She drives a silver-gray Fiat sedan," I said.

"Dull," murmured Grant.

"I don't care about her car," Charles protested. "I want to know what the woman looks like."

"I'd place her in her late fifties, maybe her early sixties," I said. "She's short — about my height — and plump. Not fat, not skinny, just nicely rounded. Gray hair, blue eyes, no makeup. She'd bundled her hair into a loose knot on the back of her head, the kind that leaks wisps and tendrils and comes undone three times a day. Her complexion was a little ruddy. I think she must be outdoorsy."

"Ruddy, wispy, and outdoorsy," said Grant, with a faint shudder. "A rambler, I'll wager. She probably owns a backpack, a walking staff, and a pair of stonking great hiking boots."

"Attire?" Charles said primly, ignoring his partner.

"Casual," I replied, "but not cheap. An oversized shirt in a pretty Liberty print, worn open over a pale blue silk T-shirt and a pair of loose-fitting khaki trousers. She was directing the decorators," I reminded them, "so she wouldn't be wearing her Sunday best."

"Shoes?" said Charles.

"Tasseled loafers," I said. "Conventional, but pricey. And the double strand of pearls she was wearing didn't come from a cereal box."

"Ergo," Charles murmured reflectively, "Mrs. Thistle is monied, but not showy." He smiled. "I like her already."

"I'll reserve judgment," said Grant.

The buzz of conversation ceased as the front door opened and Bree Pym strode into the tearoom. Nineteen-year-old Bree was from New Zealand, but she'd inherited a lovely old house as well as a pot of money from her great-grandaunts, the late and much lamented Ruth and Louise Pym, who'd lived on the outskirts of Finch. Though Bree had made their house her own, she hadn't yet been embraced by everyone in the village.

The most narrow-minded among us objected to her tattoos, her pierced nose, and her skimpy attire, but almost everyone was wary of her sly wit. Bree could throw verbal darts with great accuracy, a skill she displayed shortly after she closed the door behind her.

" 'Morning, Henry," she called to Henry

Cook, who'd emerged from the kitchen bearing four plates piled high with buttery crumpets.

" 'Morning, Bree," he called back, smiling delightedly.

Bree appealed to Henry's sense of mischief. He loved to hear her say aloud what most of us said only to ourselves.

"Full house today," Bree commented cheerfully, gazing around the room. "No surprise there. Best spot in town to spy on the new woman. I'm glad her gear hasn't arrived yet. I can't wait to see if she's filthy rich or just rich enough to look down her nose at the rest of us."

Henry's face split into a broad grin as he served the crumpets to the Handmaidens, but the ladies were not amused.

"*Spy?*" Elspeth Binney hissed indignantly.

"The very *idea,*" huffed Opal Taylor.

"Of all the *nerve,*" grumbled Millicent Scroggins.

"So *rude,*" muttered Selena Buxton.

"So true," Grant said under his breath.

Charles and I nodded our agreement. The Handmaidens could protest until they were blue in the face, but they knew as well as we did why half of Finch's population had chosen that particular morning to visit Sally's tearoom or to take the air on the village green.

"I'll keep a lookout, shall I?" Bree asked the room at large. She glanced in the direction of the church and smiled brightly. "And none too soon. Here they come, ladies and gentlemen. Let the show begin!"

A moment later, a silver-gray Fiat sedan passed the tearoom, followed by a medium-sized moving truck. The short, nicely rounded, ruddy-faced woman driving the Fiat parked it in the narrow shed beside Pussywillows, then walked to the rear of the truck to have a word with the movers.

"There she is," I murmured. "Mrs. Amelia Thistle."

She was dressed for the brisk weather in a knee-length brown cardigan, brown tweed trousers, and a vermillion silk blouse with a round collar. I was about to comment on the absence of her pearls when I heard Charles gasp.

"What's wrong?" I asked, startled.

"It can't be," Charles whispered. He bent forward to stare hard at Mrs. Thistle.

"It can't be what?" I asked.

"It *is*," he said, clapping a hand to his mouth.

"It is *what?*" I demanded.

Grant, too, was gaping at Mrs. Thistle as

21

if she were stark naked and dancing a jig. The two men exchanged meaningful looks and rose abruptly.

"Please excuse us, Lori," said Grant, throwing a handful of coins on the table. "We left the kettle on the hob. Must dash."

I stared after my departing friends, mystified. Grant and Charles had lain in wait for Mrs. Thistle for well over an hour. Why, I asked myself, would they run off as soon as she appeared? Did they know something about her they wished to keep under wraps — something shocking, sensational, scandalous?

The scent of intrigue was in the air and I responded to it like a wolf scenting raw steak. Although it would be a pity to miss the unveiling of Mrs. Thistle's worldly goods, it would be downright galling to let a juicy morsel of gossip slip from my grasp. After the briefest of hesitations, I jumped to my feet, grabbed my jacket, added a few coins to Grant's, and ran out of the tearoom, calling, "Wait for me!"

Bree Pym, Mrs. Sciaparelli, Annie Hodge, Mr. Barlow, George Wetherhead, Christine Peacock, Sally Pyne, Henry Cook, and the Handmaidens watched intently as I followed Grant and Charles across the green, racing to keep up with their longer strides while they made their way hotfoot to Crab-tree Cottage. By the time we darted into the foyer I was too winded to speak, but Charles's voice had lost none of its power as he slammed the door shut and wheeled around to face me.

"That woman," he thundered, "is *not* Amelia Thistle!"

Two

The sound of high-pitched barking assaulted our ears as Goya and Matisse scampered into the foyer to find out who'd slammed the front door. While I leaned against the wall to catch my breath, Charles scooped his golden Pomeranian into his arms and Grant bent low to give his overexcited Maltese a reassuring cuddle. Charles and Grant might own Crabtree Cottage, but their friendly little dogs ruled it.

"What are you talking about, Charles?" I asked, when the canine chorus had subsided. "I spoke with the estate agent myself. She told me that the woman who bought Pussywillows is Mrs. Amelia Thistle."

"The estate agent was bamboozled," Charles stated flatly. "And I can prove it."

He placed Goya gently on the floor and led the way into the front parlor, a sunny, simply furnished room that served as his office. Goya and Matisse bounced around us happily, pausing only to sniff our shoes, while Grant sank dazedly into one of the upright wooden chairs provided for clients. I stood with my back to the bay window, thanking my lucky stars that instinct had prompted me to chase after the two men. I had a feeling that I was about to learn something extremely interesting about our newest neighbor.

Charles took a fat folder from a wooden file cabinet, placed it on his desk, and began to riffle through its contents.

"As you know, Lori," he began, "Grant restores works of art and I appraise them. We may not be artists, but art is our life."

"We eat, drink, and breathe it," Grant put in, nodding.

"We read about it, of course," Charles went on, "but we also attend gallery openings, exhibitions, auctions, sales, private viewings —"

"I know," I interrupted. "The two of you are always haring off to London to see the latest works by the newest geniuses."

"Grant and I attend shows by established artists as well," Charles countered, "and we never throw anything away." He pulled three colorful brochures from the folder and spread them across the desk. "We collected these publicity pieces from three solo exhibitions mounted by a *very* well established artist." He laid the folder aside and extended his arm toward me with a dramatic flourish. "I invite you to examine the evidence."

I crossed to the desk, peered down at the brochures, and read the exhibition titles aloud. " 'Mae Bowen: Nature's Servant,' 'Mae Bowen: Nicotiana by Moonlight,' 'Mae Bowen: The Lost Glade.' " I looked inquiringly at Charles. "I don't get it. What does Mae Bowen have to do with Amelia Thistle?"

He flipped each brochure over and smiled triumphantly. I looked down again and saw three identical black-and-white portrait photographs of a woman who was the spitting image of the woman I'd seen speaking with the movers in front of Pussywillows.

"I present to you," Charles announced, "incontrovertible proof that the woman calling herself Amelia Thistle is, in fact, the well-known and highly respected English painter, Mae Bowen."

"The resemblance is uncanny," I acknowledged, "but I wouldn't call your proof incontrovertible." I folded my arms. "I've heard it said that everyone has a double. Amelia Thistle could be Mae Bowen's double. Or they could be identical twins. I can hardly tell my own sons apart in dim

26

light and Ruth and Louise Pym were carbon copies of each other."

Grant left his chair to stand beside me at the desk, taking care to avoid tripping over Goya and Matisse as they frisked at his heels.

"We're not dealing with twins or doubles," he said. "Charles and I have seen Mae Bowen in person on three separate occasions, Lori. The gestures, the stance, the walk, the tilt of the chin — they're unmistakable." He gazed from one photograph to the next and shook his head. "I'm willing to swear that Amelia Thistle and Mae Bowen are one and the same person."

I groaned softly as I recalled the chaos that had ensued when Sally Pyne had temporarily assumed a false identity.

"Are you telling me that we have another impostor on our hands?" I asked wearily.

"Amelia Thistle isn't just another impostor," Charles expostulated. "She's Mae Bowen, England's greatest botanical artist!"

"She paints plants and flowers," Grant put in.

"I know what a botanical artist does," I said irritably.

"She's insanely gifted," Charles gloated. "A child prodigy. I believe she first put brush to paper when she was ten years old.

27

Entirely self-taught, as a naturalist as well as a painter. Everything she knows, she knows from firsthand observation."

"Her face is weathered because she works *en plein air,* painting directly from nature," Grant explained. "Yet her paintings aren't merely photographic. They're . . . they're . . ." He squinted toward the ceiling as he searched for the right word, then shrugged helplessly. "You'll think I'm waxing lyrical, Lori, but Bowen's paintings are simply . . . magical."

"Prints don't do them justice," Charles said emphatically. "One must stand before an original Bowen to fully comprehend her brilliance."

"She's not terribly prolific," said Grant, "but each work of art she produces is a masterpiece."

"Do you own any?" I asked.

"Only in our dreams," Grant replied ruefully. "Her paintings sell for thousands of pounds, Lori. Connoisseurs the world over compete to collect them."

"Why haven't I heard of her?" I asked, frowning.

"Artists like Mae Bowen seldom make headlines," said Grant. "Art critics spend most of their time fawning over self-promoting poseurs. They tend to ignore self-effacing geniuses like Bowen, who contribute something of lasting value to the world."

"Fair dues," Charles protested. "Far be it from me to defend the critics, but it must be said that Bowen doesn't go out of her way to make herself accessible to the press." He gave me a sidelong, knowing look. "Truth be told, she's a bit of a recluse."

"Then why did she move to Finch under an assumed name?" I asked, perplexed. "If she's already a recluse, and if the press doesn't pester her, why would she feel the need to change her address *and* her name?"

"Why, indeed?" said Charles. "It's more peculiar than you can possibly imagine, Lori, because Mae Bowen —" He broke off, interrupted by the doorbell, which triggered another round of frantic barking as the dogs raced each other into the foyer.

"We're not expecting a client, are we?" Grant asked quietly.

"No," Charles replied. "And we *do not* want visitors. See who it is, will you, Lori?"

I tiptoed over to peer cautiously through the bay window and saw Millicent Scroggins standing on the doorstep. The skinny spinster lived next door to Crabtree Cottage, but I'd last seen her in Sally Pyne's tearoom, conversing volubly with the rest of the Handmaidens.

"It's Millicent," I whispered over my shoulder.

"What's she doing here?" whispered Grant, looking annoyed.

"Go and find out," Charles whispered to him. "And for heaven's sake, don't tell her about Mae Bowen."

Grant shushed him and went to answer the door. Charles and I moved closer to the hallway, the better to eavesdrop.

After greeting Grant and praising "the dear little puppies," Millicent got down to business.

"I do hope you'll forgive the intrusion," she said in an overly solicitous tone of voice. "I wanted to make sure that you and Lori and Charles were all right."

"She's snooping," Charles murmured, his eyes narrowing.

"Naturally," I murmured back.

"I couldn't help but notice your rather abrupt exit from the tearoom," Millicent continued. "I was afraid that one of you might have been taken ill."

"No, no," Grant assured her airily. "We're quite well, thank you."

"I *am* pleased," said Millicent, but she wasn't about to let Grant off the hook so easily. "You gave us quite a scare, you know, running away as you did. Selena said you looked as though you'd seen a ghost." Millicent's tinkling laugh set the dogs off again, but she simply talked over them. "Selena has quite a vivid imagination."

"You can tell Selena that we didn't see a ghost," said Grant. "We saw something far more disturbing."

"Did you?" Millicent prompted eagerly.

"Oh, yes," Grant said gravely. "We saw ourselves sitting there, staring at Mrs. Thistle as if she were a monkey in a zoo. And suddenly, we felt ashamed."

Charles emitted a snort of suppressed laughter and I smiled wryly. Grant had apparently decided to have a little fun with his inquisitive neighbor.

"Ashamed?" Millicent echoed, sounding bewildered. "Of what?"

"Of ourselves," Grant answered solemnly. "What is the world coming to, we asked ourselves, when a respectable woman can't move into a respectable house without being gawped at by a crowd of strangers? We were sickened, I tell you, *sickened* by our own despicable behavior, so we came away, before we could lose any more of our self-respect."

"I *see.*" Millicent hesitated, then said, "I hope you don't think *I* was there to . . . to *gawp* at Mrs. Thistle."

31

"The possibility never occurred to me," Grant told her.

"Because I can assure you that I had no such intention," Millicent stated militantly. "I went there, as I often do, to have a cup of tea and to visit with my friends. I can't speak to *their* intentions, of course. They may have gone to the tearoom to gawp, but I most certainly did not."

"Of course not," said Grant.

"Dear me," Millicent said fretfully. "I seem to have left my gloves behind. If you'll excuse me, Grant, I'll pop back to the tearoom to fetch them. Please give my best to Charles and Lori, won't you?"

"I will," said Grant.

I heard the sound of footsteps scurrying down the front walk, then the click of the latch as Grant closed the front door. Charles and I gave him a brief round of applause when he stepped into the office.

"An inspired performance," I said.

"Grant has a gift for improvisation," Charles said proudly.

"So does Millicent," I said. "If she came here to inquire after our health, I'll eat my sneakers. She was fishing for scraps of gossip to bring back to her cronies."

"And you sent her away with a flea in her ear," said Charles, beaming at his partner.

32

"Shall we celebrate your victory with a tot of brandy?"

Grant nodded, but I declined. I wasn't a teetotaler, but the thought of sipping brandy in the middle of the day made me feel slightly queasy. While Charles and Goya bustled off to the kitchen, Grant resumed the chair he'd occupied earlier. I took a seat in the chair next to his and bent to scratch Matisse behind the ears.

"You parried Millicent's thrusts beautifully," I commented.

"I put her on the defensive by taking the moral high ground," Grant allowed, "but I'm not sure she believed me. I've lived in Finch for too long to have scruples about minding other people's business."

I sat up and turned to face him. "Why didn't you come straight out and tell Millicent about Mae Bowen?"

"Because the longer we keep Mae Bowen's secret, the better off we'll be," Grant replied. "Don't misunderstand me, Lori. It's an honor to have such a distinguished artist in our midst, but it's an honor that could cost us dearly."

He was about to elaborate when Charles returned with two oversized snifters containing generous tots of brandy. He handed one to Grant, then seated himself behind the desk and drank from his own.

"Thank you, Charles," said Grant, after taking a restorative sip. "Shall we carry on where we left off before we were so rudely interrupted?"

"Certainly," said Charles. "I was about to explain to Lori why Mae Bowen's behavior seems so particularly peculiar." He cupped his hands around his snifter and leaned back in his chair. "You see, Lori, Mae Bowen has become something of a cult figure. Her acolytes have developed a philosophy of life based on her art."

"They call themselves Bowenists," Grant elaborated, "and their philosophy is based on the direct perception of the universe. They regard Bowen as a sort of guru whose paintings demonstrate the correct way to view nature."

"They're a great nuisance," said Charles, with a disparaging sniff. "They show up at every exhibition and stand for hours before each painting, meditating. One has to elbow them aside in order to view the painting oneself."

"Bowen has never done anything to encourage them," said Grant, "but in a strange way, her lack of encouragement has strengthened their faith in her. They see her reticence as a form of integrity."

"The filthy hypocrites," Charles said disgustedly. "They *say* that they respect her need for privacy, yet they follow her everywhere, pelting her with questions and requests. She has to have a security escort whenever she makes a public appearance."

"Do her acolytes follow her home?" I asked.

"I'm afraid they do," said Grant. "Before she moved here, she evaded them by living on a gated estate similar to your father-in-law's."

I stared at him, dumbfounded. "Mae Bowen gave up a gated estate for *Pussywillows?* I mean, it's a sweet little cottage, but it's no Fairworth House. Why would she make such a radical change?"

"Peculiar, eh?" Charles clucked his tongue sadly. "Pussywillows offers her no protection whatsoever from her worshipers. She's made herself a sitting duck."

"Not necessarily," I said. I was proud of my village, but I was also aware of its limitations. "Finch isn't exactly the center of the art world. Finch isn't the center of any world, except ours. She may feel safer here than she did on her estate."

"If so, she's deluding herself," said Grant. "Finch may be a backwater, but it doesn't have a moat. Once word gets out that Mae

Bowen is here, the Bowenists will flock to Finch."

"They're not dangerous, are they?" I asked.

"No," Charles said. "They may be nutters, but they're law-abiding nutters."

"They wouldn't harm her physically," Grant agreed. "But emotionally? Psychologically? Spiritually? They could destroy her. And they could do a great deal of harm to Finch."

"How could they harm Finch?" I asked, suddenly alert.

"By changing it out of all recognition," Grant replied. "Finch could become a center for New Age pilgrims."

"Hippies camping on the green?" I suggested tentatively. "Rainbow-colored RVs parked along the lanes?"

"Worse than that," Grant said grimly. "The Bowenists aren't all penniless vagabonds, Lori. Some of them are wealthy enough to buy property. A millionaire chap named Myron Brocklehurst bought a small farm across the road from Bowen's estate and turned it into a Mother Earth–worshiping Bowenist commune."

"Hold on," I said. "Are you telling me that Mae Bowen's followers might move to Finch *permanently,* just to be near her?"

"It's a possibility," said Grant. "She's removed the walls that used to stand in their way. They'll want to take advantage of her accessibility."

"If the Bowenists drive up housing prices," said Charles, "they could drive out the locals."

"And the village we know and love," Grant concluded, "would cease to exist."

We lapsed into a prolonged and heavy silence. The men sipped their drinks, the dogs rested from their exertions, and I stared into the middle distance, contemplating a future without Finch.

"You're overreacting," I said at last.

"Perhaps," Grant acknowledged. "But what if we're not? What if the scenario plays out exactly as we've described it?"

"I don't see what we can do to stop it," said Charles. "It's a free country. We can't prevent loonies like Myron Brocklehurst from coming here."

"They won't come if they don't know she's here," I said slowly. I thought for a moment, then sat forward in my chair. "I'll bet you just about anything that we're the only people in Finch who know who Amelia Thistle is. If we keep our mouths shut, no one else will find out about Mae Bowen."

"This is Finch," Grant reminded me, "the

Olympic training center for the sport of nosey parkering. The truth is bound to come out sooner or later. Bowen herself will slip up or a piece of forwarded mail will arrive, with her real name on it. Something will give her away."

"We'll cross that bridge when we come to it," I said decisively. "In the meantime, we button our lips, for her sake as much as our own. We don't refer to her as Mae Bowen, even among ourselves. We don't hang out near Pussywillows, hoping to catch a glimpse of her, and we don't grin like Cheshire cats every time we see her."

"We're not Bowenists, Lori," Grant said loftily. "Charles and I know how to maintain our composure in the presence of greatness."

"We've been given the opportunity to protect a national treasure," Charles declared. "I, for one, will not shirk my responsibility."

"I'll have to tell Bill," I said.

"Understood." Grant inclined his head graciously. "There should be no secrets between husband and wife. Apart from that, Bill's legal expertise may prove useful."

"Very useful indeed," Charles concurred. "If there *are* laws to prevent rampaging hordes of Bowenists from trampling Finch into the dust, Bill will know how to enforce them."

"I suggest you consult with him immediately, Lori," Grant advised. "It's best to be prepared."

"I'll go straight from here to Bill's office," I promised. I pointed to the brochures on the desk. "May I borrow these? They'll help me to explain the situation to him."

"Be my guest," said Charles.

I slipped the brochures into my jacket pocket, bent to give Matisse and Goya farewell pats, then straightened and looked puzzledly from Charles to Grant.

"One more thing before I go," I said. "Why did you let me catch up with you? Why didn't you slam the door in my face and keep Mae — er, I mean, *Mrs. Thistle's* secret all to yourselves?"

The two men exchanged amused glances.

"If we'd slammed the door in your face," said Grant, "you would have knocked it off its hinges. Our other neighbors may be pests when it comes to gossip gathering, but you, my friend, are a veritable pit bull."

I grinned sheepishly, but accepted the remark as a compliment. Like a pit bull, I was tenacious, and I could be fiercely territorial, something the Bowenists would find out if they were foolish enough to invade my village.

THREE

My departure from Crabtree Cottage coincided with the moving truck's departure from Pussywillows. By the time it lumbered past me on its way out of the village, the tearoom had emptied and small knots of chattering villagers had formed on the green. I knew for a fact that my neighbors were discussing Mrs. Thistle's furnishings, and though I longed to hear every delicious detail, I resisted the urge to join them and scurried across the green to my husband's place of business, Wysteria Lodge.

Bill had transformed Wysteria Lodge into a thoroughly modern law office. He'd retained the undulating flagstone floors, the rough stone walls, the mullioned windows, and the gnarled vine that gave the lodge its rustic charm, but he'd filled the rooms with the tools of his trade — tons of legal tomes, mountains of paperwork, and the multitude of electronic devices that allowed him to serve his wealthy, international clientele from a modest building in a tiny English village.

Since Bill's profession frequently took him away from home, it was a treat to pay him an impromptu visit in the middle of a workday. I found him behind his desk with a half-eaten apple in one hand, poring over a sheaf of densely printed legal papers. He dropped the apple when he saw me and came around the desk to envelop me in a hug.

My husband was a fine figure of a man, quite literally tall, dark, and handsome. He'd had a scraggly beard and a paunch when I'd first met him, but he'd gotten rid of both within a few years of our marriage, and replaced his heavy, horn-rimmed glasses with contact lenses. I'd loved Bill before his transformation and I would have gone on loving him if he hadn't changed at all, but I had no strong desire to turn back the clock.

"What's the verdict?" he asked, sitting on the edge of his desk. "Did Mrs. Thistle pass muster? In my estimation," he continued before I could answer, "she acquitted herself admirably in the furniture department: a tasteful collection of simple, solid antiques as well as a few custom-made pieces. What she didn't inherit, she purchased from reputable craftsmen. Either way, I think it's safe to assume that our new neighbor isn't poor, which should make the vicar happy. If Mrs. Thistle is a churchgoer, she should be able to make a hefty donation to the church roof fund."

I scrutinized him carefully. My husband had never displayed the tiniest crumb of curiosity about Mrs. Thistle. He had, in fact, teased me mercilessly for being overtly interested in her, yet here he was, delivering a learned dissertation on all things Thistle. I couldn't imagine what had come over him.

"You didn't watch them unload the moving truck, did you?" I asked.

"From start to finish," he said with gusto. "First the rugs, then the furniture, and finally, the boxes." He heaved a melodramatic sigh. "Boxes are cruelly tantalizing. Do they contain songbooks, ferrets, clown shoes? It's impossible to tell. Our new neighbor prolonged the agony by bringing with her quite a few boxes — far too many for a small place like Pussywillows — which led me to my first deduction."

"Which is?" I asked.

"Mrs. Thistle is downsizing from a much larger home, but hasn't yet realized what downsizing means," Bill replied. "Which leads, in turn, to my second deduction."

43

"Out with it, Sherlock," I said with a bemused smile.

"The next few bring-and-buy sales will enjoy an infusion of new wares as Mrs. Thistle gradually unloads the items she can't squeeze into the cottage. They should be quality items, too, if the furniture's anything to go by, which will make for a nice change from the chipped teacups, the stained ashtrays, and the hideous lamps offered at the last few sales." He cocked his head to one side and eyed me expectantly. "Well? How did I do? Will I be able to hold my own in the pub?"

I laughed delightedly and gave him a kiss.

"You could go toe-to-toe with Peggy Taxman," I assured him, "and she's the busiest busybody in Finch."

Peggy Taxman ran the Emporium, the greengrocer's shop, and nearly every village event. Since she also ran the post office and had unlimited access to postcards, semi-translucent envelopes, and return addresses, she knew a lot more about her neighbors' private affairs than she should have and maintained an air of omniscience the rest of us both envied and despised.

"I'm no Peggy Taxman," Bill said humbly, "but I try."

He left his perch on the desk and drew

me over to sit beside him on a button-backed leather sofa he used occasionally for client consultations but more often for post-lunch power naps.

"When did you develop an interest in Mrs. Thistle?" I asked.

"When I realized that she would be the main topic of conversation in Finch for the next few weeks," Bill said. "I didn't wish to seem ill informed. But you must have seen more than I did." He gestured toward his windows. "The view from here isn't nearly as good as the view from the tearoom."

"How did you know I was in the tearoom?" I asked.

"Where else would you be on moving day?" he retorted. "I also saw you sprint across the green after you dumped the groceries in the Rover."

"I didn't sprint," I protested.

"You sprinted like a manic gazelle," Bill said imperturbably, "which leads me to believe that you landed a window seat. So? What did you see?"

"Nothing," I replied.

Bill's eyes narrowed. "What happened? Concussion? Narcolepsy? Hysterical blindness? Or did the Handmaidens wrestle you to the floor because you were blocking their view?"

"None of the above," I replied, smiling. "I didn't see anything because I left the tearoom before the movers opened the truck."

"Impossible," said Bill. "I'd have noticed if you'd . . ." His voice trailed off and he frowned in concentration. "I had to leave the window for a few minutes to take a call from Gerard Delacroix. He rang as the movers pulled up to Pussywillows."

"That's when I left the tearoom," I confirmed. "Grant and Charles reacted oddly when they spotted Mrs. Thistle, so when they took off for Crabtree Cottage, I took off after them. I knew in my bones that they had some sort of inside knowledge about her and I wanted to know what it was."

"Did your hunch pay off?" Bill asked.

"I hit the jackpot." I swung around on the sofa to face him. "Have you ever heard of an English artist named Mae Bowen?"

"Yes," he replied. "I've never met the woman and I don't know much about her, but Father owns one of her paintings."

"Does he?" I said, very much surprised. "Have I seen it?"

"I doubt it," said Bill. "Father keeps it upstairs, in his private sitting room. It's a pretty thing. No, I take it back. It's more than pretty. It's . . ." He caught his breath and left the sentence hanging, as if he, like

46

Grant, couldn't find the right words to describe Bowen's work. "Why are you asking me about Mae Bowen?"

"Brace yourself for a major news flash," I warned him. "According to Grant and Charles, Amelia Thistle is Mae Bowen."

Bill's eyebrows shot up. "Are they sure?"

"They're positive," I said. "They've seen her in person several times. Here . . ." I pulled the exhibition brochures from my pocket and handed them to Bill. "Take a look at the photos and tell me what you think."

Bill studied the black-and-white photographs in silence, then stroked his chin thoughtfully.

"I can't argue with Grant or Charles," he said. "I've spent the past two hours ogling Mrs. Thistle. She does seem to be a dead ringer for Mae Bowen." He passed the brochures back to me and peered speculatively toward the windows. "How strange. Why would Mae Bowen pretend to be someone she isn't?"

"To preserve her privacy. Charles and Grant explained it all to me," I said and went on in a rush, "Through no fault of her own, Bowen has attracted a cult following, a rabid pack of New Age crazies who call themselves Bowenists and pester her, like a

47

gang of spiritual paparazzi. One of them bought a farm across from her gated estate —"

"So I was right," Bill interrupted. "She *is* downsizing."

"In a major way," I said, nodding. "According to Grant, her old house was the size of Fairworth. The gates ensured her privacy, but one of her followers bought a farm nearby to make it easier for the rest of the gang to camp out on her doorstep. Now that she's here, Grant and Charles are afraid her acolytes will overrun Finch and turn it into a crazies commune."

"We're getting a little ahead of ourselves, aren't we?" Bill said. "The woman moved here under an assumed name. How will her fans find her?"

"Fan is short for fanatic," I reminded him, "and fanatics don't rest until they track down the object of their obsession. I think we can count on their showing up in Finch at some point and I dread to think of what will happen when they do." I gripped his arm. "Remember what it was like during the Renaissance Fair, when the tourists trashed the green? The Bowenists will be a hundred times worse because they won't be passing through — they'll want to stay. Are there any legal maneuvers we can use to

48

keep Mae Bowen's fans from ruining Finch?"

"We could erect barricades, issue village passports, and hire security guards to man checkpoints," Bill suggested.

"Are you serious?" I said, eyeing him suspiciously.

"Of course I'm not serious," he said, with an exasperated chuckle. "We can't build a wall around Finch and we wouldn't want to."

"Wouldn't we?" I said, releasing his arm.

"No, we wouldn't," he said. "There are laws against trespassing, harassment, loitering, littering, and so forth, but if the Bowenists behave themselves, our hands will be tied. We can't ask the police to arrest a group of peaceful visitors."

"What if they try to buy property near here?" I asked.

"Our hands are still tied," Bill said firmly. "The law doesn't allow us to pick and choose our neighbors, Lori. If it did, Peggy Taxman would have nowhere to live."

I sighed forlornly and flopped back on the sofa.

"In that case," I said, "we'll have to rely on Plan A."

"Which is?" Bill inquired.

"Amelia Thistle is Amelia Thistle," I said

firmly. "If anyone asks, we've never heard of Mae Bowen."

"Mae who?" said Bill, feigning ignorance.

I acknowledged his jest with a wan smile.

"It won't work forever," I said, "but if Grant and Charles and you and I keep Amelia Thistle's true identity to ourselves, we may be able to keep Finch safe . . . for a while." I glanced at my watch. "I'd better go. I haven't had lunch yet and the laundry awaits."

"As do my clients." Bill got to his feet and pulled me to mine. "Be of good cheer, my love. The worst hardly ever comes to pass."

"As a lawyer," I said bleakly, "you should know better."

FOUR

Had I known what the day would bring, I would have parked my Range Rover directly in front of Bill's office. As it was, I'd parked it near the Emporium, which meant that I would have to cross the green to reach it.

I faced the journey with no little trepidation. I was certain that Millicent Scroggins had broadcast Grant's facetious explanation for our exit from the tearoom, which meant that my neighbors had had ample time to digest his tale and to decide, quite rightly, that it was a big fat lie. I fully expected one or more of them to fling truth-seeking missiles at me as I made my way to the car, and I wasn't in the mood to dodge them.

Much to my relief, the attack failed to materialize. By the time I left Wysteria Lodge, the knots of chattering villagers had dispersed, and though a few curtains twitched as I strode across the leaf-strewn grass, I made it to the Rover unmolested. I climbed in, shoved the key into the ignition, and sped away before the boldest of my inquisitors could abandon their chores and interrogate me.

I planned to drive straight home, toss a load of laundry into the washing machine, and sit down to a much-needed bite of lunch, but when the gated entrance to my father-in-law's estate came into view, I slowed to a crawl, then stopped. Though my stomach was rumbling, I was overcome by a sudden craving to know more about Mae Bowen.

What kind of woman, I asked myself, could inspire a philosophy, attract a cult following, and silence both Grant Tavistock and my husband? What was it about her work that sparked faraway looks and faltering speech in two strikingly intelligent and exceptionally articulate men? More to the point: Would her paintings have the same effect on me?

According to Charles Bellingham, one had to "stand before an original Bowen to fully comprehend her brilliance." Since the only original Bowen within my reach belonged to my father-in-law, I clicked the gate-opener clipped to the Rover's sun visor and turned onto the tree-lined drive leading to Fairworth House.

Lunch, I decided, could wait. I would first appease my appetite for art.

Fairworth House was a relatively modest eighteenth-century Georgian mansion. A succession of former owners had allowed it to fall into disrepair, but my father-in-law had rescued it from oblivion and restored it to its former glory. I often thought that Fairworth had a lot in common with its present owner. Like Willis, Sr., it was restrained, elegant, and immaculate.

I parked the Rover on the graveled apron in front of the house and ran up the front stairs to ring the doorbell. Deirdre Donovan answered it, clad in the crisp white shirtdress that served as her housekeeper's uniform. Deirdre was a tall, exotic beauty, with chestnut hair, almond-shaped eyes, and an air of competence I valued highly. I slept better at night, knowing that Willis, Sr., had someone of her caliber to look after him.

I stepped into the entrance hall and handed my jacket to Deirdre to hang in the cloakroom. I could have hung it there without her help, but Deirdre had strict rules about who should and shouldn't enter the cloakroom. Bill claimed that the cloakroom was the nerve center of Deirdre's top secret security system, but he knew as well as I did that Deirdre merely regarded coat management as part of her job.

"Is William in?" I asked.

"He is," Deirdre replied. "You'll find him in the conservatory, communing with the orchids. Any news on the new woman?"

"Mrs. Thistle?" I said sharply. "Why should there be news about her?"

"Because . . . she's . . . new," Deirdre said slowly, as if a scatterbrained gnat could have worked out the answer. "I thought you might have introduced yourself to her, welcomed her to the village, that sort of thing."

"No," I said, forcing myself to calm down. "In Finch, we usually give a newcomer a few days to unpack before we welcome her."

"A sensible tradition," said Deirdre. "I've heard she's a well-to-do widow."

"So have I," I said. "But I haven't heard anything else."

"The Handmaidens must be dying to meet her," said Deirdre, smiling. "They'll want to size up the competition."

"The poor woman doesn't know what she's let herself in for," I said, shaking my head. "But she'll find out soon enough."

Deirdre nodded her agreement. "Can I get anything for you, Lori, or shall I leave you to it?"

"Go," I said. "If you need me, I'll be with William and his orchids."

Deirdre bustled off to attend to her many duties and I gave myself a mental kick.

"You're a fine one to lecture Grant and Charles about behaving normally," I muttered as I crossed the morning room. "Deirdre asks a simple question about Mrs. Thistle and you bristle like a startled cat. Get a grip, Shepherd."

I wasn't having an identity crisis. I'd kept my own last name when I'd married Bill, so while my father-in-law, husband, and sons were Willises, I was and always would be Lori Shepherd.

The patriarch of the Willis clan greeted me warmly when I entered the conservatory. Willis, Sr., was a slightly built, impeccably attired, white-haired gentleman of the old school. He stood when a lady entered a room, he never left home without a pristine pocket handkerchief, and he worshiped the ground his grandsons galloped over. I loved him dearly and I was one hundred per cent certain that the feeling was mutual.

"Lori," he said. "What a delightful surprise. I did not anticipate a visit from you today. What brings you to Fairworth?"

"Curiosity," I said. "I'd like to take a look at one of your paintings."

His eyebrows rose in surprise. "My home is yours, my dear. You are free to come and go as you please."

"I think I'll need your permission to look at the painting I have in mind," I said. "You keep it in your private sitting room."

"Ah," he said, nodding. "The Bowen. Yes, of course, you may see it. Come with me."

It was refreshing to encounter someone who could mention a work by Bowen without losing the ability to speak. As Willis, Sr., and I made our way upstairs to the master suite, he continued to talk about the painting quite matter-of-factly.

"I presume Bill mentioned the Bowen to you," he said.

"Well," I began carefully. I refused to lie to Willis, Sr., but I saw no need to tell him the whole truth, either. "Grant Tavistock and Charles Bellingham mentioned Mae Bowen to me and I mentioned her to Bill and he told me that you owned one of her paintings." An unsettling thought occurred to me and I asked quickly, "Have you ever met Mae Bowen?"

"I have not," said Willis, Sr. "I am not a Bowen aficionado, Lori. I own only one of her paintings and I did not purchase it. It was given to me."

We walked through his splendidly appointed bedroom to a chamber I hadn't entered since the earliest phase of the renovation. It had been a blank canvas back then. It was now the most personal space in all of Fairworth House.

Willis, Sr., hadn't furnished his private sitting room with exquisite period pieces, but with familiar odds and ends he'd brought from the Willis mansion in Boston — an old leather reading chair and an ottoman that had molded themselves to his body; a glass-fronted cabinet filled with trinkets and trophies from his son's childhood; a row of mahogany bookcases laden with family photographs and favorite books; and a jewel-toned Persian carpet I remembered from the mansion's library.

I gave a soft gasp of pleasure when I glanced to my right and saw a nineteenth-century map of the Arctic wilderness framed in intricately carved wood. I'd presented the map to Willis, Sr., as a gift before I'd known that I would become his daughter-in-law. I was delighted and slightly flabbergasted to find it hanging among the rest of the treasures in his inner sanctum.

"The Bowen is here," Willis, Sr., said quietly.

I turned around and caught my breath again.

The Bowen was a small and simple water-color: three purple crocuses emerging from the snow. The blossoms were disheveled and the snow was smudged with dirt, but the imperfections gave the painting life. I felt as if I were watching the crocuses in motion, bursting forth from the frozen earth, rising through the snow to find the sun, defeating winter's darkness with the promise of spring. The flowers, too, would be defeated, the painting seemed to say, but while they lived, they would raise their arms, rejoicing, to the light.

I stood wordlessly before the watercolor for many minutes before saying, half to myself, "Bill was right. It's more than pretty. Your heart breaks for the beauty of it."

"Yes," said Willis, Sr. "One need not know the story behind it to be aware of its power."

"Charles called Mae Bowen a genius, but I had no idea . . ." I turned to Willis, Sr. "Who gave it to you?"

"Jane," he replied. "My wife."

"Ah," I said softly, and looked away. I felt as if I'd intruded on sacred ground.

Willis, Sr., had been a widower for many years before I'd met him. He rarely spoke of his wife and I respected his reticence, sensing the grief that lay behind it. I wanted to kick myself for blundering blindly into a memory that could only cause him pain. I wished I hadn't asked to see the Bowen.

"There is no need to avert your eyes, Lori," he said. "Mine are quite dry, I assure you."

"Bill didn't tell me where the painting came from," I mumbled awkwardly.

"He did not tell you," said Willis, Sr., "because it is not his story to tell. I would like to share it with you now, however, if you would be so kind as to listen."

He gestured for me to sit on the ottoman and lowered himself into the reading chair. The watercolor, I noted, hung directly opposite his chair. I wondered how often he looked up from a book to contemplate it.

"I was ten years older than my wife," he began, "but she was wiser than I will ever be. She was a bundle of boundless energy until the age of thirty-two, when she fell ill with pancreatic cancer. She died three months later."

"Bill told me," I whispered. "I'm so sorry."

"Some said it was a merciful release," Willis, Sr., continued, "but I do not remember Jane as a sickly woman. I remember only her bright eyes and her enchanting smile. Her body was frail, but her spirit was radiant. It is her radiance I remember."

59

"It's a fine way to remember her," I offered.

"Indeed," said Willis, Sr.

"And the painting?" I asked. "How did she buy it for you if she was so desperately ill?"

"Jane met Miss Bowen during one of our frequent trips to London," Willis, Sr., explained. "While I attended a conference, Jane visited one of Miss Bowen's exhibitions. Years later, after Jane was diagnosed with her fatal illness, she commissioned Miss Bowen to create a painting for me. Jane gave it to me the day before she died." He paused. "Are you familiar with the language of flowers?"

"Vaguely," I said, straining to recall what little I knew of the arcane subject. "It started in the Middle East, I think, as a sort of code. Each flower had a distinct meaning and lovers used them to communicate secretly with each other. In *Hamlet,* Ophelia is speaking the language of flowers when she says, 'There is rosemary, that's for remembrance.' "

"Yet Jane did not commission Miss Bowen to paint rosemary, for remembrance, or yew, for sorrow, or the willow, for mourning," said Willis, Sr. "She specifically requested a painting of the spring crocus."

"What does the spring crocus signify?" I asked.

"Youthful gladness," Willis, Sr., answered, his eyes fixed on the watercolor. "I believe Jane gave the Bowen to me for a reason. She hoped it would teach me that the certainty of illness, pain, and death compels us to live life with youthful gladness. It took me many years to learn the lesson, but as I said before, Jane was wiser than I will ever be." He paused, then said quietly, "I would like one day to meet Miss Bowen, to thank her for fulfilling my wife's commission with such grace."

I opened my mouth to speak, then shut it again and turned to look at the painting, wondering if Mae Bowen would remember Jane Willis, the bright-eyed, enchanting woman who'd lived with her face turned to the sun.

FIVE

I left Fairworth House in a somber mood, all thoughts of lunch forgotten, and drove straight to Morningside School in Upper Deeping to pick up the boys. Will and Rob were somewhat taken aback by the ferocious hugs and kisses I bestowed upon them before depositing them in the Rover, but I couldn't help myself. Jane Willis's tragic death had reminded me of how fortunate Bill and I were to have robustly healthy children.

I listened while the twins rattled on about their day at school, fed them milk and homemade cookies when we got home, then turned them loose in the garden to blow off steam while I prepared dinner. My preparations were interrupted by no fewer than seven telephone calls from villagers who regarded it as their civic duty to describe to me each and every item that had come out of Mrs. Thistle's moving truck. I stemmed the tide by telling my informants that Bill had already filled me in, and with a truly heroic effort succeeded in rescuing the roast from the oven before it was burned to a crisp.

Since Bill had spent half the morning peering through his windows instead of sitting at his desk, he brought work home from the office. After he demolished dinner and put his sons to bed, he repaired to his favorite armchair in the living room with his cell phone, his laptop, his briefcase, and his cat. Stanley made several sneaky attempts to insinuate himself between the computer and Bill's lap, but finally settled for a lesser perch, draped across the back of the chair.

I stretched out on the sofa, feeling as if the day had been a thousand hours long.

"I stopped at Fairworth on my way home from the village," I said.

"I thought you might," said Bill. "Did Father show you the Bowen?"

"Yes," I said. "He also told me who gave it to him."

"I hoped he would." Bill opened his computer and began tapping away at the keyboard. "I would have given you a heads-up, Lori, but —"

"It wasn't your story to tell," I broke in,

nodding. "It's okay. I preferred hearing it from him."

"What did you think of the painting?" Bill asked.

"It took my breath away," I replied. "Literally. I can understand why people get worked up about Mae Bowen. She sees the world in a very special way." I hesitated before adding, "Your father wants to meet her."

"Then an introduction will be made," Bill declared, in a tone of voice that brooked no contradiction.

"Of course it will," I said. "If William can't keep a secret, no one can."

The laptop *dinged.* Bill glanced down at the screen, then looked at me apologetically.

"It's from Gerard Delacroix," he said. "The latest codicil to his ever-evolving will. I should probably give it my undivided attention."

"Go ahead," I told him, hauling myself into an upright position. "I'll be in the study."

"Enjoy your reading," he said, giving me a wink.

I smiled as I strolled up the hallway. Bill was one of a scant handful of people who knew about the curious book I kept on a shelf beside the mantelpiece in the study.

The book had been — and was still being — written by the cottage's previous owner. Her name was Dimity Westwood and her tale provided irrefutable proof that truth was much stranger than fiction.

Dimity Westwood had been my late mother's closest friend. The two women had met in London while serving their respective countries during the Second World War, and the bond of affection they forged during those dark and turbulent years was never severed.

After the war ended and my mother sailed back to the States, she and Dimity strengthened their friendship by sending hundreds of letters back and forth across the Atlantic. When my father died unexpectedly, those letters became my mother's refuge, a retreat from the everyday pressures of working full-time as a teacher while raising a boisterous daughter on her own.

My mother was extremely protective of her refuge. She told no one about it, including me. As a child, I knew Dimity Westwood only as Aunt Dimity, the heroine of a series of bedtime stories invented by my mother. I didn't learn about the real Dimity Westwood until both she and my mother were dead.

It was then that the fictional heroine of my favorite stories became very real to me.

To my everlasting astonishment, the woman I knew as Aunt Dimity bequeathed to me a considerable fortune, the honey-colored cottage in which she'd grown up, the precious correspondence she'd exchanged with my mother, and a blue-leather-bound journal filled with blank pages.

It was through the blue journal that I finally came to know my benefactress. Whenever I opened it, her handwriting would appear, an old-fashioned copperplate taught in the village school at a time when the only book most cottagers owned was a family Bible. Although I had a minor fit of hysteria the first time it happened, I soon came to realize that there was no reason to fear and every reason to love Aunt Dimity's unconventional means of communication.

I still had no idea how Aunt Dimity managed to bridge the gap between life and afterlife, and she wasn't too clear about it herself, but I didn't require a technical explanation. It was enough for me to know that she was as good a friend to me as she'd been to my mother.

The study was dark, but not silent when I entered it. The wind moaned in the chimney and rattled the dried strands of ivy criss-crossing the diamond-paned windows above the old oak desk. Shivering, I switched on the mantel lamps and knelt to light a fire in the hearth. It wasn't until the flames caught that I stood to greet Reginald.

Reginald was a small rabbit made of powder-pink flannel. He had black button eyes, hand-sewn whiskers, and a faded purple stain on his snout, a memento of the day I'd shared my grape juice with him. Reginald had entered my life soon after I'd entered it, and he'd been my companion in adventure ever since. He'd absorbed more tears than any handkerchief I'd ever owned and he'd kept every secret I'd ever shared with him. Another woman might have folded him in tissue and stored him in a trunk as a cherished relic of her childhood. I kept him close at hand, because I never knew when I'd have more tears to shed or deep dark secrets to share.

"It's been a strange day, Reg," I said. "A famous artist has moved to Finch under an assumed name and we have to conceal her true identity or we'll end up chin-deep in lunatics." I raised an admonitory finger to him. "Everything I say from now on is strictly confidential."

Reginald kept his mouth shut, as if to demonstrate his trustworthiness. I twiddled his ears fondly, then took the blue journal down from its shelf and sat with it in one of the pair of tall leather armchairs facing the fireplace.

"Dimity?" I said, opening the journal. "I hope you haven't made any plans for the evening. I can guarantee that you'll want to hear the lowdown on our new neighbor."

I grinned as the familiar lines of royal-blue ink began to loop and curl sinuously across the page.

Let me consult my appointments diary. Hmmm . . . No, I have nothing scheduled for this evening and even if I did, I'd cancel it. I've been waiting all day to hear about Mrs. Thistle. Do tell!

I kicked off my sneakers, curled my legs beneath me, and began, "As I told you last night, today was move-in day at Pussywillows."

A regrettably twee name for such a lovely cottage. The original owner was no doubt inspired by the pussywillows growing along the riverbank, but I can't help wishing he'd given the place a more sensible name. Plain old "Willows" would have done nicely.

"Er, yes," I said, momentarily distracted from my train of thought. "Willows would have worked, but it's too late to rename the cottage now."

Nonsense. Mrs. Thistle could simply hire someone to paint a new sign for her.

68

"She could do it herself," I countered. "Mrs. Thistle knows how to use a paint-brush."

Is she a decorator?

"No," I replied. "She's an artist and her name isn't Amelia Thistle, it's Mae Bowen."

The botanical artist? The child prodigy?

My eyebrows rose. "Did you know her?"

I never met her, but I knew of her. In my day, everyone who appreciated flowers and watercolors knew about Mae Bowen, and I'm particularly fond of both. I attended her very first exhibition and was astounded by the talent she displayed at such a young age. Youthful gifts can fade over time, but hers never deserted her. She was one of the lucky few who go on to make a tidy fortune doing something they love. Why has she chosen to call herself Amelia Thistle? Another regrettably twee name, I might add. I would have expected Mae Bowen to have better taste in pseudonyms.

"Twee or not," I said, "Amelia Thistle is the name she's using, possibly for self-defense."

I leaned back in the chair, planted my stockinged feet on the ottoman, and launched into a detailed recap of everything Grant and Charles had told me about Mae Bowen, her fanatical followers, and the

69

threat they posed to Finch.

"The hoopla surrounding Mae Bowen seemed kind of silly to me," I concluded, "until William showed me one of her paintings. It's a little thing — a small watercolor of spring crocuses — but it packs a punch. She made it seem as if crocuses have souls."

Who's to say they don't? Be that as it may, I do know what you mean. When I first saw her work, I was instantly reminded of some lines from William Blake's "Auguries of Innocence":

To see a world in a grain of sand,
And a heaven in a wild flower,
Hold infinity in the palm of your hand,
And eternity in an hour.

Mae Bowen sees to the heart of every living thing she paints and she helps us to see what she sees. Although I felt no need to create a belief system based on her works, it doesn't surprise me to hear that others have. I must say that I feel terribly sorry for Miss Bowen. Her worshipers sound positively pestilential.

"According to Grant and Charles, they're like a plague of locusts," I agreed, "and I don't want them nesting in Finch."

Finch's hypothetical troubles seem to me to be of less importance than Mae Bowen's verifiable trials. Imagine yourself in her place, Lori. Imagine being mobbed by strangers making demands they have no right to make — demands on your time, your wisdom, your passion, your privacy. It would drive the sanest woman mad.

"Which is precisely why Mae Bowen should have stayed on her gated estate," I reasoned. "She was safe there. Why would she decide to live in Pussywillows, where she's anything but safe?"

Some things are more important than safety, Lori. Perhaps Miss Bowen is tired of living in isolation. Perhaps she craves the stimulation of village life.

"If the Bowenists find out where she lives," I grumbled, "she'll have all the stimulation she can handle."

If her secret is kept, however, the Bowenists need never know she's here.

"Never is a long time," I said glumly, "especially in Finch, where news spreads faster than wildfires. Peggy Taxman's whispers can be heard around the world — and *she* has access to Mae Bowen's *mail!*" I frowned worriedly at the fire. "Call me a stick-in-the-mud, Dimity, but I like Finch the way it is. I don't want to see Sally's tea shop turned into a vegetarian café. I don't want Peacock's pub to become a wine bar. I want the Emporium to sell tea and sugar and milk, not dowsing rods and crystal balls and tarot cards. And, yes, I would like Mae Bowen to live in peace, but peace is exactly what she won't have if the loonies come looking for her. They'll be able to knock on her door at any time, day or night. She's totally unprotected. And so is Finch."

There was a pause, as if Aunt Dimity were marshaling her thoughts. Then the handwriting continued, flowing calmly and steadily across the page.

It's clearly too late to keep you from working yourself into a froth over Mrs. Thistle, but I'm not convinced that she is froth worthy.

"If the destruction of Finch isn't froth worthy, I don't know what is," I retorted.

But you have no reason to believe that Finch will be destroyed. You have no reason to believe anything. You do not yet know that Amelia Thistle is, in fact, Mae Bowen.

"Charles and Grant swore up and down that she is," I protested.

Charles and Grant could be mistaken. As you yourself pointed out, the two women could be doubles or identical twins. Before you take up arms to defend Finch from Mae Bowen's overzealous admirers, don't you think it would be wise to find out if Grant and Charles are correct?

"I could ask Bill to run a background check on Mrs. Thistle," I offered.

You'll do no such thing. Mae Bowen is not a criminal and she doesn't deserve to be treated like one.

"You're right," I conceded equably. "I'd be acting like a Bowenist if I pried into her private life without her knowledge, so a background check is out. I suppose you have a better idea?"

I believe I do. It's a risky proposition, though. It might even be dangerous. It will almost certainly require courage and cunning.

Intrigued, I glanced toward the hallway, then hunched secretively over the journal and lowered my voice. "Are you by any chance suggesting that I break into Pussy-willows and rifle through Mrs. Thistle's papers?"

I most certainly am not. However much it might appeal to your sense of adventure, Lori, such a course of action would be an even greater invasion of privacy than a background check. I would never advise you to burgle a home unless it was absolutely necessary, which, in this case, it is not.

"What *are* you suggesting, then?" I asked.

I am advising you to speak with Mrs. Thistle.

"Speak with her?" I repeated, feeling a bit deflated. The adventurous side of me would have preferred burglary. "That's it?"

That's it. Ask Mrs. Thistle if she is Mae Bowen. The rest of the conversation will follow naturally from her answer.

"The direct approach, eh?" I said ruminatively.

It's usually the best approach. It's certainly less risky than breaking and entering.

"Where does the danger come in?" I inquired.

To ask questions is to risk rebuffs. Mrs. Thistle may tell you to mind your own business. She may faint or shriek or slap your face. She may even see you to the door. Courage will be needed to ask the question. Cunning may be needed to gain an answer. I suggest that you bring a selection of tea biscuits with you.

"To use as a defensive weapon?" I said, smiling.

In a manner of speaking. Mrs. Thistle will feel obliged to offer you a cup of tea in return for your kindness. Once she sits down to tea with you, she'll have to behave in a civilized manner. You might bring a quiche as well, or any other dish that can be refrigerated, then warmed through when needed. It's a bother to cook when one's pots and pans are inaccessible. She'll appreciate a quiche.

"So," I said, "I should bring Mrs. Thistle

some cookies and a quiche, wait for her to make tea, then spring the big question on her."

Yes, and the sooner, the better. The longer you speculate, the more likely you are to do something you, Bill, William, and I will regret. You have been known to behave rashly, Lori.

"If I were blessed with impulse control," I responded, "I wouldn't have torn out of the tearoom to chase after Charles and Grant. The only reason we know about Mrs. Thistle's little secret is because I followed a hunch."

But we don't know for certain that Mrs. Thistle has a secret, Lori, not yet, though I'm sure you'll find out all about it tomorrow. I wish you the best of luck, my dear,

"Thanks, Dimity," I said. "I'll keep you informed."

I know you will and I'm grateful. Good night, Lori. Sleep well.

I waited until the lines of royal-blue ink had faded from the page, then closed the journal and looked up at Reginald.

"Sleep will have to wait," I said to my pink bunny. "I have to make cookies and a quiche tonight, because I intend to visit Pussywillows first thing tomorrow morning, right after I take the boys to school."

Reginald's black button eyes glimmered a

warning and I understood why. I would be breaking a village tradition by calling on a newcomer so soon after her arrival — a transgression that would earn me a month's worth of dirty looks from the Handmaidens, among others — but I didn't care. The quest I was about to undertake was of vital importance to the entire community. Neither slaps nor shrieks nor dirty looks would keep me from seeking the truth.

SIX

I awoke the following morning to a leaden sky and the drumming of autumn rain on the slate roof. Having stayed up until the wee hours baking three separate batches of cookies as well as a quiche lorraine, I felt almost as leaden as the sky when I rolled out of bed, but a hearty breakfast and the bracing company of my menfolk perked me up. By the time I reached Pussywillows, with the fruits of my night's labor tucked safely in a canvas carryall, I was ready for battle.

Mrs. Thistle answered my knock almost instantly, as if she'd been sitting near the door, hoping someone would come to call. Her blue eyes seemed enormous in a face that had grown pale, the gray hair bundled on the back of her head was on the verge of falling down around her ears, and she appeared to be wearing the same clothing she'd worn the day before — knee-length cardigan, tweed trousers, and vermillion blouse. She looked, in short, like a woman who'd been shipwrecked on foreign shores without a hairbrush, a hairpin, or a change of clothes to call her own.

"Good morning," I said brightly. "My name is Lori Shepherd and I live just up the lane." I held the canvas carryall out to her. "I've brought a little something to welcome you to the village."

"Is it edible?" she asked, her eyes fixed on the bag.

"Quiche and cookies," I replied. The question seemed a little strange to me, but I was willing to go with the flow.

Mrs. Thistle licked her lips and released a tremulous sigh before asking, "Is the quiche cooked?"

"All you have to do is warm it up," I assured her.

"No need for that," she said. "I *adore* cold quiche. *Do* come in."

She seized my wrist, drew me across the threshold, and kicked the door shut with her foot. I had a brief glimpse of a front room littered with crumpled newspaper and cardboard boxes before she whisked me through to the kitchen, at the rear of the cottage. Once there, she relieved me of the carryall, placed its contents on a scrubbed

78

pine table, and began rummaging through yet another cardboard box.

"I've unearthed the cutlery and my tea things," she said, "but I haven't been able to locate the crockery, and my pots and pans are nowhere to be found. I suppose I should have labeled the boxes, but after living in the same place for ten years, one loses the knack for moving house." She pulled two exquisite antique forks out of the box and offered one to me. "Care to join me?"

"No, thanks," I said. "I've already had breakfast."

"How I envy you," she said. "I didn't think to bring provisions with me. By the time I abandoned the unpacking last night, the local shops were closed, and I didn't know where else to go. Dinner was a packet of crisps left behind by the removals men and breakfast was a cup of tea brewed from one of the desiccated tea bags I found at the bottom of my tea caddy. Thank heavens my predecessor left behind a roll of loo paper or I would have been in real trouble. As it is, I'm famished."

"Dig in," I said, gesturing to the quiche. "I'll make a fresh pot of tea."

"You are an angel of mercy." She pulled a chair out from the table, sat down, and attacked the quiche, scooping bites of it directly from the pie plate with her fork.

I slid out of my dripping rain parka and hung it to dry in the scullery, then turned my attention to tea. The kitchen had been thoroughly updated — stainless steel appliances, birch countertops and cabinetry — but the rustic stone sink, the exposed beams, and the flagstone floor softened its modern edges, and the view of the river meadows from the window over the sink was timeless.

The tea caddy sat between an electric kettle and a chubby cherry-red teapot on the counter next to the sink. The only drinking vessels in sight were a dozen jam jars, one of which contained traces of Mrs. Thistle's spartan breakfast. I'd never drunk tea from a jam jar before, but evidently Mrs. Thistle had.

I had no cream or sugar to offer my hostess, but she didn't seem to mind. Once she'd quelled the worst of her hunger pangs, she accepted a jar of weak, unadulterated tea with a grateful smile. After a careful sip, she held the jam jar at arm's length and examined it.

"I usually use these for cleaning my paintbrushes," she said philosophically, "but needs must."

I froze, with my jar of tea halfway to my lips.

"I rinsed them thoroughly," Mrs. Thistle said, taking note of my startled reaction. "And the paints I use are nontoxic."

"Do you paint?" I asked offhandedly, as if the thought of her wielding a paintbrush was new to me.

"I dabble," she replied, and before I could press her for details about her "dabbling," she was off and running again, taking the conversation in an entirely different direction.

"You're an American," she observed. "Your accent gave you away, as did your use of the word *cookies*. An Englishwoman would have said *biscuits*. Your informality betrayed you as well. An Englishwoman wouldn't have urged me to 'dig in.' She would have insisted on searching high and low for a proper plate. Americans are, as a rule, much more easygoing about such matters, especially in an emergency, and I can promise you, it *was* an emergency." She lifted her chin and gave me a searching look. "You've known what it is to be hungry."

I froze again, this time in surprise. It was true that I'd gone through some lean years after my mother's death, but Amelia Thistle couldn't have known it. If she was Mae

Bowen, however, and could see into a crocus's heart, perhaps the human heart was open to her as well.

"Yes," I said. "I've known what it's like to be hungry. It's the kind of thing a person doesn't forget."

"You'd be surprised by the number of people who do." She opened one of the food storage boxes I'd filled with cookies, bent over it, and inhaled deeply. "Heavenly. What kind of, er, *cookies* are they?"

"Oatmeal," I said. "My mother made them for me when I was little."

"And now it's your turn to make them," she said. "My mother taught me to make brown bread. It's my most special recipe. Perhaps I'll bake a loaf for you after I've tamed my kitchen. Let's enjoy your lovely oatmeal cookies in comfort, shall we?"

She stood, crossed to rummage through the cardboard box again, and came up with a Victorian silver salver engraved with an intricate floral motif.

"I can't imagine why I put the tea tray in with the cutlery," she said, shaking her head, "but it's just as well I did. If I'd put it in with the crockery, we'd have to dig through who-knows-how-many boxes to find it." She handed the salver to me and retrieved a broom and a handful of trash bags from a corner cupboard. "If you'll bring the tea and the oatmeal cookies, I'll put the parlor to rights and build a fire. I found some dry logs in the shed last night, before the rain set in. I should be able to coax a friendly flame or two out of them. Heaven knows I have enough tinder."

"Don't be silly." I put the salver on the table and took the broom and the bags out of her hands. "I'll see to the parlor and the fire. You'll sit down and relax. You've had a rough night, Mrs. Thistle. You've earned a breather."

"Not Mrs. Thistle, dear," she said, and my ears pricked alertly until she added, "Amelia, please. Guardian angels are allowed to use first names."

"I'm no angel," I said, "but if I'm to call you Amelia, you must call me Lori. Everyone does. Have a seat and a cookie, Amelia. Leave the parlor to me."

I was a bit disappointed in myself for failing to nail down Mrs. Thistle's true identity within the first thirty minutes of my arrival at Pussywillows, but my disappointment was replaced by a tingle of excitement as I entered the front room. Although I would have lent a helping hand to anyone in Mrs. Thistle's situation, I couldn't deny the special pleasure it gave me to see up close what Bill and my neighbors had seen only from a distance.

I quickly cleared the room of packing debris, pushed the half-emptied boxes into a neat row along one wall, and lit a fire in the hearth. I piled the bulging trash bags near the front door for later delivery to the recycling bin, then paused to take in the scene my cleanup work had revealed.

I saw what Bill had seen: a pleasing mix of the old and the new. Burgundy silk taffeta drapes hung at the windows and a colorful Turkish rug warmed the polished plank floor. A *secretaire* bookcase made of lustrous cherrywood served as a focal point for the interior wall — an efficient use of space on Mrs. Thistle's part, since the *secretaire* combined the virtues of a small desk with those of a display cabinet.

A brass floor lamp with a vellum shade cast a soft glow over a plump love seat and a pair of armchairs grouped around a low rosewood table before the hearth. The love seat was covered in a reddish-brown tweed and the armchairs were upholstered in a glorious brown, gold, and burgundy paisley. The dark furnishings looked well against the room's whitewashed walls and complemented the smoke-blackened oak beam that had been set into the chimney breast to serve as a mantel.

Mrs. Thistle's pots and pans might still be among the missing, but a selection of smaller, less practical items had clearly been found. The *secretaire*'s shelves were filled with pretty and possibly revealing ornaments — porcelain posies, blown-glass blossoms, bone-china bouquets — and a charming, enameled carriage clock sat upon the mantel. A pair of photographs flanked the clock, silver-framed color portraits of two different men, both smiling, one blue-eyed, clean-shaven, and balding, the other sporting horn-rimmed glasses, a dark beard, and long, dark hair. I wondered who the men were, realized that Mrs. Thistle could probably tell me, and returned to the kitchen with the broom resting on my shoulder.

I could tell upon entering the room that my quiche — and a handful of oatmeal cookies — had revived Mrs. Thistle. She'd pinned her hair more securely in place, the color had returned to her cheeks, and her eyes had lost their mildly desperate gleam.

"Have you finished already?" she said, brushing crumbs from her fingertips.

"As the mother of two little boys," I said, "I've learned how to deal with messes. Not that your room was a mess —"

"It was," she interrupted amiably as she

pushed herself to her feet. "Let's take our tea to the parlor and see what you've accomplished."

I could almost hear a Victorian silversmith rotate in his grave as Mrs. Thistle used his splendid creation to convey a chubby red teapot, two jam jars, and a plastic box filled with oatmeal cookies to the front room. Smiling, I put the broom back in the cupboard and followed her.

She deposited the tray on the low table, clasped her hands to her bosom, and turned in a circle to survey a room she hadn't yet seen decluttered.

"I can't thank you enough, Lori," she said finally. "It would have taken me a whole day to do what you did in twenty minutes." She sat in one of the armchairs and motioned for me to take the other. "Please, dear, you must tell me all about your little boys."

It wasn't easy to refuse an open invitation to brag about my sons, but I managed. I was ready to get down to business.

"I'll introduce you to Rob and Will whenever you wish," I said. "Right now I'd like to ask you a question."

"Of course," she said.

"Are you Mae Bowen, the famous artist?" I slid back in my chair and gripped the armrests, braced to withstand roars, rants, and recriminations, but none of Aunt Dimity's dire predictions came true. Though Mrs. Thistle's face fell, she seemed to be more vexed with herself than with me.

"Drat," she said quietly. "I knew I'd be found out eventually, but to be unmasked by my very first visitor is extremely discouraging." She shrugged helplessly. "I'm simply not cut out for this sort of thing."

"What sort of thing?" I asked.

"Subterfuge," she answered. "I've no head for it. My late husband used to say that I was as guileless as a kitten, but he was wrong. A kitten would have concealed herself better than I have."

"You invented a new name," I said encouragingly.

"No, I didn't," she retorted glumly. "You'd think that an artist would have the imagination to create a proper pseudonym, but I couldn't even do that. I was so flustered by the house sale and the auction and packing up my bits and pieces that I simply couldn't concentrate on anything else."

"If you didn't come up with a pseudonym," I said slowly, "whose decision was it to call you Amelia Thistle?"

"It was my decision," she replied, "but I didn't invent Amelia Thistle. I am Amelia Thistle."

"I thought you were Mae Bowen," I said, in some confusion.

"I'm Mae Bowen as well," she said. "I'm Mae Bowen *and* Amelia Thistle." She took a deep breath and went on, "I was christened Amelia Bowen, but my family called me Mae, so I've always signed my paintings as Mae Bowen. Years later, when I married, I took my husband's last name and became Amelia Thistle, but I continued to use the name Mae Bowen professionally because my paintings had become rather well known by then and I would have created a muddle if I'd begun signing them with a name hardly anyone associated with me."

"I see," I said, though my head was spinning slightly. "Amelia Thistle is your married name and Mae Bowen is your professional name."

"I prefer to think of Amelia Thistle as my private name and Mae Bowen as my public name," she said. "I hoped using my private name would give me more privacy, but it was a foolish hope. Both names are a matter of public record, so anyone can look them up and connect them to me. Honestly," she said with a wistful sigh, "a half-witted badger could see through my ruse. As I said, I have no head for subterfuge."

She seemed so depressed by her lack of

guile that I felt compelled to comfort her.

"It's hardly surprising that someone who paints the way you do would find it difficult to lie," I said. "How did Keats put it? 'Beauty is truth, truth beauty — that is all ye know on earth and all ye need to know.' "

"Beauty? Truth?" she exclaimed. "Oh, dear." She turned her head to gaze dispiritedly into the fire. "I hoped we would become fast friends, Lori, but if you insist on throwing Keats at me before ten o'clock in the morning, it can mean only one thing: You must be one of *them*."

"One of —" I broke off as the penny dropped. "Are you accusing me of being a *Bowenist?*"

"I could be mistaken," she said timidly.

"You are spectacularly mistaken," I declared. "I am *not* a Bowenist. I'd never even heard of you until yesterday, when my friends told me about you. Charles Bellingham and Grant Tavistock live in Crabtree Cottage, right here in Finch, and they're much more knowledgeable about the art world than I am. They recognized you when you showed up with the moving truck."

"Are they . . . ?" She glanced anxiously toward the windows, as though she expected to see two sets of eyes peering at her through the gap in the draperies.

"Absolutely not," I said. "I can assure you that Grant and Charles would like nothing better than to see all Bowenists take a running leap into a bottomless bog. Please believe me when I tell you that my friends and I want to *protect* you from the Bowenists."

"Protect me?" she said faintly.

"As best we can," I said. "We don't want your followers to infest Finch and we don't want them to hound you, so we're prepared to do whatever it takes to keep your secret from reaching their ears."

"You came here this morning to protect me?" she said, her face softening.

"I came here to find out if Grant and Charles were right about you," I said. "Now that I know who you really are, well, yes, I'd like to do what I can to protect you, if you'll let me." I leaned forward. "I'd advise you to take me up on my offer, Mrs. Thistle. I don't mean to toot my own horn, but I'm *great* at subterfuge."

"So are my followers." She folded her hands in her lap and gazed steadily at me. "If you're fibbing, Lori . . ."

I stuck out my arm and held my palm over the plastic box. "I swear on my mother's oatmeal cookies that I'm telling you the truth, Mrs. Thistle."

She hesitated for a brief moment, then reached out to take my hand in hers.

"Amelia," she said, smiling. "Please call me Amelia."

SEVEN

"You can have no idea," said Amelia, "what my life has been like for the past ten years. I've been constantly pecked, poked, and prodded in public by people who are, as far as I can tell, mentally unhinged. Me? A great spiritual guide?" She gave a short, unhappy laugh. "I can't even find my tea-cups!"

"You will," I soothed, topping up her jam jar. "What happened ten years ago? Is that when the Bowenist movement started?"

"It kicked into high gear ten years ago," she informed me. "It was founded a few years earlier by a well-to-do crackpot named Myron Brocklehurst. When Mr. Brocklehurst began to upend my dustbins in his search for sacred relics, Walter decided to buy Highburn Park, up near the Scottish border." She gazed tenderly at the silver-framed photograph of the clean-shaven, balding man. "Walter Thistle was my dear husband. He passed away four years ago, believing he'd created a safe haven for me. I had two hundred wild acres in which to wander," she added, with a reminiscent smile. "I knew every inch of it by heart, yet it never failed to surprise me. Each season brought an endless succession of fresh delights."

It was pleasant to sit indoors on a wet Tuesday morning and listen to Amelia reminisce, but I couldn't help wondering why she'd chosen to leave a place that had clearly meant so much to her.

"You must have been lonely after your husband died," I ventured, kneeling to stir the fire. "Living all by yourself on such a large estate —"

"Oh, but I didn't live there by myself." She gestured to the second photograph, the portrait of the bespectacled, bearded man. "My brother Alfred lived at Highburn with me until he passed away, nearly a year ago."

"First your husband, then your brother . . ." I shook my head sadly as I returned to the armchair and picked up my jar of tea. "The past few years haven't been easy for you, Amelia."

"No, they haven't," she agreed, "and the Bowenists haven't made them any easier. You may find it hard to believe, Lori, but a gang of them had the unmitigated gall to invite themselves to Walter's funeral! A nice constable shooed them away, but I'd learned my lesson. I held Alfie's memorial service at Highburn, behind locked gates."

"If you'd learned your lesson," I said, mystified, "why did you leave Highburn? Why did you trade your safe haven for Pussywillows?"

"I thought I'd be safe here, too," she admitted sheepishly. "It was naive of me, I suppose, but . . . Are you familiar with Homer's tale about Odysseus and the oar?"

I nodded. "After many tumultuous years at sea, Odysseus wandered inland, carrying an oar, until he found a place where no one knew what an oar was. He took it as a sign that his seafaring days were over and settled down to the peaceful life of a gentleman farmer."

"An excellent summary," said Amelia. "I visited Finch several months ago in much the same spirit. I spent time in the pub, the tearoom, the Emporium, and the greengrocer's, and I didn't hear anyone mention the word *art,* apart from four women who were taking painting lessons from a Mr. Shuttleworth in Upper Deeping, and they were far more concerned with the local art show than they were with the London art scene." She grimaced ruefully. "Your knowledgeable friends must have been out of town."

"Grant and Charles are rather fond of the London art scene," I told her.

"I couldn't have known," Amelia said resignedly. "I came away from Finch with the impression that, to the villagers, the professional art world was as distant as the moon. Better still, not once did I hear anyone mention a television program, a film, a pop song, or a so-called celebrity. Instead, I heard about Mr. Barlow's broken furnace, the new curtains Mrs. Peacock had made for the pub, which, I might add, most people thought were rather garish —"

"They are," I put in.

"— and the joke Henry Cook had told about the chicken, the juggler, and the man in the top hat," she went on. "It was as if the world beyond Finch didn't exist, not because the villagers were backward or isolated, but because they were so caught up in real life that they had no time to spare for fantasies concocted by the media. I found it immensely refreshing to be among such well-grounded, sensible people."

A snort of laughter escaped me when I heard Amelia's generous — and generally erroneous — description of my neighbors, but I turned it into a cough. I didn't want to be the one to disillusion her.

"I thought I'd be safe here," she reiterated, "which was a great relief, because I had to come here, regardless of my safety."

"Why?" I asked.

Amelia's gaze drifted toward her brother's photograph. "I have to complete a task Alfie was unable to complete."

"What task?" I asked, sitting forward and listening closely.

Still gazing at her brother's smiling, bearded face, she answered: "I need to find a witch."

My eyebrows shot up in surprise. "Do you mean Miranda Morrow? For pity's sake, Amelia, you didn't have to buy a cottage in Finch to meet Miranda. Her phone number's in the book. She'll be in Spain for the next two weeks — the vicar's wife is cat sitting for her and taking care of her indoor plants — but I'll be happy to introduce you to her when she gets back. She lives two doors down from Grant and Charles, in Briar Cottage. It's a five-second stroll from here."

"Who," Amelia asked, "is Miranda Morrow?"

"She's a witch," I replied, as if the answer were obvious, "though you wouldn't know it to look at her. I mean, who expects a freckle-faced strawberry blonde to be a witch?" Before Amelia could respond, I continued, "Miranda does most of her work over the telephone and on the computer — horoscopes, psychic readings, spell castings, that sort of thing — but she won't mind meeting with you in person."

"I don't wish to meet with her," Amelia protested, "not unless she knows something about Gamaliel Gowland."

"Gamaliel . . . who?" I said, brought up short.

"Gamaliel Gowland," she repeated. "He's the man who wrote the secret memoir."

"What secret memoir?" I asked. I was beginning to feel a familiar spinning sensation in my head.

"The secret memoir that tells the story of Mistress Meg," said Amelia.

"And Mistress Meg is . . . ?" I said.

"She's Gamaliel's witch, of course," said Amelia, sounding mildly exasperated. "Mistress Meg was also known as Margaret Redfearn. Do either of the names mean anything to you?"

"No," I said, eager to hear more.

"Oh, well," she said with a soft sigh. "I didn't expect to find her on my first full day in Finch."

She refilled her jar of tea and sipped from it placidly, as if she intended to move on to other subjects, but I refused to budge. As a member in good standing of the Finch Busybody Society, I couldn't bear the thought of a newcomer knowing more about my village than I did.

"Did Mistress Meg live in Finch?" I pressed. "Why did Gamaliel Gowland write a secret memoir about her? Who, for that matter, is Gamaliel Gowland?"

Instead of answering my queries directly, Amelia deposited her jar on the tray, stood, and crossed to the cherrywood *secretaire.* She reached into the top drawer beneath the slanted desk lid and returned to her chair carrying a gaudily decorated biscuit tin commemorating Queen Elizabeth II's coronation.

She placed the biscuit tin on the low table, prized it open, and withdrew from it what appeared to be a handwritten note encased in a protective envelope of transparent plastic. Without saying a word, she passed the mysterious document to me.

I gazed down at the small sheet of parchment — no more than four inches by six inches — covered with a densely written Latin text. The text was punctuated by a curious symbol, a black cross within a shield-shaped lozenge.

"If you're familiar with Keats and Homer," Amelia said, "you must be a well-educated woman. What can you tell me about the writing you see before you?"

"I can't translate it," I admitted readily, "because I don't read Latin. And I don't know what the glyph at the end of the text means because I've never seen anything like it before." I studied the script more closely. "I can tell you that the writer used a quill — most likely a goose quill — and iron gall ink, made from oak galls and a few other components. At a rough guess, I'd say that whoever wrote it lived sometime in the mid-seventeenth century. Handwriting styles are difficult to date precisely because old styles continue to be used long after new styles come into fashion."

"I'm impressed," Amelia admitted.

"I used to work with rare books and manuscripts," I explained, handing the piece of parchment back to her. "Do you know what it says?"

"Yes, I do, thanks to Alfie. He studied and translated the . . ." Her words trailed off and she peered at me diffidently. "I don't wish to bore you, Lori. You will tell me when I've droned on too long, won't you?"

"Don't worry about it," I said, waving off

her concern. "Some people like comic books and some like paperback thrillers. I like the old, dusty stuff." I pointed to the parchment. "This is my idea of pizza and a movie."

"Very well, then." Amelia returned the document to the biscuit tin, moistened her throat with a sip of tea, and began, "My brother Alfred never married and he had no children. As his only sibling, I inherited all of his possessions. I discovered the parchment after his death, when I was sorting through his things." She touched the biscuit tin. "He kept it in the tin, under his bed, along with a notebook containing his English translation of the text and all the information he'd been able to gather about it."

"How did he come by it?" I asked.

"He found it among the papers of one of our great-grandfathers," said Amelia, "an eccentric antiquarian named John Jacob Bowen. John Jacob was an interesting character — a typical Victorian magpie. He collected all sorts of curiosities, simply for the pleasure of having them about. He purchased the parchment from a cobbler who claimed that it had fallen out of his chimney."

"A strange place to store parchment," I

commented.

"Is it?" Amelia smiled enigmatically, then continued, "John Jacob examined the parchment before he bought it, of course. I believe it interested him because the man who wrote the text identified himself as Gamaliel Gowland. Gowland is a family name, you see. John Jacob may have believed that Gamaliel Gowland was a distant relation."

"Was he?" I asked.

"As it turns out, yes," said Amelia, with a satisfied air. "John Jacob was too busy accumulating oddities to give the parchment the attention it deserved, but Alfie wasn't. He discovered that the memoir's author, Gamaliel Gowland, was a many-times-great-granduncle of ours who served as the rector of St. George's Church from 1649 to 1653." She gave me an approving nod. "Your guess wasn't so rough after all, Lori. The memoir was indeed written in the mid-seventeenth century."

"Hold on," I said. "Let's back up a step. Are you telling me that your many-times-great-granduncle Gamaliel was a rector at St. George's Church in *Finch?*"

"Yes, I am," said Amelia.

"Wow," I marveled, almost spilling my tea in my excitement. "I'd give my eyeteeth to read his memoir — and I'm terrified of the dentist. It'd be worth it, though, to read a firsthand account of everyday life in seventeenth-century Finch. The vicar and his wife will go *bananas* when they find out what you have. Where's the rest of it?" I shrank back in my chair as a dreadful possibility occurred to me. "Please don't tell me it was lost or destroyed, Amelia. I don't think I could stand it."

"I can assure you that it wasn't lost or destroyed. Here." Amelia took an ordinary, spiral-bound notebook from the biscuit tin, opened it to a specific page, and passed it to me. "It will save time if you read Alfie's translation for yourself."

I took the notebook from her and read her brother's spiky, cramped scrawl silently.

I, Gamaliel Gowland, rector of St. George's Church in Finch, writing alone at night in my private study, record in a secret memoir that which is too dangerous to speak. I tell the forbidden tale of Mistress Meg, known to some as Margaret Redfearn, a fearsome and most potent witch. To write the witch's tale is to risk calamity for me and for my congregation. I will, therefore, divide and hide my memoir in hopes that it will be found by one who does not fear retribution, long after I and those I serve are with Our Lord. If you would seek the truth, follow the signs (clues?).

Alfred's English translation ended with a faithfully copied rendition of the glyph I'd observed at the end of Gamaliel's Latin text: a cross within a shield-shaped lozenge.

I handed the notebook back to Amelia and she laid it in her lap.

"The memoir wasn't lost or destroyed," she said. "It was hidden. Gamaliel hid it because it contained a tale that might spell trouble for him and his congregation, namely, the story of Mistress Meg."

I nodded sagaciously. "Witchcraft was a pretty touchy subject in the seventeenth century."

"Witchcraft was regarded as a crime punishable by death," Amelia stated firmly. "To praise it would be to risk dire punishment by church or civil authorities — sometimes both. To condemn it would be to risk a witch's retribution. It's not clear whether Gamaliel was afraid of the authorities or of Mistress Meg. All I know for certain is that he separated the pages of his forbidden tale and concealed them in various hiding places."

"Such as a cobbler's chimney," I said, as

comprehension dawned. "Did the cobbler live in Finch, too?"

"He lived directly across the lane from St. George's," Amelia informed me, "in Plover Cottage."

"Gamaliel hid the first page of his memoir in Plover Cottage?" I said, astonished. "Opal Taylor lives there now. She'll be gob-smacked when she hears what was stuffed up her chimney."

"As rector, Gamaliel would have had ready access to Plover Cottage," Amelia went on. "It would have been a simple matter for him to place the parchment in the chimney." She glanced at her brother's photograph. "Alfie believed that Gamaliel hid all of the pages in and around Finch. He was convinced that they're still in their hiding places, waiting to be found."

"It'd be a tall order to find them now," I said. "You'd have to poke your arm up an awful lot of chimneys."

"Not necessarily." Amelia tapped her finger on the spiral notebook. "Gamaliel states explicitly that he left behind a series of clues that would lead a truth seeker to the rest of the memoir." She held up the notebook and pointed to the curious symbol at the end of the text. "Alfie believed that the glyph, as you called it, was the first of

Gamaliel's clues. Unfortunately, he was unable to decipher it."

"Did your brother ever come to Finch?" I asked. "He might have understood the glyph better if he'd seen the village with his own eyes."

"Alfie was unable to visit Finch," said Amelia. "My brother was severely handicapped, Lori. He used his computer and the Royal Mail to carry out his research because travel was all but impossible for him. It was the fondest dream of his heart to read Mistress Meg's story, but illness prevented him from completing his life's work." She turned her head to gaze up at her brother's smiling face. "I intend to complete it for him."

I sat in silence, touched by the bond that seemed still to exist between Amelia and Alfred, a bond that I, as an only child, had never known. I was humbled by her willingness to share her home with him, despite his disabilities, and I admired her determination to carry out what appeared to be a fairly daunting task. I was about to ask her where she planned to start when a knock sounded on the front door.

"I'll answer it," I said promptly.

I placed my jam jar on the silver tray and hastened to the door, wondering if the infamous Myron Brocklehurst had already solved the riddle of Amelia Thistle. I heaved a sigh of relief when I saw Sally Pyne and Henry Cook peering at me through the rain, holding an oversized wicker hamper between them.

"Good morning, Lori," Sally said brightly. "Henry was convinced he'd seen you here earlier. I told him he must have been mistaken, because you of all people would know better than to bother a new neighbor on her first day in the village, but I can see now that he was right."

It required very little effort on my part to translate Sally's words into Finch-speak. *If you can break a village tradition,* she was saying, *so can I.* I suspected that a good many others would feel the same way.

"Is Mrs. Thistle at home?" Sally asked.

"Yes," said Amelia, appearing at my elbow. "Won't you come in?"

Sally accepted the invitation with alacrity and let Henry make the introductions while her head swiveled this way and that, taking in every detail of the front room. Henry had to nudge her with his elbow to get her to stop gawking long enough to offer the hamper to Amelia.

"Henry and I made up some sandwiches and a few other tidbits to tide you over until you've stocked your pantry," she explained. "And Henry's taken the rest of the day off."

"I'm under orders from my Sally to get you settled in." Henry patted his broad chest. "If you need help with the heavy lifting, I'm your man."

"You're on," I said, clapping Henry on the shoulder.

"Is he?" said Amelia.

"Of course he is." I turned to Sally and Henry. "Why don't you bring the hamper through to the kitchen? Amelia and I will join you in a minute."

I expected Sally and Henry to leap at the chance to inspect Amelia's kitchen and they didn't disappoint me. They sped down the narrow passageway as if they were on rocket-propelled roller skates, leaving me and my hostess alone in the front room.

"Amelia," I said quietly. "Unless I'm very much mistaken, you're about to get an influx of visitors."

"N-not . . . ," she faltered.

"No, not Bowenists," I said hastily. "Just your normal, everyday neighbors. Don't mention Mistress Meg or Uncle Gamaliel to them just yet. They might think you're a little crazy. But *use* them," I urged. "Send Sally to the Emporium with a shopping list. Let *her* stock your pantry. Put everyone else to work unpacking your boxes and organizing your new home. I promise you, they'll be willing to oblige."

"Such a *friendly* village," she said with a contented sigh. "One question, though: Why must we do everything at once?"

"Because you won't be able to think straight until you tame your cottage," I said. "And you'll need to think straight while we're searching for Uncle Gamaliel's forbidden memoir."

"We?" she said hopefully. "You mean, you'll help me?"

"Try stopping me," I said, grinning. "Put your house in order today, Amelia. Tomorrow you and I launch a witch hunt!"

EIGHT

While Sally and Henry exchanged views on the kitchen's decor, Amelia and I exchanged telephone numbers. I promised to call her as soon as I'd devised a plan of action, left her to make the most of her volunteer work force, and headed for home.

As I drove over the humpbacked bridge, I spotted Millicent Scroggins, Opal Taylor, Elspeth Binney, and Selena Buxton in my rearview mirror, bobbing along under a cluster of black umbrellas, toting a covered casserole dish apiece. I didn't have to be clairvoyant to figure out where those casserole dishes would end up. Having watched Sally Pyne, Henry Cook, and me enter Pussywillows, the ladies had plainly decided that it was their turn to shatter a time-honored village tradition by paying a premature call on their newest neighbor.

"Reinforcements are on their way, Amelia," I muttered. "Let *them* find your pots and pans!"

I had no doubt whatsoever that the Hand-maidens would regard pawing through Amelia's possessions as a golden opportunity to gauge her chances in the Willis, Sr., marriage sweepstakes. In return for allowing them to gather vital information about her furnishings, finances, and fashion sense, Amelia would gain four energetic helpers and a week's worth of nutritious nosh. It seemed like a fair trade to me.

I would have turned back to give Amelia a few pointers on how to handle the Hand-maidens, but I had other fish to fry. I wanted to squeeze in an hour or so of historical research before I sat down to lunch. Fortunately, I knew exactly where to find an expert on local history.

Rain was streaming from the slate roof when I reached the cottage. Rivulets raced down the graveled drive, the flagstone path was strewn with soggy leaves, and fat drops dripped from the rose trellis onto my head as I opened the front door. It was such a great day for playing in puddles that I made a mental note to bring a few bath towels with me when I went to pick up the boys.

I shed my wet parka and sneakers in the front hall, said hello to Stanley, who was keeping Bill's armchair warm in the living room, and padded damply up the hallway to the study. My cold feet compelled me to stoke a blazing fire in the hearth before sharing the morning's headlines with Reginald.

"Miranda Morrow isn't the first witch to live in Finch," I told my pink bunny. "Her predecessor was called Mistress Meg, but whether Mistress Meg was a good witch or a bad witch remains to be seen."

I could tell by the glimmer in Reginald's eyes that he was riveted. Smiling, I touched a fingertip to his snout, reached for the blue journal, and sat with it in one of the tall leather armchairs near the hearth.

"Dimity?" I said. "I have met Amelia Thistle!"

The fluid lines of royal-blue ink began to scroll across the page, but they didn't get very far.

And?

"And I asked her if she was Mae Bowen," I said.

And?

"No shouting, no slapping, no demands for my departure," I replied.

I repeat, somewhat impatiently: AND?

"And, yes, Amelia Thistle is Mae Bowen," I said. "Or, to put it another way, Mae Bowen is Amelia Thistle."

Ah-ha! She's using her maiden name.

"Bingo," I said, nodding.

It's not what I would call an impenetrable disguise.

"She claims she's not very clever," I said, "but I think she's underselling herself. I don't know how, but she knew I'd been through hard times, Dimity. She looked into my eyes and stated flat out that I knew what it was to be hungry."

She may be sensitive rather than clever. They're two very different traits, and I know which one I prefer. Do you still believe she poses a threat to Finch?

"I'm more concerned with protecting her than the village," I admitted. "I like her, Dimity, and I think she could do with some serious TLC."

Why?

"She's had a lot on her plate lately," I said. "Not just selling her old house and buying a new one, but dealing with her brother Alfred's death. He lived with her and her late husband, Walter Thistle, at Highburn, the estate they bought to keep the Bowenists at bay. Amelia and Alfred were very close and he died less than a year ago. To lose him so soon after losing her husband must have knocked the wind out of her sails. If you ask me, she simply didn't have the energy to create a completely false identity."

The poor woman. Did she leave Highburn because it was filled with so many painful memories?

"Not exactly," I said. "It sounds to me as though she still loves the place. She called it her safe haven."

Why did she trade her safe haven for Pussywillows?

"You told me last night that some things are more important than safety," I said. "Amelia came to Finch to do one of those things. . . ." I settled back in the armchair, stretched my chilled toes toward the fire, and recounted everything Amelia had told me about John Jacob's purchase, Alfred's research, Gamaliel Gowland's forbidden memoir, and the as-yet unfinished story of Mistress Meg. "Alfred's disabilities kept him from following the clue Gamaliel drew on the memoir's first page," I concluded, "so Amelia intends to follow it for him, once she figures it out."

A treasure hunt! How wonderful! What a pity Alfred couldn't participate in it. Did Amelia describe the nature of his handicap?

"No," I said, "but he was housebound, so he must have had mobility issues." I shook my head. "Thank heavens his mind was unaffected. If his notebook is anything to go by, he was a first-rate scholar."

He was certainly devoted to his subject. I find it very interesting that the memoir's first page was found in Plover Cottage. I need hardly point out that the house next door belongs to Finch's current witch-in-residence, Miranda Morrow.

"It's quite a coincidence," I agreed. "Miranda picked the wrong time to go to Spain. She'll kick herself when she finds out that we've been hunting for Mistress Meg without her. And if one of Gamaliel's clues points to Briar Cottage, I'll be in there like a shot, whether she's home or not."

Your treasure hunt may still be in progress when Miranda returns. I suspect it will be rather challenging to find documents that have remained hidden for centuries.

"Did any of your neighbors discover an odd bit of parchment stuffed up a chimney when you were, um, around?" I asked awkwardly. Aunt Dimity was so vibrantly present that it seemed impolite to speak of her in the past tense, but she responded without hesitation.

Not to my knowledge. It's possible that someone found a page and kept mum about it, but I think it highly unlikely. As you know, secrets don't last long in Finch. If a neighbor had made such a discovery, I'm sure I would have heard about it.

"I'm sure you would have, too," I said confidently. "Since you didn't, I think it's safe to assume that the rest of the memoir's pages are still in their original hiding places. Are all of the buildings in Finch as old as Plover Cottage?"

There are a few exceptions — the schoolhouse, for example, is Victorian and Fairworth House is Georgian — but generally speaking, Finch's building boom ended in the first decade of the seventeenth century.

"Well, you've reduced the search area a tiny bit," I allowed. "If a building wasn't here in Gamaliel's day, he couldn't have hidden anything in it, so we can eliminate the schoolhouse and Fairworth from our inquiries. What about Mistress Meg? Do you know anything about her?"

In an odd way, I may. When I was a small child, I lived in dread of a loathsome creature called Mad Maggie. I envisioned her quite clearly as a snaggletoothed, warty old hag who prowled the shadows in my bedroom with a bloodstained axe.

"Good grief," I said, wincing. "And you accuse *me* of having a wild imagination."

I was a child, Lori. You are an adult. There is a difference.

"So I've been told." I hunkered down

more comfortably in the chair, glad that I'd lit the fire. It seemed to me that a story starring an axe-wielding hag deserved to be told by firelight. "Tell me more about Mad Maggie."

Mad Maggie was a bogeyman — a bogeywoman, to be more precise — conjured by adults trying to frighten unruly children into good behavior. If, for example, one failed to wash one's hands before tea, one was told that Mad Maggie would chop them off.

"How quaint," I said weakly.

Parents were more demanding in those days, Lori, and children were tougher. If we were naughty, we expected to be spanked, to have our ears boxed, or to be sent to bed without our suppers. If all else failed, we knew we would be threatened with Mad Maggie. Most of us were bright enough to realize by the age of six that Mad Maggie was nothing more than a make-believe monster used by tired grown-ups to keep peace in the home. I can assure you that no one in Finch ever amputated a child's soiled hands.

"I'm relieved to hear it," I said, casting an appalled grimace at Reginald.

What interests me is that Mad Maggie belonged exclusively to Finch. I never heard her mentioned beyond the bounds of St. George's parish, not even in Upper Deeping.

Since Mistress Meg once lived in Finch, and since she was regarded as a witch, it seems reasonable to ask: Was Mad Maggie a latter-day version of Mistress Meg?

"The names are related," I said. "Both Maggie and Meg come from Margaret, and Mistress Meg was also known as Margaret Redfearn."

My thoughts exactly. Furthermore, myths often have a basis in reality. If the villagers in Gamaliel's time feared their local witch, they'd invent horror stories about her. The stories could have traveled down through the ages until they reached my tender ears.

"Gamaliel describes Mistress Meg as *fearsome* and you point out a possible link between her and the horrible hag of your childhood." I gazed into the fire reflectively. "Do you know what, Dimity? I'm beginning to think that Mistress Meg must have been a wicked witch. Gamaliel wrote his memoir at night, in his private study, because he was afraid of what she'd do to him if she found out about it." I shrugged and looked down at the journal. "Who wants to be turned into a toad?"

It would be a disconcerting experience, I'll grant you, but I'm not yet convinced that Gamaliel was afraid of Mistress Meg or that Mistress Meg was wicked. We don't know enough about their relationship to describe it accurately. If we're to do so, we must first read the rest of the memoir. Thankfully, the second page will be relatively easy to locate.

"Will it?" I said dubiously.

Of course it will. The first glyph isn't very subtle. You must have deciphered it by now.

"I haven't given it much thought," I admitted. I closed my eyes for a moment and pictured the glyph. "A cross in a shield-shaped lozenge . . . Now that you mention it, it does seem *vaguely* familiar." I opened my eyes in time to see the next line of fine copperplate zip speedily across the page.

Of course it seems familiar! You see it every Sunday.

"Do I?" I said, bewildered. "Where?"

Since the rain has evidently rusted your brain, my dear, we'll take it one step at a time. To which saint is the church in Finch dedicated, Lori?

"St. George," I replied. "That's why it's called St. George's."

Aunt Dimity ignored my weak attempt at humor and continued, *What scene is depicted in the medieval wall painting above the church's north aisle?*

"St. George, slaying the dragon," I said.

What is strapped to St. George's left arm?

"A shield." I closed my eyes briefly, then

118

sat bolt upright and cried, "A shield with a red cross!"

I knew you'd get there in the end.

"The glyph must refer to the wall painting!" I said animatedly. "Uncle Gamaliel must have hidden the second page of his memoir in the church! It makes perfect sense, Dimity. He was the rector at St. George's. He would have known every square inch of the church by heart. He'd know exactly where to stash a piece of parchment." I thumped the arm of the chair with my fist. "Dimity, you are a genius!"

If a talent for pointing out the obvious makes me a genius, then I will accept the accolade. I'm sure you would have seen it for yourself once you'd put your mind to it.

"I should call Amelia," I said, glancing at the telephone on the old oak desk. "We should go to the church right this minute and start looking for hiding places."

No, you should not. Amelia has quite enough to do today, Lori. She'll be better equipped to commence the search tomorrow.

"You're right," I acknowledged reluctantly. "I'll call her after lunch. We can meet up tomorrow morning, after I do the school run."

If I may make a suggestion? Speak with the vicar and his wife before you enter the church.

Lilian loves to root around in the church archives and the vicar is as familiar with St. George's as Gamaliel Gowland would have been. The Buntings may be able to save you and Amelia a great deal of time and effort.

"Very true," I said, nodding. "I'll give Lilian a buzz after lunch, too, and find out if she and the vicar will be at home tomorrow. If so, Amelia and I will stop at the vicarage before we tackle the church."

Excellent. Haven't you had lunch yet?

"No," I said. "I wanted to speak with you first."

No wonder your brain is functioning at half speed! Go. Eat. And try not to wear yourself out with too much speculation.

"I can't promise not to speculate," I said, "but I'll try not to wear myself out."

Good enough. Until tomorrow, my dear.

"Until tomorrow, Dimity."

I waited until the graceful lines of royal-blue ink had faded from the page, then closed the journal, returned it to its shelf, twiddled Reginald's ears, and made a bee-line for the kitchen. I helped myself to some barley soup and a thick slice of buttered bread, but I could have been chewing old boots and I wouldn't have noticed.

In my mind I was already in the church, gazing up at St. George's shield.

NINE

I awoke from my speculative daze an hour later and telephoned Lilian Bunting, who assured me that she and the vicar would be at home to visitors the following morning and invited me to drop in at any time with Mrs. Thistle.

I called Amelia next. She promised to be up, dressed, and ready to go at nine o'clock the next morning. To avoid distracting her from the all-important job of unpacking, I said nothing about Aunt Dimity's interpretation of the glyph. I told her only that I wished to introduce her to the vicar and his wife.

"What a good idea," she said. "They may be able to provide us with useful information about Gamaliel. I'll be on the doorstep at nine o'clock sharp. You'll have to excuse me now, though, Lori. Mrs. Binney, Miss Buxton, and Miss Scroggins are engaged in a rather heated debate about how best to arrange my Staffordshire flatbacks. I must mediate."

I would have thought long and hard before throwing myself into the middle of a Handmaiden brawl, but Amelia seemed unfazed by the challenge. I ascribed her courage to blissful ignorance and returned to the kitchen to prepare a beef stew for dinner.

While the stew simmered, I drove to Upper Deeping to pick up the boys. Predictably, Rob and Will made a point of jumping in every puddle between the school's front door and the Rover, so I blotted them with towels and brought them home to hot chocolates and hot baths. I had dinner on the table when Bill arrived and spent the rest of the evening sharing with him everything I'd learned at Pussywillows and everything I hoped to learn at St. George's.

I may have overdone it. Bill listened attentively for the first hour, then withdrew to the twins' bedroom, where he read aloud a record-breaking number of bedtime stories. Will and Rob were asleep long before he finished and I found him asleep in the master bedroom when I came upstairs. I gazed at him ruefully as I readied myself for bed, then removed Stanley from my pillow, crawled under the covers, and vowed to keep my mouth shut about the secret memoir until Bill specifically requested a progress report.

"I didn't wear myself out with speculation, Dimity," I murmured as I drifted into sleep. "I wore Bill out instead!"

The sun must have risen on Wednesday morning, but it was hard to tell. Though it wasn't actively raining, the sky was a solid mass of grim, gray clouds. Even the colorful autumn leaves seemed mildly depressed and the Little Deeping's ripples were devoid of sparkles.

Pussywillows, by contrast, shone like a new penny. There wasn't a trace of packing material in sight when I stepped into the front room and Amelia looked as fresh as a daisy. Her cheeks were pink, her eyes were bright, her hair was pinned in a more or less tidy bun, and she'd swapped her moving-day attire for a pale blue blouse that floated softly over a pair of wide-legged black trousers. I'd elected to face the day in a fairly drab brown sweater and a faded pair of jeans, but Amelia defied the gloom by draping a lemon-yellow scarf around her neck and slinging a multicolored carpet bag over the shoulder of her voluminous beige trench coat.

"You look great," I said as we left the

house and strolled toward the vicarage.

"I feel great," she responded ebulliently. "My new home is in apple-pie order and I couldn't be happier. Everyone was so *helpful,* Lori. Henry hauled boxes as if he were a navvy, Sally shopped for groceries as if she were my personal assistant, and Mrs. Binney, Miss Buxton, Mrs. Taylor, and Miss Scroggins took it upon themselves to do everything else. Other neighbors popped in to help, but the ladies wouldn't hear of it."

She glanced across the green, caught sight of Millicent and Selena standing in the Emporium's doorway, and gave them a friendly wave. They smiled, nodded, and waved back, then put their heads close together and, murmuring, disappeared into the Emporium.

"I've lived under siege for too long," Amelia continued. "I've forgotten what it's like to interact with pleasant people. It was wonderful, Lori. The four ladies were interested in every little thing."

I was about to retort "I'll bet they were!" but I swallowed the uncharitable remark before it could escape. Setting ulterior motives aside, the Handmaidens had put in a hard day's work at Pussywillows. Even I had to admit that they'd earned Amelia's plaudits.

As we walked along, I pointed out Crab-tree Cottage, Briar Cottage, and the notice board outside the old schoolhouse, and described the many activities that took place inside the schoolhouse throughout the year. I was about to issue a gentle word of warning to Amelia about getting involved in the nativity play — the competition for roles could be vicious — when she paused to gaze intently at the three semidetached cottages that stood across the lane from St. George's Church.

"The cottage nearest us is Plover Cottage," she observed. "Alfie used old maps to pinpoint its location. How I wish he could have seen it. I imagine it looks much as it did when John Jacob's cobbler lived in it."

"I imagine it looks much as it did in Gamaliel's time," I countered, and with Aunt Dimity's comments still fresh in my mind I added, "Architecturally speaking, Finch hasn't changed much since the seventeenth century."

"It's lucky for us that it hasn't," said Amelia. "Our chances of finding the rest of the memoir would be sadly diminished if we were faced with buildings that had been demolished or radically altered."

"Let's hear it for stability," I said, and came to a halt. "Here we are, Amelia. The vicarage."

The Buntings' rambling, two-story house was set back from the lane and shaded by chestnut trees. A low stone wall separated it from the churchyard surrounding St. George's and an unkempt front garden testified to the fact that neither the vicar nor his wife were blessed with green thumbs. A midnight-blue Jaguar parked on the grassy verge told me that my father-in-law was nearby.

Lilian Bunting answered the doorbell, greeted us warmly, and ushered us into the foyer. A respected scholar in her own right, Lilian was also an exemplary vicar's wife — sympathetic, well-organized, and virtually unflappable. She routinely disarmed bickering browsers at our bring-and-buy sales, soothed disgruntled losers at our flower shows, and pacified irate parishioners with the calm efficiency of a trained diplomat. Since I possessed the finely honed diplomatic skills of a belligerent toddler, I admired her greatly.

"I'm delighted to meet you, Mrs. Thistle," she said as she hung our coats on the Victorian coat tree in the foyer. "I feel as if I ought to apologize for the miserable weather, even though I don't believe I'm responsible for it."

"There's no need to apologize," said Amelia, clasping her carpet bag in her arms. "If not for rain, England's green and pleasant land would be less green and therefore less pleasant."

"Since I have no desire to live in a desert, I'm forced to agree with you," said Lilian. "Come through to the study," she added, leading the way up the corridor. "We're very popular this morning. Teddy — my husband — is already in the study, entertaining another visitor."

"We don't wish to intrude," said Amelia.

"Our guest won't mind," said Lilian. "It's only William — William Willis, that is — Lori's father-in-law. He's come to return a book he borrowed from Teddy."

As soon as Lilian mentioned Willis, Sr., I recalled the painting of spring crocuses he kept in his private sitting room at Fairworth House. There was no reason to suppose that the name "Willis" would mean anything to Amelia after so many years, but I couldn't help wondering if she would, eventually, remember the dying woman who'd commissioned the exquisite watercolor.

The men, being gentlemen, stood when we entered the study, a spacious room with a lofty ceiling, book-lined walls, and comfortably shabby furniture. Lilian stuck

127

around long enough to introduce Amelia, then went to the kitchen to prepare tea.

With his wavy iron-gray hair, mournful gray eyes, and predominantly gray attire, Theodore Bunting could have blended in with the lowering sky, but his greeting was as warm as his wife's had been and he insisted that Amelia and I sit in the faded chintz armchairs closest to the fire.

Willis, Sr., was dressed as immaculately as ever, in a black three-piece suit, a crisp white shirt, and an understated silk tie. He remained standing after the vicar had lowered himself into the worn leather armchair opposite Amelia.

"If you wish to speak privately with Mr. Bunting —" Willis, Sr., began.

"You needn't leave on my account," Amelia interrupted. "In fact, it might be better if you stayed. You and the vicar look like intelligent men and intelligence will be needed if my search is to succeed."

"Your search?" Willis, Sr., inquired politely, taking the chair beside the vicar's.

"Let's wait for Mrs. Bunting, shall we?" Amelia proposed. "Otherwise, I'll have to repeat myself and repetition is tiresome for the speaker as well as the audience. In the meantime, please allow me to say, Mr. Bunting, that you are fortunate indeed to tend such a warmhearted and generous flock. . . ."

Willis, Sr.'s years of legal training enabled him to maintain a neutral expression while Amelia sang the Handmaidens' praises, and the vicar hid his emotions admirably, but the two men couldn't help exchanging a single, fleeting glance that hovered somewhere between incredulity and pity. They, too, realized that Amelia's impression of the Handmaidens would become considerably less rosy once the four women unsheathed their claws, and they were as reluctant as I was to disillusion her.

"They're much better housekeepers than I am," Amelia concluded. "I doubt that Pussywillows will ever again be as tidy as it is now."

Mr. Bunting and Willis, Sr., responded with innocuous comments, then retreated to safer ground with remarks about the weather, a conversation that lasted until Lilian returned, bearing the black lacquer tea tray she'd inherited from her paternal grandmother. She was accompanied by Angel, the fluffy white vicarage cat, who peered at each of us in turn before leaping onto the vicar's lap and draping herself languidly over his knees.

While Lilian served the tea and handed

around a plate filled with her irresistible lemon bars, Mr. Bunting brought her up to speed.

"Mrs. Thistle is engaged in a search," he informed her. "We don't yet know the nature of her search because she wanted you to be present when she enlightened us."

"How intriguing," said Lilian, sitting cautiously on the wobbly settee that faced the hearth. "Please, carry on, Mrs. Thistle. You have my undivided attention."

"I suppose you could say I'm on a quest," Amelia began, "though it's my late brother's quest, really. . . ."

I sipped my Earl Grey and savored a lemon bar while Amelia repeated the remarkable story she'd related to me at Pussywillows. She'd evidently decided not to advertise the name Bowen and the complications that went with it because she spoke of her brother only as Alfred or Alfie, with no last name. She finished her account by delving into the colorful carpet bag for Alfred's spiral-bound notebook and the first page of Gamaliel's memoir, both of which were examined closely by Lilian, the vicar, and my father-in-law.

The Buntings didn't go bananas, as I'd predicted, but they were clearly thrilled by the discovery. Willis, Sr., as if conscious that their interest in the subject matter carried more weight than his own, allowed them to take the lead in the discussion that followed.

Lilian spent a considerable amount of time comparing the original Latin text to Alfred's translation before passing them to Willis, Sr.

"Does the translation pass muster?" the vicar inquired.

"Oh, yes," said Lilian. "It's colloquial, but accurate."

"I approve of Alfred's use of common speech," said the vicar. "It brings the Reverend Gowland to life. I can almost see him, lit by the light of a single candle, alert to the sound of approaching footsteps, moving his quill hurriedly from ink pot to parchment as he writes late into the night."

"He seems real to me, too," Amelia agreed. "It's as if I were hearing one of my ancestors speak directly to me from the past."

"And what a turbulent period of the past it was," said Lilian. "England wasn't a peaceful kingdom in those days. To the contrary, the country was racked with strife throughout much of the seventeenth century — civil war, sectarian violence, outbreaks of the plague, Cromwell's thugs plundering churches, and the Witch-finder General

131

committing appalling atrocities in the name of God." She compressed her lips into a thin, disapproving line, then added in clipped tones, "In England, women found guilty of witchcraft weren't burned at the stake. They were hanged."

"You've quite put me off my tea," said Amelia, gazing sadly at her cup.

"I'm sorry," said Lilian, "but it would be dishonest to sugarcoat the facts. Witch-hunting was a pernicious practice."

"Religion was sadly abused in those days," said the vicar. "People used it as an excuse to murder, maim, and torture those whose beliefs differed from their own. The ongoing conflict between the Roman Catholic Church and the Church of England called everyone's allegiance into question."

"It was a dangerous time to be a clergy-man," Lilian confirmed, "yet the Reverend Gowland survived and prospered. The lowly rector of St. George's Church eventually became the archdeacon of Exeter."

"I know," said Amelia. "Alfie devoted three pages in his notebook to Gamaliel's rise through the ecclesiastical ranks. Did you read it there just now, Mrs. Bunting, or are you familiar with the careers of each of your husband's predecessors?"

"My wife takes an interest in church history," the vicar explained. "She wrote a splendid monograph on selected members of St. George's clergy. It's available in the church for a small donation. The roof fund . . ." His voice trailed off delicately.

"I shall purchase a copy today," said Amelia.

"And I shall rewrite it," Lilian declared, "because it doesn't include what may be the most interesting chapter in the Reverend Gowland's career." She fastened her gaze on the plastic-covered piece of parchment in Willis, Sr.'s hand. "I pride myself on my intellectual rigor, Mrs. Thistle, but your late brother's quest has inflamed my imagination as well."

"The complete memoir could alter our understanding of the Reverend Gowland," the vicar explained.

"It certainly could," said Lilian, nodding. "What secrets did he have to tell? How could telling them endanger his flock? Who was Mistress Meg? If she was regarded as a witch, what happened to her? Did the Reverend Gowland bring about her torture and her death? Or did he sell his soul to her in a misguided attempt to gain preferment in the church?"

"Good heavens," said Amelia, her eyes widening. "The notion of soul selling never occurred to me."

"I'm sorry to say it," said the vicar, "but an atmosphere rife with fear and superstition can infect the mind of the most devout cleric."

"I can't imagine such evils infecting your mind, Mr. Bunting," said Amelia.

"I do my best to guard against them," the vicar responded, "because I'm well aware of my own frailty."

"How frail was the Reverend Gowland, I wonder?" Lilian asked. "I must confess that I shall find it difficult to concentrate on mundane matters until we find the rest of his memoir." She eyed Amelia speculatively. "Forgive me, Mrs. Thistle. I may be assuming too much. Will you allow Teddy and me to help you with your search?"

"I'm counting on your help, and Lori's," Amelia exclaimed. "I haven't been able to make heads or tails out of Gamaliel's first clue."

It was my cue to jump in with Aunt Dimity's guess about the glyph. Since I didn't know how to explain the inexplicable, I would have taken the credit for her contribution, but before I could open my mouth to speak, Willis, Sr., decided to break his long silence.

"Were you familiar with St. George's,

Mrs. Thistle," he said, "you would have no trouble interpreting the Reverend Gowland's clue."

Amelia gazed at him attentively. "Do you claim to understand it, Mr. Willis?"

"I do," he replied. "I believe, however, that a demonstration will be more efficient than an explanation." He slipped the piece of parchment into his breast pocket and stood. "Shall we repair to the church, Mrs. Thistle?"

"By all means, Mr. Willis," said Amelia, getting to her feet.

"We'll come, too," Lilian said quickly.

There was a flurry of activity as the vicar dislodged a dozing Angel from his knees, Amelia returned the notebook to the carpet bag, and Lilian retrieved an armload of raincoats from the foyer.

"It's begun to drizzle," she reported as we followed Willis, Sr., to the front door.

"No matter," said Amelia. "It would take a flood of biblical proportions to keep me from finding out if Mr. Willis is as intelligent as he seems."

TEN

The Buntings allowed the soft rain to dampen their heads on the way to the church, but I pulled up the hood on my parka and Willis, Sr., sheltered Amelia beneath his black umbrella. While the vicar and his wife hurried forward, I hung back and listened with interest as my father-in-law struck up a conversation with his new acquaintance. Unsurprisingly, it was she who did most of the talking.

"Please allow me to offer my sincere condolences on your brother's death," he said.

"Thank you," said Amelia. "Alfie was my only sibling and I miss him terribly. He was five years older than I, but he always treated me as an equal. He introduced me at a very young age to many of the things I still enjoy — Japanese films, Thai cuisine, Chinese poetry, Bhangra music. I owe a great deal to Alfie. He opened my eyes to the world."

"What is Bhangra music?" Willis, Sr., asked.

"It's Indian — from the Punjab originally — and very cheerful." Amelia stopped beneath the lych-gate's shingled roof and said quietly, "What a lovely church."

My heart warmed to her. I, too, loved my church's modest charms.

St. George's was squat and sturdy and its only external decorations were the chevron patterns incised in the stone moldings above the doors and windows. The window embrasures were filled with leaded panes of wavy clear glass rather than stained or painted glass, and the embrasures themselves were relatively small. The church boasted a square bell tower, but the bells hadn't been heard since the 1970s, when they'd been replaced by an automated recording device that chimed the hours and half hours with unfailing, if inhuman, regularity.

St. George's wasn't spectacular or glamorous. It didn't soar heavenward, stirring the soul with the intricacy of its design. It was a simple parish church, a humble friend whose door was always open, but no one who saw its golden walls rising from the graveyard's lush green grass could deny its loveliness.

"Alfie adored old churches," Amelia went

on as we left the lych-gate and walked up the gravel path to the south porch. "When we were young, we'd cycle for miles to see an interesting font or a curiously worded memorial tablet. He would have loved St. George's. It's Norman, isn't it? The rounded arches, the thick walls, the zigzag stonework over the doors . . . They're hallmarks of Norman architecture, aren't they?"

"Indeed they are," said Willis, Sr. "St. George's was built in the twelfth century by Sir Guillaume des Flèches, a Norman nobleman whose castle no longer exists. The stones from Sir Guillaume's castle were used in the construction of many of the buildings in and around Finch."

"Those who think recycling is a modern concept should spend more time studying history," Amelia commented.

Willis, Sr., smiled and left his umbrella on the south porch to drip while Amelia and I preceded him through the iron-banded oak door to join the Buntings.

The church smelled of beeswax, furniture polish, and damp. The wooden pews had been buffed to a gleaming finish by the same rota of village women who arranged the flowers. Christine Peacock, who liked to experiment, was responsible for the asymmetrical bouquets of bare branches, shiny

138

berries, and crab apples that graced the altar and the baptismal font. I found them attractive, but I knew of at least four ladies who were itching to pitch them and who would, as soon as their turns came around, revert to traditional arrangements of mums, asters, and dahlias.

The Buntings stood in the north aisle, gazing up at the faint, rust-colored image of a larger-than-life St. George brandishing his shield while thrusting his lance into a writhing, wormy-looking dragon. Amelia crossed to join them, looking everywhere but up, with Willis, Sr., and I trailing in her wake.

"My compliments on your beautiful church," she said to the vicar.

"Thank you," he said. "Our sexton, Mr. Barlow, looks after the church building and the grounds. He's Finch's odd-job man as well. If you need anything done around the house, Mrs. Thistle, Mr. Barlow is the man to call."

"Yes, I met Mr. Barlow yesterday," said Amelia. "He came to Pussywillows to introduce himself and to —" She broke off as she caught sight of the faded image on the north wall. "A medieval wall painting," she breathed rapturously. "What a fortunate survival! So many were plastered over or whitewashed in Victorian times."

"Ours was whitewashed," the vicar informed her. "It was uncovered a little over a decade ago by Derek Harris, a local man who specializes in restoration projects."

"Derek Harris," Amelia repeated thoughtfully. "Does he live at Anscombe Manor with his second wife, Emma — the American woman who runs the riding school — and his daughter, Nell, who married the stable master, Kit Smith, a man who's twice her age?"

"Y-yes," stammered the vicar, who looked as nonplussed as I felt. Newcomers to the village usually required more than twenty-four hours to learn the complex ins and outs of the Harris family.

"Miss Scroggins mentioned him to me," Amelia said airily.

Lilian and I exchanged startled looks. I couldn't be certain of her thoughts, but I was wondering what the heck Millicent Scroggins had told Amelia about *me.*

"Mr. Harris must be good at his job," Amelia continued, "and he should be proud of the work he's done here. It's a pity to think that such a striking image went unseen for so many years."

"The image would, however, have been plainly visible to the Reverend Gowland," Willis, Sr., reminded her. He took the first page of the memoir from his pocket and held it up for all to see. "I would ask you to compare the Reverend Gowland's glyph to St. George's shield," he suggested, sounding for all the world like an attorney instructing a jury.

Amelia looked from the piece of parchment to the painting and emitted a fretful little huff.

"How very disappointing," she said, frowning.

"In what way have I disappointed you?" Willis, Sr., inquired, lowering the parchment.

"It's not you, Mr. Willis." Amelia patted his arm absentmindedly while she continued to frown at the wall painting. "You were quite right. Had I been familiar with the church, I would have understood the glyph immediately. That's the problem, you see. I expected something a bit more devious from Gamaliel, something cunning and labyrinthine." She flung her arm out toward the painting. "I didn't think his clue would lead us to a great huge billboard stuck up on a wall for everyone to see."

"He may have led us to the painting," Lilian allowed, "but I, for one, have no idea where to go from here."

"My dear Mrs. Bunting," said Amelia,

"it's as plain as the nose on your face. There must be a loose stone or a thin layer of plaster behind the shield. When we remove one or the other, we'll find a recess containing the second page of the memoir. The solution to Gamaliel's first clue is, I regret to say, painfully obvious."

"It's not obvious at all, Mrs. Thistle," Lilian protested. "Derek Harris tested the wall thoroughly while he was removing the whitewash, to make sure the surface was stable. I can promise you that there are no recesses behind the painting."

"No cracks?" said Amelia. "No fissures?"

"There's nothing behind the shield but a large block of solid limestone," Lilian answered firmly.

A smile wreathed Amelia's rosy face as she peered heavenward.

"Forgive me, Gamaliel," she said. "I underestimated you."

"Am I reading you correctly, Amelia?" I said, eyeing her bemusedly. "Do you *want* the search to be challenging?"

"Of course I do," said Amelia. "If a secret's worth hiding, it's worth hiding well. Now, let's see . . ." She began to pace back and forth before the wall painting, tilting her head and squinting at the shield from different angles. "Could the cross on the shield be our next clue? Could it, perhaps, direct us to a hiding place?"

"The cross points in four directions," Willis, Sr., observed. "The salient reference points appear to be the rafters above, the floor below, the pulpit to the east, and the font to the west."

"We'll need one of Mr. Barlow's ladders to check the rafters," said the vicar.

"We can test the floor, though," said Lilian. "If we extend the cross's vertical bar downward . . ." She drew her finger through the air and pointed at a spot on the floor directly below the painting.

I walked to the place she indicated and stomped on it a few times, then crouched down and ran my palm over it.

"It doesn't sound hollow to me," I said, "and I can't feel a crack in it or a patch where a hole might have been filled in."

"I think we can scratch the floor off the list of potential hiding places for the moment," said Lilian. "Since we must postpone our survey of the rafters, we're left with the pulpit and the font. Teddy and I will take the pulpit. Lori? William? Mrs. Thistle? The font, if you please."

Whipped into action by Lilian's commands, our assigned teams headed in opposite directions.

The baptismal font was as old as the church. The rough bowl and the stumpy square post beneath it had been sculpted from a single block of stone. A raised relief of leafy vines encircled the bowl's exterior, and each side of the post featured a primitively carved symbol of one of the four evangelists: an angel for Matthew, a winged lion for Mark, a winged ox for Luke, and an eagle for John. The carvings were timeworn and indistinct in places, but there were still plenty of nooks and crannies to explore.

I moved Christine Peacock's non-floral arrangement from the font to a nearby windowsill, and Willis, Sr., removed the font's wooden lid and leaned it against the side of a pew. Amelia ran her hand around the bowl's smooth wooden liner, then began rapping on it with her knuckles. Willis, Sr., bent to examine the vines and I knelt before the eagle.

I tugged on the eagle's wings, stuck my fingers in its eyes, twisted its talons, pounded its beak, and pressed hard on the stone panel, to no avail. I went through a similar routine with the angel, the lion, and the ox, with the same results. Willis, Sr., and I swapped places to double-check each other's work, and Amelia took a turn as well, but nothing budged.

After forty-five minutes of intensive poking, prodding, pushing, and pulling, our separate parties regrouped in the center aisle to compare notes. We had to raise our voices to be heard above the rain hammering the roof because, while we'd been busy searching, the drizzle had turned into a deluge.

"Anything?" Lilian asked.

"Zip," I replied. "How about you?"

"No joy," said the vicar. He tipped his head back to peer at the rafters. "It looks as though we'll have to ring Mr. Barlow."

A gust of wind ruffled the hymn books as Bree Pym pushed the south door open and walked into the church, clad in a camouflage-print rain poncho and a very wet pair of Wellington boots.

"I was chatting with the aunties when the sky let loose," she said, striding toward us. Bree's great-grandaunts had been laid to rest beneath a single headstone in St. George's churchyard. She liked to keep them abreast of village news. "I stepped onto the porch to get out of the storm and I heard people shouting, so I thought I'd investigate. I'm afraid Mr. Barlow's gone to Upper Deeping to pick up his new drill, Mr. Bunting, so there's no point in ringing him. You're the new woman," she went on, extending her hand to Amelia. *"Kia ora!"*

Kia ora was a Maori greeting I'd learned during a trip to New Zealand. Bree used it to declare her loyalty to her native land and, I suspected, to throw unsuspecting innocents off balance. If she hoped to wrong-foot Amelia, however, she was in for a big surprise, as were the rest of us.

"Kia ora!" Amelia replied, without missing a beat. *"Ko wai to ingoa? He iti noa iho taku reo Maori,* so be gentle with me."

Bree froze in midstride. Her hand dropped to her side and her mouth fell open. It was refreshing to see someone turn the tables on her for once, but she bounced back almost instantly.

"My name is Bree Pym," she said, presumably in response to Amelia's question, "and I don't speak much Maori either, so we'll have to be gentle with each other." She stepped forward and shook Amelia's hand enthusiastically. "I'm very pleased to meet you, Mrs. Thistle."

"Please, call me Amelia," said Amelia.

"Have you been to New Zealand?" Bree asked.

"Once, years ago," Amelia said. "It was heaven on earth. You're a Kiwi, I take it?"

"I am, but I'm over here exploring my Pommie roots," said Bree. "What brought

146

you to Finch?"

"A riddle," Amelia replied.

"Is it a private riddle or can anyone have a whack at it?" Bree asked.

Amelia nodded to Willis, Sr., who produced the first page of the memoir and handed it to Bree.

"Sorry," she said, shaking her head. "I can't read Latin."

"We're trying to figure out what the symbol at the end of the text means," I told her.

Bree took a closer look, then handed the parchment back to Willis, Sr.

"I don't know what the symbol means," she said, "but I can tell you where to find another one just like it."

"Are you referring to the wall painting?" Amelia asked.

"Not the wall painting." Bree pointed at the ceiling. "The bell tower."

"The bell tower," Amelia said exultantly. "Much more secretive than a billboard. Dear Gamaliel, I *knew* you wouldn't disappoint me."

ELEVEN

Since the bell tower was too small to accommodate six over-excited adults, and since nothing short of sedation could have prevented Amelia, Lilian, and me from going up there with Bree, the gentlemen volunteered to stay below. The vicar retrieved a ring of keys from the sacristy, unlocked the tower door, and stood aside to avoid being trampled.

Bree led the charge up the spiral staircase, throwing warnings over her shoulder about the uneven stone steps.

"Wouldn't want you to stumble," she said, adding for Amelia's benefit, "Mr. Bunting lets me sit in the tower during Sunday services. I know the staircase by heart."

"You must know the tower by heart, too," said Amelia.

"I wish I'd known it when it had real bells," said Bree. "The tower never had a separate room for the bell ringers. The bells hung in the bell chamber, but the ropes hung down through the tower all the way to the ground floor. The bell ringers stood on the same level as the worshipers when they rang peals. Very simple, very communal."

It was as good a description of St. George's as I'd ever heard.

The rain's drumming became louder as we climbed higher, and when Bree paused to push open a trap door, a gust of wet wind sailed down the spiral staircase, dampening our upturned faces. Bree hauled herself into the bell chamber, then gave each of us a hand up as we clambered through the trap door after her.

The chamber was a sounding box, a square room with a pair of louvered openings set side by side in each stone wall. The oak beams that had once supported the bells were still in place overhead, but the floor had been covered with modern sheets of plywood.

A metal stand holding four megaphone-shaped loudspeakers stood in the center of the chamber. The metal stand was bolted to the floor and the speakers' cables ran through a length of plastic tubing that snaked across the weather-beaten plywood into a small opening, the only visible reminder of the holes through which the bell ropes had once dangled.

The wind curled and swirled around us, sending eddies of rain through the louvers. My fingers felt like icicles, Bree's poncho flapped, Amelia's bun began to loose its moorings, and the tip of Lilian's nose was as red as her ears, but no one complained. We were too excited to be put off by the weather.

"Here!" Bree called, squatting in the tower's northeast corner. "Look here!"

Lilian, Amelia, and I picked our way around the metal stand and bent over the crouching girl, who was pointing at something down low in the dark corner.

"That's it!" Amelia cried. "That must be it! Oh, Bree, you clever girl."

The artist's eyes were sharper than mine. I had to get down on my hands and knees and poke my face into the corner before I could see what Amelia had seen at first glance.

The bell tower's irregular blocks of limestone were held in place by a cream-colored mortar, but the stone that had provoked Amelia's outburst was outlined in dark brown. Incised in the stone's center was a cross within a shield-shaped lozenge.

"I thought it was graffiti," Bree explained.

"It *is* graffiti," I said, getting to my feet.

150

"Gamaliel must have carved it after he hid the second page behind the stone."

"We must break through the mortar," Amelia declared. "Does your husband own a hammer and a chisel, Mrs. Bunting?"

"I'm afraid not," Lilian said apologetically. "Teddy isn't one of nature's handymen."

"We may not need a hammer or a chisel," said Bree.

Her right hand vanished beneath her poncho and reappeared a moment later, grasping a flathead screwdriver. Amelia looked surprised, but Lilian and I merely smiled.

"Have you been helping Mr. Barlow again?" Lilian asked.

"He had to rehang a door for Mrs. Wyn," said Bree. "I went along to see how it's done."

"You must have been a brilliant Girl Guide," said Amelia, beaming at her.

"I earned my badges," Bree acknowledged, grinning. She raised the screwdriver and looked up at Lilian. "Do I have your permission to deface church property, Mrs. Bunting?"

"I'm sure Mr. Barlow will be able to repair whatever damage you inflict," said Lilian. "Have at it!"

Bree used the screwdriver to hack at the

brown mortar. Her hand was soon covered with muddy streaks as spritzes of rain turned the mortar dust into paste, but she kept digging.

"Gamaliel must have come up to the tower many times to create his hiding place," said Amelia.

"I hope he chose sunny days," I said, breathing on my frozen fingers.

"Oh, dear," Lilian said suddenly.

"What's wrong?" I asked.

"The bells," she said. "It's almost noon. If the recording starts while we're standing beside the loudspeakers . . ." She pressed her hands to her ears and grimaced.

"No problem." I pulled out my cell phone. "I'll call William and ask him to ask the vicar to turn the machine off."

"Teddy's not very good with machines," Lilian said doubtfully.

"Hold on," said Bree. "The mortar's only a couple of inches deep and the stone seems to be shallower than the others. There must be a cavity behind it. I'm . . . almost . . . there."

She set the screwdriver aside, inserted her fingers and thumbs into the empty space where the brown mortar had been, and gently wiggled the stone loose from its fellows.

"Oh, my," breathed Amelia, clutching my arm.

I could almost hear her heart race. Mine, too, began to gallop as Bree reached into the cavity and withdrew from it a loosely rolled scroll of parchment tied with a ribbon of black cloth. She handled it gingerly, to avoid smearing it with wet mortar, and passed it up to Amelia, who slipped it with shaking fingers into the pocket of her billowing trench coat.

"We've found it!" Bree roared, her eyes dancing. "Now, will someone please tell me what we've found?"

"Let's get clear of the loudspeakers first," said Lilian, and led the way through the trap door.

We trailed back to the vicarage looking like a pack of drowned rats, except for Willis, Sr., who was miraculously unsullied. Lilian spread towels under the coat tree to catch the water dripping from our rain gear and invited us to dry our wet shoes on the hearth in the study. Angel, roused from a nap in the vicar's chair, took one look at us and fled.

While I added a log to the fire and Amelia got her hair under control, Lilian, the vicar, and Bree cleared piles of books from the library table near the French doors and replaced them with a lamp, a pencil box, two hefty Latin dictionaries, and several pads of lined paper. Willis, Sr., added the memoir's first page to the newly created work space and the rest of us gathered around to watch Amelia place the be-ribboned scroll in the pool of light shed by the lamp.

"Before we move on," she said, "please allow me to say how grateful I am to all of you. I came to the vicarage hoping for a little information, but you've given me so much more. Thank you for applying your formidable minds and your tireless enthusiasm to my brother's quest. I would never have found the second page without you."

"You won't find the rest of the memoir without us, either," I said, "because we won't let you!"

Everyone laughed, including Amelia, but I was telling the simple truth. A quick glance at the circle of faces around the table told me that Alfred's quest had inflamed more than one imagination. If curiosity were a fatal disease, we all would have dropped dead on the spot.

"Shall we proceed?" Amelia asked.

"The scroll should be opened in a controlled environment," I advised. "Parchment is more durable than paper, but it can become brittle over time."

"Nonsense," said Amelia. She pressed the scroll lightly with a fingertip and watched it spring back into shape when she released it. "It seems quite supple to me."

"Ours is a damp climate," Lilian reasoned.

"Humidity can mitigate brittleness," I allowed.

"For pity's sake, ladies . . ." Amelia clucked her tongue impatiently and reached for the scroll. She discarded the black ribbon, spread the scroll flat on the table, and laid the Latin dictionaries across its top and bottom edges to keep it from rolling up again like a window shade. "There. What do we think?"

We peered down at the flattened scroll in silence. The memoir's second page was twice the width and nearly three times the length of the first page, and the writing on it was even smaller and more compact. The slanted downstrokes on the *F*'s and the odd curls appended to the *S*'s indicated to me that both pages had been written by the same hand — Gamaliel's.

The scroll featured two drawings, one at the beginning of the text and one at the end. The first depicted a tiny bird with a mask-like stripe across its eyes and a black ring around its neck. Amelia immediately identified it as a plover.

"Gamaliel must have included it," she said, "in case the person who found the second page hadn't yet discovered the first. The plover refers, of course, to Plover Cottage, where the first page was hidden."

"Well-reasoned," murmured Willis, Sr.

"The rector left a new clue as well," said the vicar, pointing to the second drawing. "What do you suppose it is?"

"A plant?" I suggested. "A stem with long, thin, oval leaves?"

"What are the three little circles at the bottom of the stem?" asked Lilian.

"Grapes?" Bree ventured.

"Grapevines don't have long, skinny leaves," I pointed out.

"Then what are the circles?" Bree retorted.

"Olives," said Willis, Sr. "The new clue appears to me to be an olive branch. The olive tree has attenuated leaves and the olive branch is an ancient Christian symbol with which the Reverend Gowland would have been familiar."

"I believe you've hit the nail on the head," said Amelia, nodding. "You're very good at this game, Mr. Willis."

"Thank you," said Willis, Sr., acknowledging the compliment with a courtly half bow.

"An olive branch," the vicar said slowly.

"Are there any olive branches in the church?" I asked.

"None," said Lilian.

Amelia turned to Bree. "Have you seen an olive branch in the bell tower?"

"No," Bree replied.

Brows were wrinkled, lips were pursed, and a ruminative silence permeated the room until Lilian cleared her throat.

"While we ponder the new glyph's meaning," she said briskly, "why don't we translate the text? Teddy reads Latin, as do I. Anyone else?"

Bree, Amelia, and I shook our heads, but Willis, Sr., raised his hand.

"I read both Latin and Greek," he said diffidently. "If I may be of some assistance . . ."

"Take a pencil and a pad of paper," said Lilian. "Let's get to work."

Amelia remained in the study to watch the scholars duke it out, but Bree and I repaired to the kitchen to make tea and sandwiches. Lunchtime had come and gone and if I was hungry, I was sure the others would be, too. While we plundered the Buntings' pantry, I told Bree about the Reverend Gamaliel

Gowland's secret memoir. By the time I finished, the food and drink were ready for distribution.

"Any guesses on where the olive branch leads?" Bree asked as we carried two heavily laden trays to the study.

"Ask me again after I've eaten," I replied. "I've been told that my brain doesn't function well on an empty stomach."

The vicar's eyes lit up when he saw the sandwiches, but Lilian wouldn't allow him or anyone else to eat until she'd slipped the scroll into a clear plastic bag to protect it from crumbs, drips, and sticky fingers. Once the bag was sealed, the trays and the teapot emptied rapidly.

The light meal seemed to stimulate our translation team. Bree and I returned from straightening the kitchen to find Lilian attempting to present Amelia with an English-language version of the memoir's second page.

"No, no," said Amelia, waving her off. "I wouldn't dream of stealing your thunder, Mrs. Bunting. You and the gentlemen did the work. One of you must read it to the rest of us."

"As I wrote it, I'd better read it," said Lilian. "I can read my handwriting, but I'm not sure Teddy or William can." She waited until we were all seated around the fire before explaining, "Teddy, William, and I followed Alfred's example and translated the Latin text rather loosely."

"It's a personal recollection, not a scholarly treatise," the vicar interjected. "We wanted it to sound . . . personal."

"In the first two sentences," Lilian continued, "the Reverend Gowland reiterates his hints about the trail of clues he left behind. He then goes on to say . . ." Lilian bent her head over the notepad and began to read aloud.

"Mistress Margaret Redfearn, spinster, known by all as Mistress Meg, dwelt in a wooden house she built with her own hands in a forest clearing. There she raised goats and her goats were to her like her children. Visitors often heard her speak to them, telling them to mind their manners, to come when called, to be less greedy, and many other things. She bartered goat's milk and cheese for the things she needed, but she needed little, for she was wise in wood-lore. Of root and bark, leaf and blossom she made potions, unguents, and tisanes, and those who went to her for help, she helped."

Lilian turned to the next page and looked up. "What follows is a list of the people Mistress Meg cured and their illnesses.

'Master Cobb's stertorous breathing, Mistress Bell's headaches, Farmer Hooper's stomach pains, Young Jonah's skin complaint' and so on. It's a rather extensive list. Shall I read it or skip ahead?"

"Skip ahead, please," Amelia said promptly. "If I hear a long list of illnesses, I shall begin to feel ill myself."

"Very well." Lilian flipped past the next page and resumed her narration. "Mistress Meg tended women in their time of pain and brought many children safely into the world. All this she did for no payment or reward nor did she look for praise or thanks or seek fellowship with her neighbors. She came not to the village save to barter milk and cheese and to help those who could not come to her." Lilian lowered the notepad. "There it ends."

"Good," I said. "If it went any further, I'd develop an inferiority complex."

"So would I," Amelia said, laughing. "No one could accuse Mistress Meg of frittering her time away in idle pursuits. She was a naturalist, a chemist, a doctor, a midwife, a carpenter, a goatherd, and heaven knows what else. Her range of knowledge was truly impressive."

"Impressive," Lilian acknowledged, "but also dangerous."

"Dangerous?" I said. "How?"

"An unmarried woman, living on her own, without a male relative's protection, would have been the exception rather than the rule in those days," said Lilian. "It's not always a good thing to be exceptional."

"In the seventeenth century both men and women believed that male sovereignty was ordained by God," said the vicar. "They may have tolerated independent noble-women, but they almost certainly would have frowned upon an independent peasant like Mistress Meg."

"Until she cured their tummy-aches," I observed tartly.

"They might have resented her all the more for curing them," said the vicar. "A powerful man would have found it rather vexing to be at the mercy of a seemingly powerless woman."

"Some believed," said Lilian, "that women like Mistress Meg derived their healing powers from Satan. If a patient lived, it was because the healer was in league with the devil."

"And if a patient died," the vicar contin-ued, "Mistress Meg would be accused of cursing rather than curing."

"So Mistress Meg would be in trouble whether her cures worked or not?" I said.

"Talk about a no-win situation."

"She was an outsider as well," Bree piped up. "Outsiders always arouse suspicion. Some of the looks I get from Peggy Taxman are positively poisonous."

"We all get those looks from Peggy Taxman," I assured her. "It has nothing to do with being an outsider."

"Bree makes a good point, though," said Lilian. "A woman who lived apart from the community could arouse suspicion, especially if she talked to goats. I'm sure you've all heard of a witch's familiar — a satanic spirit disguised as an animal. If a superstitious person heard Mistress Meg speak to her goats, he might have suspected her of witchcraft."

"Unfortunately," said Willis, Sr., "Mistress Meg would have reinforced those suspicions by refusing to attend church services."

"Gamaliel doesn't say a word about her churchgoing habits," I objected.

" 'She came not to the village save to barter milk and cheese and to help those who could not come to her,' " Willis, Sr., recited. "In other words, Mistress Meg came to Finch only to conduct business and to heal. She did not come to Finch to listen to the Reverend Gowland preach."

I looked at the scroll, sitting safely in its

plastic bag on the lamp-lit table. The story it told sounded innocent, even admirable, to modern ears, but a seventeenth-century reader might have regarded it as a damning indictment of a godless reprobate.

"It's as though the rector is building a case against her," Lilian said, staring pensively into the fire.

"I realize that Mistress Meg has been dead for several centuries," said Amelia, "but I fear for her nonetheless. She was an independent woman in a patriarchal world. She lived outside the prevailing social structure. She brewed potions, spoke with animals, and rejected conventional religion." Amelia bit her lower lip and glanced worriedly at the scroll. "I have a terrible feeling that the memoir's third page will contain a trumped-up charge of witchcraft."

"We won't know until we find it," I said. "Has anyone had a blindingly brilliant insight about the olive branch?"

"I don't know about blindingly brilliant," said Bree, "but I may have had an insight." She leaned forward, her elbows on her knees, her nose ring glinting in the firelight. "Gamaliel hid the first page near the church, in Plover Cottage, and the second page in the bell tower. He didn't stray too far from home, did he? So my idea is to check out the churchyard. I think some of the older headstones have olive branches on them."

"It's true," Lilian said, emerging from her pensive reverie. "They're so weathered they seem like abstract shapes, but they could be olive branches."

"We're not talking about grave robbing, are we?" I said, eyeing her uncertainly.

"Of course not," said Lilian. "The third page may be hidden inside a headstone, or the headstone may somehow direct us to another hiding place."

Bree jumped to her feet. "Shall we take a look at them now?"

Five older heads, including mine, swiveled in unison toward the waves of rain sluicing the French doors.

"Tomorrow, I think," said Amelia. "We'll be able to see the headstones more clearly after the storm passes. I propose that we reconvene in the churchyard at nine o'clock tomorrow morning, weather permitting."

"Fair enough," said Bree, "but wear your Wellies. The grass'll be sopping."

The Buntings and Willis, Sr., glanced toward the French doors again, then announced regretfully that, due to prior engagements, they would be unable to join Amelia, Bree, and me in the churchyard. I couldn't blame them for excusing themselves from the excursion. The prospect of traipsing through a graveyard on a damp October morning didn't fill me with delight, but my desire to find the memoir's third page was too strong to resist. Mistress Meg wouldn't have let a little wet grass dampen her spirits, I reasoned. I owed it to her to hang tough.

Lilian promised to search the parish archives for further information about Margaret Redfearn, then brought the meeting to a close. She and the vicar accompanied us to the foyer, where Willis, Sr., turned heads by offering to drive Amelia home in his Jaguar.

"You're very kind, Mr. Willis, but I'd rather walk," she said, throwing her yellow scarf around her shoulders and picking up her carpet bag. "It's no distance at all and I could do with a breath of fresh air."

I'd have accepted a lift to my car — my sneakers weren't designed to repel rain — but Willis, Sr., didn't offer one to me. He simply drove off by himself, leaving me to trudge through the tempest with Amelia, clamber squelchily into the Rover, and head for home. As I passed Fairworth's wrought-iron gates, I found myself wondering what the Handmaidens would make of a woman who'd turned down a drive with their dream date.

"If Amelia isn't careful," I said to the rearview mirror, "she'll have a whole new fan club."

TWELVE

I had no intention of boring Bill stupid with a blow-by-blow account of the day's events, but when he asked about them after dinner, I could hardly refuse to answer. A generous impulse prompted me to provide him with the highlights and to save the extended version for Aunt Dimity. As a result, I had the satisfaction of keeping my husband up to date without putting him into a coma, and I sailed into the study feeling like an exemplary wife.

Aunt Dimity, unlike Bill, wanted me to describe the day in excruciating detail and I was happy to oblige. By the time I finished telling her about the helpful Handmaidens, the church search, the bell tower's long-concealed secret, and the light it shed on Mistress Meg, my voice was hoarse.

"Well?" I croaked. "What do you think?"

I curled my legs beneath me as the familiar copperplate scrolled gracefully across the journal's blank page.

I must confess that the Mistress Meg portrayed by Gamaliel is not the Mistress Meg I envisioned.

"If you mean to say that Mistress Meg wasn't a horrible hag who maimed toddlers, I'm forced to agree with you," I said dryly. "Mistress Meg was a healer, not a hacker, Dimity. It would take a lot of distortion to transform her into Mad Maggie."

Perhaps Mistress Meg changed. The next page of the memoir may reveal her dark side. By the same token, it may reveal Gamaliel's dark side. As the local clergyman, his testimony would carry a great deal of weight in a witch trial. If he was, as Lilian suggested, building a case against Mistress Meg, his words may have led to an innocent woman's torture and execution.

"How could he be so cruel?" I asked, baffled. "How could he vilify a woman who delivered babies and helped sick people?"

Ignorance breeds fear and fear breeds cruelty. It's as true today as it was in Gamaliel's time. Open any newspaper and you'll find appalling instances of people railing against things they don't understand.

"Yet another reason to avoid newspapers. Newspapers," I repeated thoughtfully as the word sparked a fresh idea. "Are there written records of witch trials?"

Of course. Witch trials were formal court proceedings. They were recorded in much the same manner as other court proceedings.

"Imagine a civil court docket listing witchcraft along with grand theft and homicide." I snorted derisively. "The good old days, eh?"

For women like Mistress Meg they were more likely to be the grim old days.

"Maybe Lilian will find a record of Mistress Meg's witch trial in the church archives," I said. "I hope she does. I don't like waiting around and wondering whether or not Gamaliel Gowland sent Mistress Meg to the gallows."

If he did, you won't find her grave in the churchyard. Witches weren't buried in consecrated ground.

"Persecuted even after death," I said bitterly. "What a cheerful thought." I stretched my legs out on the ottoman and leaned back in my chair. "On a brighter note, I'm pleased to report that Amelia's as fond of old churches as I am. When William was escorting her though the graveyard, she told him that she and Alfred used to cycle for miles when they were young, exploring country churches."

If Alfred cycled for miles when he was

young, he must have become disabled later in life.

"The poor guy," I said, shaking my head. "Amelia makes him sound like an ideal big brother, Dimity. He introduced her to all sorts of cool stuff — Japanese films, Thai food, Indian music."

He must have spent a lot of time with her. Didn't he have any friends?

"He probably spent time with them, too," I said. "I think it's great that Alfred and Amelia got along so well. I can see why she was willing to turn her life upside down to complete his quest. If I'd had a brother like Alfred, I would have done the same thing."

She must have been pleased to find the memoir's second page so rapidly. I thought it would take weeks, perhaps months, to locate it.

"Teamwork," I said, nodding decisively. "That's the secret."

There was a pause, as though Aunt Dimity were contemplating her next comment, and when the handwriting continued, it flowed in carefully measured loops and curls.

I've never thought of William as a team player.

"Nor have I," I admitted. "He does like puzzles, though, and Gamaliel has provided him with a whole raftload of puzzles to solve."

Even so, William's willingness to join Amelia's team, to shelter her beneath his umbrella, and to drive her the ludicrously short distance from the vicarage to Pussywillows suggest to me that he may be under the spell of something other than the secret memoir.

"He's not under Mae Bowen's spell," I asserted, "because he still doesn't know that Amelia Thistle *is* Mae Bowen. I promised Bill I'd introduce them, but the right moment didn't present itself."

I strongly advise you to rescind your promise to Bill. I'm shocked that you made it in the first place. Amelia's secret isn't yours to share, Lori, nor is it Bill's. She must be allowed to reveal herself as Mae Bowen in her own good time. I doubt that it will make any difference whatsoever to William. If he's smitten by Amelia Thistle, he won't be put off by her alter ego.

"Smitten?" I said doubtfully. "William seems to like Amelia well enough, but I wouldn't describe him as smitten. He's not a love-at-first-sight kind of guy, Dimity. He thinks things through and through before he acts on them."

When the heart is engaged, the brain is frequently disengaged.

"Amelia hasn't given him the slightest encouragement," I pointed out. "She sort of patted him on the head when he deciphered the glyphs, but she paid more attention to Bree than she did to him."

William is accustomed to being hunted. He may prefer being the hunter.

A slow smile spread across my face and I gave a satisfied nod.

"As a matter of fact," I said smugly, "the same thought had occurred to me. I kept it to myself because I was afraid you'd accuse me of jumping to conclusions."

I've drawn no conclusions, Lori. I simply feel that the situation merits monitoring.

"Don't worry," I said, laughing. "Experience tells me that the entire village will monitor this particular situation." I glanced up as the mantel clock chimed eleven. "Time for me to hit the sack, Dimity. I want to be wide-awake among the headstones tomorrow."

An unusual aspiration, but an appropriate one, given the circumstances. Sleep well, my dear. Good luck finding the olive branch!

"Thanks," I said. "We'll need it."

As the curving lines of royal-blue ink faded from the page, I gazed contentedly into the fire. Distressed though I was by distant thoughts of Gamaliel's treachery and

Mistress Meg's gruesome demise, I simply could not keep myself from jumping to a few gleeful conclusions about Amelia and my father-in-law.

Amelia emerged from Pussywillows the following morning dressed for the great outdoors — a chunky blue turtleneck beneath a much-used rain parka, a pair of brown corduroy trousers tucked into mud-stained Wellington boots, and a tweed fishing hat into which she had tucked her flyaway hair.

"It's my tramping gear," she explained, noting my admiring glance. She looked over her shoulders, as if she were checking for eavesdroppers — a wise precaution in Finch — then said quietly, "A botanical artist can't do fieldwork wearing stilettos and a frock. Not that I ever wear stilettos — ridiculous things, designed by sadists for masochists — but I'm sure you take my meaning."

She hoisted her carpet bag onto her shoulder and we set out for the churchyard. Our attire was almost identical — hence, my admiring glance — except that I carried my necessities in a small day pack instead of a carpet bag and wore a hand-knitted woolen cap instead of a tweed hat.

The sky was gray, the air crisp, the cobbled lane plastered with rain-soaked leaves. The

only villager in sight was Millicent Scroggins, who was making her way to Taxman's
Emporium, a wicker shopping basket
hooked over one arm. When Amelia called a
friendly greeting to her, she responded with
a glacial nod and entered the Emporium
without a backward glance. Millicent's
aloofness puzzled me until Amelia dropped
her first bombshell of the morning.

"If you'd come to Pussywillows ten minutes ago, you would have bumped into your
father-in-law," she said. "Mr. Willis knocked
on my door before I'd finished breakfast."

The matchmaker in me snapped to attention.

"Did he?" I asked, trying very hard to
sound nonchalant.

"Yes," she replied. "He was on his way to
deliver a lecture in Oxford — something to
do with Anglo-Saxon law, I believe — but
he dropped by to present me with a guide
to local walking trails. He thought I might
find it useful."

"He's a thoughtful man," I said.

"He is," she agreed. "He invited me to
explore his property as well. He was especially keen to show me a rare orchid he
discovered on his estate." She came to a halt
and gave me a searching look. "You haven't
told him about Mae Bowen, have you?"

"Not a word," I said, relieved that I hadn't kept my promise to Bill.

"I just wondered . . ." She gazed at me a moment longer, then walked on. "He seemed to be aware of my passion for nature, you see, so I thought, perhaps, you might have let the cat out of the bag."

"I didn't," I stated firmly. "I had nothing to do with William's gift or his invitation. He thought them up all on his own." I glanced at Amelia's mud-stained boots and continued craftily, "A trail guide might seem like an odd gift, but William adores long walks through the countryside, so he assumes everyone does. And he's batty about orchids — his greenhouse is filled with them — so it would be natural for him to tell you about the ones he found in the woods at Fairworth."

"A greenhouse filled with orchids . . ." Amelia murmured. She lapsed into a short but dreamy silence, then heaved a sigh and peered at me contritely. "Forgive me, Lori. I've been betrayed so often that I've learned to mistrust people, but I shouldn't have doubted you."

"Why not?" I said. "You hardly know me. A little caution never hurt anyone, Amelia. But you don't need to be cautious with William," I added, spurred on by my inner matchmaker. "He's a retired attorney, you know. He used to be the head of his family's law firm. He's an expert secret keeper."

"Even so," said Amelia, "I can't afford to take Will — Mr. Willis — into my confidence. The fewer people who know my secret, the greater my chances are for a quiet life. And I crave a quiet life."

We arrived at the churchyard to find Bree Pym placing two identical bunches of bronze chrysanthemums on her great-grandaunts' graves. She was once again draped in her camouflage poncho, her spiky hair exposed to the elements.

"Aunties," she said as we approached, "here's the woman I was telling you about, the one who bought Pussywillows. Amelia? Allow me to introduce you to Auntie Ruth and Auntie Louise. They died the day after I met them, but they made a big impression. You would have liked them."

"I'm sure I would have." Amelia inclined her head toward the Pym sisters' headstone. "I'm very pleased to meet you, Auntie Ruth and Auntie Louise. Your niece is a perfect treasure."

"Great-grandniece," Bree corrected her, "but who's counting? And thank you for the kind words."

"It's nothing but the truth." Amelia smiled

back at Bree, then turned to survey our surroundings. "I wonder if Mistress Meg is buried here?"

"I'm pretty familiar with the churchyard," I said, "and I can't recall seeing Margaret Redfearn's name in it. Of course, if she was hanged as a witch," I continued, recalling Aunt Dimity's gloomy comments, "she wouldn't have been buried here. It was against the rules to bury witches in consecrated ground."

"Let's say she died of old age," Bree proposed.

"I prefer your version," I murmured.

"If Mistress Meg died of natural causes," Bree went on, "she might still be buried here. The inscriptions on seven headstones are too weathered to read. They're the ones Mrs. Bunting and I remembered, the ones that might be decorated with olive branches. Don't get your hopes up, though. I've taken another look at them and they're pretty far gone."

"We may be able to bring them back," said Amelia. She reached into her carpet bag and pulled out several large sheets of white paper and a handful of fat black crayons. "Have either of you ever done any brass rubbing?"

"I've read about it," said Bree. "It's a way

of copying brass plaques onto paper, isn't it?"

"That's right," said Amelia. "Engraved plaques were sometimes used as memorials or tomb markers. They were usually inlaid in a church's floor. Some are life-size and many are quite elaborate — engraved images of knights in armor, for instance, or ladies in wimples."

"Bill and I took the boys to a brass-rubbing center once," I put in, "but we didn't rub much brass. Will and Rob enjoyed it for about ten minutes, then started drawing great big pictures of their ponies."

"A true artist sticks to what he loves," Bree said, laughing.

Amelia flushed slightly and avoided Bree's eyes as she continued, "We can use the same technique to bring out the faded images on the grave markers. Take me to them and I'll demonstrate."

Bree led the way to a row of stumpy, lichen-dappled stone slabs that retained barely a trace of their original carvings. Amelia placed a sheet of paper flat against the face of the first slab, then rubbed a crayon gently across the paper in short, swift strokes. In seconds, an image began to appear.

"It's a cherub!" Bree exclaimed, as the

little angel's chubby face came into view. "And the olive branch isn't an olive branch."

"It's an angel's wing," I said with a sigh. "Ah, well. One down, six to go."

"Don't stop," Bree urged Amelia, who'd paused to take stock of her work. "I want to know if the cherub is hovering over Mistress Meg's name."

"As do I," said Amelia. "You and Lori can get to work on the other headstones while I finish this one."

In just over an hour, we had created legible images of everything carved on the weather-beaten grave markers of the Tolliver family — Hannah Tolliver, Josiah Tolliver, and their five children — all of whom had departed this earth in the year of our Lord 1653. Each child's headstone bore a winged cherub. The adults' featured winged skulls.

"Lots of feathers," I said, "but no olive branches."

"And no Mistress Meg," said Bree.

"Death's heads," said Amelia, pointing from one skull to the other. "Reminders of our mortality."

"Or reminders of human stupidity," I said. "If you hang the local doctor because you believe she's in league with the devil, sick people are a lot more likely to die."

"A whole family wiped out in one year," Bree said soberly. "It's a high price to pay for superstition."

Amelia rolled up our stone rubbings and deposited them carefully in her capacious carpet bag.

"We may not have found Gamaliel's olive branch," she said, closing her bag, "but I'm sure Mr. and Mrs. Bunting will be pleased to know about the Tollivers."

"Lilian may want to display our rubbings in the chu—" I broke off, startled, as Amelia gave a high-pitched yelp and flung herself to the ground.

"Amelia?" said Bree.

"Don't say my name," Amelia whispered. "And don't look at me."

"Okay," said Bree, turning her face to the sky.

Amelia crawled frantically to a wool merchant's rectangular tomb and huddled behind it, clutching her carpet bag to her chest and trying to make herself as small as possible.

"Is something wrong?" I asked, fastening my gaze on the lych-gate.

"No," Amelia replied acidly. "I *like* flopping in wet grass. *Of course something's wrong!*"

"Sorry," I muttered, reddening. "Can you

be more specific?"

"It's *him*," she said in an urgent undertone. "He's *here!* I just *saw* him!"

"Who's here?" I asked, bewildered.

"Myron Brocklehurst," Amelia answered venomously.

The morning's second bombshell burst on my brain like a thunderclap. I stiffened in alarm and scanned the churchyard alertly.

"I don't see him," I said.

"He's not *here*," she said impatiently.

"But you just said —" I began, but Amelia cut me off.

"He's in *Finch*," she whispered hoarsely. "He's at *Crabtree Cottage*. The men who live there *know who I am*."

Crabtree Cottage stood a little ways away from St. George's, on the opposite side of the green from the schoolhouse, but I could see its front door plainly from the churchyard.

"The men who live there won't give you away," I said quickly. "Grant and Charles can't stand the guy. They'll flick him off like a piece of lint."

"He fancies himself a spiritual leader," Amelia reminded me. "What if he visits the church?"

"You'll be gone by then," Bree said brightly. The girl couldn't possibly know who Myron Brocklehurst was or why Amelia Thistle wished to hide from him, but she could always be relied upon in a pinch. "I'll distract Mr. What's-It. You two hop the churchyard wall, sneak around to the back of the vicarage, and go through the French doors into the vicar's study. The doors are never locked."

"Can you manage it?" I asked Amelia.

Her eyes flashed as she said through gritted teeth, "I'd climb the Great Wall of China to escape Mr. Brocklehurst."

THIRTEEN

Bree's plan worked like a charm. She accosted Myron Brocklehurst when he emerged from Crabtree Cottage and kept him talking, with his back to St. George's, while Amelia and I fled the churchyard. Amelia had no trouble negotiating the low stone wall, but her trousers were soaked and her nerves were standing on end by the time we entered the vicar's study.

"Less than a week!" she cried, wringing her hands. "It took him less than a week to track me down!"

Privately, I agreed with her assessment of the situation. I was convinced that Myron Brocklehurst had discovered her general whereabouts and gone to our local art experts to learn the exact location of her new home, but it seemed inadvisable to tell her so while she was storming around the room and roaring like a caged lion.

"He hasn't tracked you down," I pointed out.

"He's *here!*" she exploded.

"He's in Finch," I acknowledged, "but he's at Crabtree Cottage, not Pussywillows. For all we know, he could be a client. He could have gone to Grant and Charles to have a piece of art restored or appraised. They're highly regarded in their professions."

"Are you trying to tell me that the founder of Bowenism — hateful word! — followed me to Finch *by sheer coincidence?*" Amelia demanded.

"Coincidences happen," I replied.

Amelia gave me a scathing look, then pressed a finger to her lips for silence.

Someone had opened the front door.

"Lori? Amelia?" Bree called from the foyer. "Guess who's back from visiting the sick!"

Amelia groaned, sank into a chintz armchair, and buried her face in her hands. A moment later, Bree strode into the study, followed closely by the Buntings.

I stared blankly at the newcomers, trying in vain to think of a way to explain Amelia's panic attack without mentioning Mae Bowen.

"Bree tells us that you and Mrs. Thistle

sought sanctuary in the vicarage," said the vicar, eyeing Amelia solicitously. "Is Mrs. Thistle unwell?"

I opened my mouth, but before I could put my foot in it, Lilian took charge.

"Lori, build a fire. Teddy, take Mrs. Thistle's coat and hat. Bree, help her to remove her boots, then tuck an afghan around her lap. I'll be back in a moment with tea." She raised an eyebrow and we jumped to obey.

"Are you feeling better, Mrs. Thistle?" the vicar asked.

A fire crackled in the grate. Amelia was bootless, hatless, coatless, and swathed in a red and black afghan Lilian had crocheted. Everyone except Amelia was staring at Amelia, who was staring at her cup of Earl Grey tea.

"Oh, yes, much better, thank you, Mr. Bunting," Amelia replied. "I must apologize for tracking mud all over your nice clean floor. I was in a bit of a tizzy when I came into the study."

"Why?" asked the vicar.

"Therein lies a tale." Amelia sighed dismally and went on, "The thing is, you see, I may have been a *teensy* bit dishonest with you about my true identity. I'm not an escaped convict, you understand," she

185

added hastily. "I am who I say I am. I simply haven't said who I am as fully as I might have done."

"A sin of omission," the vicar said gently.

"Precisely," said Amelia. "It's my own fault, of course. If I'd reinvented myself properly, I might have avoided . . ." She sighed again and tilted her head to one side. "But it's too late to repaint the canvas, I'm afraid. If the cat must come out of the bag, I may as well release it."

She placed her cup and saucer on a small table, spread her hands on the afghan, and proceeded to tell her rapt audience everything she'd told me at Pussywillows. She admitted to being the world-renowned botanical artist, Mae Bowen, described the Bowenist movement, and recounted how the Bowenists, led by Myron Brocklehurst, had encroached on her privacy, driven her into hiding, and made it virtually impossible for her to appear in public.

"I came to Finch to find the rest of Gamaliel Gowland's memoir," she concluded, "but I also hoped to rediscover what it is to live in peace. Hence, my rather feeble disguise. I was afraid to tell you the truth because —"

"You had good reason to be afraid," Bree interrupted. "Myron is creepy."

"Creepy?" I said.

"He talks in a soft little voice, but his eyes are like laser beams," Bree explained. "Cuckoo eyes we used to call them at school, the kind of eyes that scream: Fanatic!"

"Anything else?" I asked, thankful that Bree was such an observant young woman.

"His clothes aren't right," she replied promptly. "He dresses like a hippie — leather hat and sandals, fringed wool poncho, embroidered bellbottoms — but everything fits him too well and he's too neat, too clean. He has a pony tail and a mustache, yes, but they're trimmed and tidy when they should be shaggy and tousled. It's like he's posing for pictures at a sixties museum."

"A fanatic in designer rags," I murmured.

"Did he mention me?" Amelia asked.

"He did," Bree replied. "I told him the only Mae I knew lived in Christchurch, then talked his hind leg off about New Zealand. He tried to shut me up with his laser-beam eyes, but his looks bounced right off me. He finally gave up and climbed into his car, but before he scarpered he gave me a beginner's guide to Bowenism, written by none other than himself. Listen to this . . ." Bree pulled a bright yellow pamphlet from the back pocket of her jeans and read aloud:

Center yourself like the daisy's eye
Petals raised to the blue, blue sky
Live each and every hour in a blissful
    Bowen bower
And your heart and soul will flower, flow,
    and fly!

Bree finished her recitation with a hearty guffaw, but Amelia grimaced.

"The man should be locked up for crimes against poetry," Lilian declared vehemently.

"He should certainly be locked up for harassment," the vicar said more seriously.

"The problem is," said Amelia, "neither he nor his minions cross the line into outright harassment. They simply appear in vast numbers, gaze at me like a herd of damp cows, and ask endless questions about the universe, the search for truth, and whether vegetables should be eaten raw or cooked."

"Have you tried telling them to go away?" Lilian asked.

"I have," Amelia replied bitterly, "but I'd have better luck talking to cows. If you say 'shoo!' to a cow, it generally obeys. A Bowenist, on the other hand —" She gasped in alarm as the doorbell rang. "If it's him . . ."

"I'll see who it is," Lilian said calmly. "You have nothing to fear from unwanted callers, Mrs. Thistle."

"I almost feel sorry for Mr. Brocklehurst," the vicar commented idly as Lilian threw back her shoulders and marched out of the room. "My wife doesn't suffer fools gladly, Mrs. Thistle. If he turns his laser eyes on her, she'll be sorely tempted to blacken them."

"A sight I'd pay to see," said Amelia.

The suspense was killing me, so I tiptoed to the doorway and put my head into the hall. When I saw two familiar figures step into the foyer, I swung around and gave Amelia a reassuring thumbs-up.

"No worries," I said. "It's Grant Tavistock and Charles Bellingham."

"Your knowledgeable friends?" she inquired. "The connoisseurs who live in Crabtree Cottage?" When I nodded, she leaned back in her chair, murmuring, "Well, this should be interesting."

I'd just regained my own chair when Grant and Charles rushed into the study, spotted Bree, and crossed to stand before her. Lilian followed them into the room at a more leisurely pace, looking bemused.

"We'd like a word," Grant said to Bree.

"It's about the man you met coming out of our cottage," said Charles.

"Myron Brocklehurst," said Bree, nodding. "What about him?"

"What about him?" Charles exclaimed. "My dear girl, he's an intolerable tick!"

"We thought we'd gotten rid of him," said Grant. "Imagine our dismay when we saw you nattering away with him on our doorstep."

"You must never speak with him again," Charles said sternly. "For reasons we're not at liberty to divulge, we must insist that you —"

"It's all right, chaps," Amelia interrupted. "You can stand down. All has been revealed."

The two men wheeled around to face Amelia. Grant gaped at her in utter astonishment, but Charles stepped forward.

"Mrs. Thistle," he said, bowing low over her proffered hand. "Charles Bellingham, at your service. May I say what an honor it is to make your acquaintance?"

"You may," said Amelia, "but only once."

Charles chuckled immoderately and introduced Amelia to his partner, who seemed too overawed to speak for himself.

"Have you a bottle of sherry, Mr.

Bunting?" Amelia asked. "I believe Mr. Tavistock could use a pick-me-up."

"A brilliant suggestion," said Charles, bowing again to Amelia. "And so very considerate."

Grant was soon safely ensconced on the love seat with a small glass of dry sherry in his hand. Charles, however, continued to loom over us.

"Is it true?" he asked the room at large. "Has all been revealed?"

"Yes," I replied. "Including a vital piece of information you and Grant missed: Amelia Thistle is Mae Bowen's married name."

"Her married name!" Charles exclaimed, clapping a hand to his high forehead. "I should have guessed."

"I hope no one else does," Amelia muttered.

"And the Bowenist menace?" Charles asked. "Has it been explained?"

"It has," said Lilian.

"Then let me assure you, Mrs. Thistle," Charles said earnestly, "that Myron Brocklehurst learned nothing from us. We laughed at his suggestion that Mae Bowen might have settled in Finch, told him he was a gullible fool for believing such an absurd rumor, and sent him on his way."

"Thank you," Amelia said gravely.

191

"And what about the rest of us?" Charles said, using a tone of voice usually reserved for kindergartners. "Have we taken a vow of silence? Have we promised to protect and defend our new neighbor" — he bowed yet again to Amelia — "from Myron Brockle-hurst and his ilk?"

"Charles," I said testily, "if you don't stop bobbing up and down like a teeter-totter, we'll be forced to protect Amelia from *you*."

Grant let out a snort of laughter and Charles, blushing, retreated to the love seat.

"It goes without saying that we'll do what we can to maintain your anonymity, Mrs. Thistle," said Lilian.

"Does it?" Amelia said hopefully.

"Naturally," said the vicar. "Your secret is safe with us."

"Myron will run for his life if he sees me coming," said Bree, with an evil grin. "I have lots more to tell him about New Zealand."

"You're too kind," said Amelia, her face glowing. "First, you promise to help me with the memoir, then you offer to —"

"The memoir?" Grant said interestedly. "Are you writing a memoir, Mrs. Thistle?"

It took a while to tell Grant and Charles about the search for Gamaliel Gowland's secret memoir. Fortunately, Amelia had brought the first two pages with her, which sped the process up a bit.

"We did some major renovation work after we moved into our cottage," said Grant, examining the page we'd found in the bell tower, "but we didn't find a sheet of parchment hidden in our chimney."

"If we had," said Charles, "we would have framed it."

"What about the glyph?" I asked. "Does it mean anything to you? William thinks it's an olive branch."

While Grant and Charles studied the small drawing, Lilian turned to Amelia.

"How did you fare in the churchyard?" she asked. "Did you find another clue?"

"I'm afraid not," Amelia replied. "The carvings that might have been olive branches turned out to be feathers." She pulled the stone rubbings from her bag and passed them to Lilian, saying, "See for yourself."

Lilian unrolled the first sheet, surveyed the image, and nodded.

"The Tolliver family," she said. "I never thought to make rubbings of their headstones, but their burials are recorded in the church archives. They lived south of Finch, on a small farmstead that no longer exists. They were the only members of St. George's parish to die of the plague."

"The good old days," I said under my breath.

"May I keep the rubbings?" Lilian requested. "They'd make a splendid exhibition in the church. Visitors often ask who's buried beneath those sad and mysterious gravestones."

"Consider them donated," said Amelia.

"Has Mistress Meg surfaced in the archives?" Bree asked.

"Not yet," Lilian answered, sliding the roll of rubbings under her chair for safekeeping. "I've traced three Margarets living in Finch during the mid-sixteen hundreds, but none of them remained single. They lie buried beside their husbands in St. George's churchyard."

"Margaret Hazlitt, Margaret Green, and Margaret Waters," Bree recited. In response to a flurry of raised eyebrows, she explained, "I visit the aunties at least twice a week. I've gotten to know their neighbors."

"I'll keep looking," Lilian continued, "but so far I've been unable to verify Margaret Redfearn's birth, baptism, death, or burial. I wouldn't read too much into it, though. Some of Teddy's predecessors were better archivists than others, so our records aren't entirely reliable. Then again, Margaret Redfearn may have been born and buried in another parish."

"Have you found any reference to a witch trial?" I asked.

"No," Lilian replied, "but I wouldn't necessarily expect to find any. Witchcraft cases were prosecuted in borough courts and assizes as well as church courts, so she could have been tried somewhere other than Finch."

"There might be another explanation for Margaret Redfearn's absence from the archives," said the vicar. "If she was convicted of witchcraft, hanged, and buried in unsanctified ground, the Reverend Gowland might have chosen to purify his church by expunging her name from the records."

"Why would he create a secret memoir about a woman he'd expunged?" I asked.

"To justify the part he played in her death?" the vicar speculated. "The truth is, we won't know the answer until we find the rest of the memoir."

"Dove Cottage," Grant said suddenly.

"What?" I said, turning to him. I'd been so caught up in conversation that I'd forgotten about the two men on the love seat.

"Dove Cottage," Grant repeated, waving the memoir's second page in the air.

"Of course!" said the vicar, slapping his

knee. "I should have seen it immediately."

"What should you have seen?" I asked.

"Dove Cottage," Grant repeated insistently. "A dove brought an olive branch to Noah as a sign that the great flood was receding. Ergo, Gamaliel's olive branch could refer to Dove Cottage."

"Dove Cottage is one door down from Plover Cottage, where the first page was hidden," said the vicar. "They're both near the church. Gamaliel would have found it as easy to conceal a piece of parchment in one as in the other."

"Gentlemen," Amelia said excitedly, "you are brilliant! I'm quite sure you've cracked the code. Who lives in Dove Cottage?"

"Elspeth Binney," Charles informed her.

"Ah, yes," said Amelia, nodding. "The retired schoolteacher who enjoys bird watching and takes painting lessons from Mr. Shuttleworth in Upper Deeping."

"Correct in every particular," said Charles. "You've met her?"

"Mrs. Binney came to Pussywillows to lend a hand with the unpacking and we got to talking, the way one does with a new acquaintance," Amelia said. "Such a kind woman. She's bound to allow us to search her house. As a former schoolteacher, she'll find it intellectually stimulating."

As far as I knew, Elspeth Binney's intellect was stimulated primarily by gossip, but I kept my thoughts to myself.

"Unfortunately, Elspeth is away from home at the moment," said Grant. "She's visiting her niece —"

"The niece who lives in London and plays the violin or the niece who's married to the organic farmer with a smallholding in North Yorkshire?" Amelia asked.

"The London niece," Grant replied, clearly delighted by Amelia's display of local knowledge. "Elspeth's due home on Saturday — around noon, she told us."

"So be it," said Amelia. "What's a day's delay after four hundred years?"

It took us less than ten minutes to devise a plan. Charles and Grant agreed to bring our request to Elspeth after her return from London on Saturday afternoon. If she was amenable, they would ring Amelia, Bree, Lilian, and me, and we would converge on Dove Cottage to conduct the search. The vicar alone had to cry off because of a diocesan meeting in Cheltenham.

"We should invite Mr. Willis to join us as well," Amelia proposed. "He was instrumental in deciphering the first and second glyphs. He could be instrumental in finding the third page."

"He shall be invited." A calculating expression crossed Charles's face as he turned to address me. "Lori? Will you please ask William to be prepared to meet us at Dove Cottage on Saturday?"

I smiled inwardly. Everyone in the room, apart from Amelia, knew of Elspeth Binney's marital aspirations. It didn't take a razor-sharp mind to figure out that Charles intended to use my father-in-law as bait to secure Elspeth's cooperation.

"I'll ask him, Charles, but I can't guarantee that he'll come." I glanced furtively at Amelia as I added, "He usually spends Saturday afternoons in his greenhouse."

"You must lure him away from his greenhouse and onto the great stage of history," Charles said portentously. "I'm depending on you, Lori."

Amelia gathered the afghan into her arms and stood.

"If I might have my hat, coat, and boots, Mrs. Bunting, I'll be on my way," she said. "I've trespassed on your time — and on your property — long enough."

"Wait," I said, springing to my feet. "I'll make sure the coast is clear."

"So will I," said Bree.

"Dear me," Amelia said, regarding us affectionately. "Are you my new bodyguards?"

"No," Bree said gently. "We're your new friends."

Bree and I escorted Amelia to Pussywillows without incident, then went our separate ways. I went home to have a bite to eat, assemble a casserole for dinner, and make a few telephone calls, but I eventually ended up in the study, with my feet propped on the ottoman and the blue journal open in my lap.

Reginald was disturbed by the news of Myron Brocklehurst's arrival in Finch, but Aunt Dimity had seen it coming.

Well, it was inevitable, wasn't it? If Mr. Brocklehurst is half the fanatic I believe him to be, he would have compiled a comprehensive dossier of personal information about Amelia, derived from the rubbish he plucked from her dustbins. By studying discarded envelopes, letters, or bills, he could easily determine that Mae Bowen's married name is Amelia Thistle. It would then be a trifling matter for him to trace her movements by contacting removals companies or estate agents.

"If you're right," I said, "why didn't he go directly to Pussywillows? Why did he stop off at Crabtree Cottage?"

His information may have been incomplete or he may have misunderstood it. Whatever

199

*the case, we must assume he'll try again and
be prepared to meet him when he does.
Grant, Charles, and Bree dealt with him
admirably, but day-to-day improvisations won't
work in the long run.*

"No, they won't," I agreed. "We have to
figure out a way to rid ourselves of Myron
Brocklehurst permanently."

Any ideas?

"Loads," I said glumly, "but most of them
involve tar and feathers."

*Perhaps it would be best if you let me devise
a scheme. I'll give the Brocklehurst problem
my full attention while you focus on Dove Cottage. I suspect you'll be more successful there
than you were in the churchyard.*

"We eliminated the Tolliver headstones
from our investigation," I said, "but we
didn't accomplish much else today. Nor did
Lilian. The only thing her research has
shown so far is that Margaret Redfearn's
name is conspicuously absent from the
church archives."

Is her absence too conspicuous, I wonder?

"The vicar thinks Gamaliel censored the
records in order to cleanse the church of
the stain of witchcraft," I said. "But it
doesn't make much sense, does it? Why
would he go to all the trouble of removing
Mistress Meg from the church records, then

write a memoir about her in secret?"

It might make sense if Gamaliel were in love with Mistress Meg.

My jaw dropped.

It would be a case of forbidden love, of course, like Romeo and Juliet, only much darker. Gamaliel would have to conceal his feelings in public or risk losing his livelihood and quite possibly his life.

"But he gave vent to them in private," I said as my imagination took flight. "He couldn't keep his feelings bottled up, so he wrote about Mistress Meg in the dead of night, and he hid his writings because, though he couldn't love her openly in his lifetime, he wanted someone, someday to know about the rector and the witch." I heaved a wistful sigh. "If it isn't true, it should be."

I, too, would prefer a tragic love story to a horror story, but we shan't know which one is true until we find the rest of the memoir. Wasn't it clever of Grant to make the connection between the olive branch and the dove?

"I think the vicar wishes he'd made the connection," I said. "After all, the Bible is his bailiwick."

Theodore Bunting is too generous to begrudge Grant his moment of glory.

"He is," I acknowledged. "It's a pity he'll

have to miss the fun at Dove Cottage." Visions of true love danced in my head as I added, "Amelia wants William to be there."

Did she ask for him specifically? In front of everyone?

"Yep," I replied.

The Handmaidens will hear of it before nightfall and they will NOT be pleased.

"Millicent Scroggins has already given Amelia the cold shoulder," I said. "She must have seen William coming out of Pussywillows this morning."

What was William doing at Pussywillows?

"Courting Amelia in his own, understated way." I laughed. "He gave her a local trail guide, told her about his wild orchids, and invited her to explore his property."

Good grief. The Handmaidens have been angling for personal invitations to Fairworth ever since William moved in. I hope Amelia keeps hers under her hat. If word of her good fortune reaches Elspeth Binney's ears, Amelia may not be allowed to enter Dove Cottage, much less search it. Elspeth, as you know, has quite a few jealous bones in her body.

"Elspeth will roll out the welcome mat for us," I said, recalling the last telephone call I'd made before entering the study, "because William has volunteered to be a member of the Dove Cottage search team."

Well done, Lori! Elspeth may feel free to snub Amelia, but she won't turn William away.

"It was Charles's idea," I admitted.

Underhanded, but effective. As a matter of interest, has Amelia accepted William's invitation?

"Not yet, but she will," I said complacently. "She's fond of orchids."

FOURTEEN

A weak sun shone through the veil of high clouds covering the sky on Friday morning, but the temperature remained on the chilly side and the air felt as damp as a wrung sponge. Will and Rob were upstairs brushing their teeth and hunting for misplaced schoolbooks while Bill and I lingered over a second cup of tea at the kitchen table.

My husband seemed to be in a receptive mood and the boys were safely out of earshot, so I decided to voice an idea that had occurred to me in the night. Someone had to do something about Myron Brocklehurst, I told myself, and Aunt Dimity was in no position — literally — to stand up to him.

"Bill," I said, "would you do me a favor?"

"If you want me to run a background check on Myron Brocklehurst," he said, "I've already put the wheels in motion."

I blinked at him in surprise, then shook

my head wonderingly.

"You should trade in your law books and take up mind reading," I told him. "How did you know I wanted you to check up on Myron?"

"I didn't," said Bill, feeding Stanley a leftover scrap of bacon. "It was my idea."

"What prompted it?" I asked, intrigued.

"I saw Myron with Bree yesterday, in front of Crabtree Cottage," he replied, "and I didn't like what I saw."

"How did you know it was Myron?" I asked.

"Pure logic." Bill stroked Stanley's back to signal the end of treat time, then rested his elbows on the table and went on matter-of-factly, "Mae Bowen moves to Finch and two days later a solitary stranger appears, dressed like a latter-day flower child. Who else could it be but Mr. Bowenist himself, Myron Brocklehurst? I also found a photo of him on the Bowenist website," he added with a sly grin.

"So much for pure logic," I said, rolling my eyes. "What did you dislike about him?"

"His smile," said Bill. "His smug, superior smile. But I suppose driving a shiny red Ferrari would put a smile on any man's face."

"He has a Ferrari?" I said.

"A brand spanking new Ferrari," Bill clarified. "What kind of guru drives one of the world's priciest sports cars?"

"We already know he's rich," I pointed out.

"Yes," Bill said reflectively. "I wonder how he got that way? Don't worry, Lori," he went on. "I've made a few calls, sent a few e-mails. I'll let you know what I dig up."

"Thanks." I stacked Bill's breakfast plate on top of mine and gazed down at it for a moment before asking, "Has your father spoken to you about Amelia?"

"No," he said. "Why? Is she throwing herself at him?"

"Guess again," I said.

Bill stared at me in disbelief. "*He's* throwing himself at *her?*"

"I wouldn't say he's throwing himself at her," I said, "but he certainly appears to be leaning in her direction."

"Does he know she's Mae Bowen?" Bill asked.

"No, and we're not going to tell him," I stated flatly. "It's Amelia's secret, not ours."

"You're right," said Bill, changing his tune without missing a beat. "It's better this way. If he falls for Mae Bowen as Amelia Thistle, she'll be certain it's because of who she is, not what she does. How is she responding to his advances?"

"Early days yet," I said.

"She's keeping her distance, eh? Good for her." Bill reached across the table and put his hand on mine. "I realize that it won't be easy for you, love, but try not to meddle. Allow events to unfold at their own pace, even if they don't unfold at all."

There was no point in pretending that I didn't understand what Bill meant — he knew me too well — so I bit back a phony protest and nodded my assent.

"But keep me informed," he added, "because Father won't." He leaned back in his chair and smiled as his gaze turned inward. "I hope it works out, Lori. He hasn't looked at another woman since Mother died. She wouldn't have wanted him to be alone for so long."

I took Will and Rob to school, then whistled my way through a lengthy list of chores, knowing that the more housework I finished on Friday, the less guilt I'd feel for spending Saturday afternoon at Dove Cottage. Apart from that, Bill had brightened an otherwise dull day by responding so well to my news about Willis, Sr. A lesser man might have been troubled by it, but Bill's heart was big enough to embrace his father's return to the land of the loving.

I was folding a minor mountain range of clean laundry in the master bedroom when Amelia called.

"They've arrived," she said tersely. "I can see them from my front room."

"How many?" I asked. I didn't need to ask who "they" were.

"Seven," she replied. "Three men and four women. I recognize them. They're the same yahoos who crashed Walter's funeral."

"Is Myron with them?" I asked.

"No," she said, "but they must be following his orders. They're going from door to door. I'm sure they're looking for me."

A tower of socks toppled onto a snoozing Stanley as I sank onto the bed, thinking hard. I wasn't concerned about the Handmaidens because they wouldn't be around to answer leading questions posed by the Bowenists. Elspeth would still be in London, visiting her niece, while Millicent, Opal, and Selena would be in Upper Deeping, attending their Friday morning art class with Mr. Shuttleworth.

The villagers who were at home, however, would find it hard to resist a friendly invitation to chat about their newest neighbor. Left to their own devices, they would lead the fanatic cohort straight to Pussywillows.

"Okay, Amelia," I said. "Stay calm, keep away from the windows, and don't answer the door."

"I'm not a complete fool," she snapped. "I may be inept at inventing names, but I know how to hide from a pack of lunatics."

"Sorry," I said. "I'll get to the village as fast as I can."

I abandoned the laundry, flew down the stairs, snatched my rain jacket from the coat rack, and paused. It seemed foolhardy to face a pack of lunatics unarmed, so I dashed to a drawer filled with loose photographs, stuffed my pockets with old photos of Will and Rob, and ran for the Rover. If Bree's New Zealand monologue could force Myron Brocklehurst to flee, I reasoned, a pocketful of baby pictures — and their attendant stories — would make his minions wish they'd never come to Finch.

Cackling wickedly, I drove up the lane at a speed that would have made Bill cringe, but I slowed to a crawl when I reached the humpbacked bridge and stopped at its apex to take in the view. To judge by what I saw, I could have left the family snaps at home because my neighbors seemed to have things well in hand.

George Wetherhead stood at the back end of a rusting, daisy-stickered camper van that had been parked smack-dab in the middle of the village green. George appeared to be recording the vehicle's tag number on a pad of paper, while Mr. Barlow stood with Buster, his cairn terrier, at the van's front end, haranguing a paunchy, balding man who was, presumably, the van's driver.

I could scarcely believe what my eyes were telling me, so I opened my windows and rolled forward at a snail's pace to listen in.

"Have you left your brains at home or were you born stupid?" Mr. Barlow bellowed. "My dog would know better than to park a van on grass after a heavy rain. Who's going to repair the ruts you've made? I'll tell you, shall I?" He thrust a thumb toward his own chest. "Me! That's who! But you never thought of me when you pulled in, did you? Never think of anyone but yourself, I'll wager."

The paunchy man mumbled words I couldn't hear, but Mr. Barlow's response clarified what had been said.

"*You?* Help *me?*" Mr. Barlow scoffed. "And spoil your pretty hands? I doubt you've ever done an honest day's work in your life." He rapped his knuckles on the van's windscreen. "What do you think you're doing driving this deathtrap anyway? Bald tires, squealing brakes, blue smoke pouring from the exhaust pipe — unsafe at any speed, I'd say. Your old banger will keep my good friend Constable Huntzicker busy writing citations for quite some time when he gets here, which he will do very soon because I called him ten minutes ago to report you for illegal parking. When he sees what you've done to our green . . ."

Sally Pyne, meanwhile, stood on the teashop's doorstep, responding to an allegation that had turned her pleasantly pink face beet-red with indignation.

"Me? Exploit animals?" she retorted, as the young blonde who'd evidently made the accusation shrank away from her. "I'll have you know that my cream comes from the happiest herd of cows this side of heaven. Grass-fed, tucked up warm at night in a spotless barn, milked as gentle as you please. The pigs for my bacon don't volunteer to be slaughtered, I'll grant you, but they're treated like members of the family until their day comes and then they're put down quick and clean, which is a better end than most humans can bank on, believe me. I know my suppliers, missy, and I know how well they treat the creatures in their care, so don't you tell me I'm part of the systematic degradation of the planet. I'll have you know . . ."

As I cruised slowly past the schoolhouse, I heard Henry Cook inform a red-haired woman in a puffy down jacket that it was illegal to pin a poster on the notice board without the parish council's written permission and that anyone caught doing so would be subject to prosecution and a hefty fine. Since I'd pinned numerous notices on the board without asking for anyone's permission, Henry's words came as news to me, but I wasn't about to get out of the car and contradict him.

Eager to hear more, I rounded the green's north end and drove up the other side, pausing at Peacock's pub to watch Dick Peacock use his imposing bulk to hasten the exit of a young couple dressed in matching bellbottoms and denim jackets.

"Herbal tea?" he was saying. "Think I was born yesterday, do you? If you've been drinking herbal tea, then I'm a ballet dancer. I don't know what you've got inside you, but I doubt it's legal because your pupils are pinwheels and you're talking daft." He spread his arms wide as if to emphasize his prodigious girth. "Do I look like a daisy? *Pah!*" He flapped a hand at them dismissively. "My friend Constable Huntzicker will have something to say about your *herbal tea* when he gets here from Upper Deeping, which he should do quite soon because my good wife is ringing him right now."

While the young couple beat a hasty retreat to the van to confer with the redhead, the young blonde, and the paunchy driver, Peggy Taxman burst out of the Emporium, dragging a scrawny, gray-haired man after her.

"Mention my petals once more and I'll have you up on a charge of public indecency," she thundered. "A man of your age should know better than to speak of such things to a lady. My petals are no one's business but my husband's and if you know what's good for you, you'll make yourself and your nasty leaflets scarce before he comes out here and bloodies your nose."

Had the gray-haired man been familiar with Peggy's husband, he would have recognized how profoundly hollow her threat was. Jasper Taxman would no more bloody a man's nose than he would speak curtly to his formidable wife, but the stranger took Peggy at her word and sprinted for the van.

I stopped snickering long enough to count heads and realized with a jolt of apprehension that only six Bowenists were clustered around the van. I craned my neck to find the missing minion and gasped in alarm when I saw a pale-faced brunette in a gypsy skirt and a bulky red sweater raise her fist to knock on Amelia's door.

I cut the engine, leaped from the Rover, and raced across the green, but I was still ten yards away from Pussywillows when my father-in-law opened the front door. Astonished, I skidded to a halt in a pile of wet leaves and waited with bated breath to see how he would handle a direct frontal assault on Amelia's unsafe haven.

"May I help you?" he asked politely.

"I hope so," said the brunette. "My friends and I are looking for a woman who recently moved to your village. Her name is Mae Bowen, but she sometimes calls herself Amelia Thistle."

"And your name is . . . ?" Willis, Sr., inquired.

"Daffodil Deeproots," the brunette replied with a tranquil smile.

"How very floral," Willis, Sr., observed. "Is Daffodil a family name or have you adopted it informally?"

"I am a child of the sun and the earth," Daffodil answered, "and I was christened by the rain." She batted her eyelashes at Willis, Sr. "My spirit guide told me I would find Mother Mae here. Be a lamb and bring her out, won't you? Her children crave her wisdom."

"Your spirit guide is misinformed, Ms. Deeproots," said Willis, Sr. "I do not know Mae Bowen, nor do I know where she lives. I do, however, know Constable Huntzicker and I would advise you and your companions to leave Finch before he arrives. I have overheard my neighbors' accusations and I can assure you that the constable takes a dim view of those who drive poorly maintained vehicles, flout parking regulations, imbibe illegal substances, post bills without permits, distribute offensive literature, and practice deception by using assumed names. Good day, Ms. Deeproots," he concluded pleasantly and closed the door in her face.

Daffodil's serene smile faltered. She shuffled her feet indecisively, then looked over her shoulder. When she saw her confederates huddled in the van, she trudged across the green to join them.

After a great deal of backing and forthing, accompanied by a chorus of catcalls from disgruntled onlookers, the paunchy driver managed to extricate his vehicle from the rain-softened ground. He'd evidently taken the villagers' threats to heart, because he headed for the Oxford road instead of Upper Deeping, to avoid a possible run-in with the law. He couldn't have known — and no one had deigned to tell him — that Consta-

215

ble Huntzicker was enjoying a well-earned holiday in Majorca.

I waited for the van to cross the bridge, then darted over to Pussywillows and tapped on the front door until Willis, Sr., opened it and invited me in. He waited for me to kick off my damp sneakers and perch on the edge of the tweed-covered love seat before lowering himself into the armchair opposite Amelia's. The items on the coffee table — a teapot, a pair of teacups, and a few slices of buttered brown bread on two crumb-littered plates — suggested that he had been there for some time.

"Would you like a cup of tea?" Amelia inquired.

"No, thanks," I said, eyeing her uncertainly.

"You must sample Mrs. Thistle's brown bread," Willis, Sr., urged. "I do not exaggerate when I say that it is by far the best brown bread I have ever tasted."

"You're too kind, Mr. Willis," said Amelia.

"Not at all," said Willis, Sr.

"Mr. Willis arrived mere seconds after I rang you, Lori," Amelia explained, topping up Willis, Sr.'s cup. "He brought a lovely orchid to brighten my empty windowsill. Little did he know that he would be called upon to bar the gate to barbarians."

"Have you . . . ?" I wasn't sure how to pose my question, so I left it dangling.

"Have I introduced myself properly to your father-in-law?" Amelia placed the cherry-red teapot on the table and clenched her hands together in her lap. "I was on the verge of doing so when I was distracted by the rumpus on the green. It sounded as though World War III had begun, so of course I crept to the window to find out what was going on and once there I couldn't tear myself away. In the end it proved to be a delightfully one-sided battle, with my neighbors vanquishing all who stood before them. Then Daffodil came to the door and . . . and rendered my introduction superfluous." She bit her lower lip and looked shyly at Willis, Sr.

"Are you Mae Bowen?" he asked.

"I am," she replied, lowering her eyes.

"My late wife commissioned you to paint a watercolor for me," he said.

Amelia looked up, an arrested expression on her face. She gazed intently into Willis, Sr.'s gray eyes, then nodded.

"Jane Willis," she said. "Spring crocuses in the snow."

"Yes," he said softly. "Thank you."

The silence that followed had more layers than a wedding cake. I sat stock still and pretended to be invisible, but I needn't have bothered. Amelia and Willis, Sr., were in a world of their own. As far as they were concerned, I *was* invisible.

The magic moment ended when a mighty fist crashed against the front door.

"I'll get it," I said, jumping to my feet. "If it's Daffodil, I'll give her a good pruning."

The mighty fist did not belong to Ms. Deeproots, however, but to Peggy Taxman, who stood, arms akimbo, at the head of a small but determined-looking delegation that included Sally Pyne, Henry Cook, Dick Peacock, George Wetherhead, Mr. Barlow, and Buster.

As I searched my mind for an appropriate greeting, each member of the delegation — except for Buster — held up a bright yellow leaflet, which they opened simultaneously to reveal black-and-white portrait photographs identical to the ones I'd seen in the brochures advertising Mae Bowen's exhibitions.

"Someone," Peggy boomed, "owes us an explanation."

FIFTEEN

"We wish to see the lady of the house," Peggy thundered. "And we wish to see her *now.*"

There was no pruning Peggy Taxman. Postmistress, business owner, and chair of the all-important village affairs committee, Peggy ruled Finch with an iron hand, a stentorian voice, and an imposing physique. Though she wore flowery dresses and pointy, rhinestone-studded glasses, she behaved like a human bulldozer, flattening anyone foolish enough to stand in her way.

Since I wanted to see my sons grown to manhood, I stood aside.

The delegation swept past me and into the front room, where they fanned out behind the love seat and peered avidly from their leaflets to Amelia, as if to confirm their suspicions. I scuttled in after them to hover near the fireplace while their fearless leader planted herself in front of the love seat, folded her meaty arms, and surveyed the lady of the house from head to foot. Peggy took great pride in her gossip-gathering skills. She would have been irked to discover that a particularly tasty tidbit had escaped her notice.

"Either you have an identical twin," she roared, "or you've been playing games with us, Mrs. Whoever-You-Are. Which is it?" She brandished a threatening index finger at Amelia. "The truth, this time, and make it snappy. I don't know how it is where you come from, but we're honest, law-abiding folk around here and we don't appreciate being lied to."

Willis, Sr., flew from his chair as if catapulted and placed himself between Peggy and Amelia. Though Peggy could have snapped him in two over her knee, the fire in his eyes forced her to fall back a step.

"You will speak courteously to Mrs. Thistle," he said evenly, "or you will leave."

"If she's attracting undesirables to our village," Peggy declared, "we're within our rights to question her."

"You are not questioning her," Willis, Sr., countered. "You are badgering her. I will not permit —"

"Thank you, Mr. Willis," Amelia intervened. "I'd prefer to speak for myself."

"As you wish," said Willis, Sr., but he shot another fiery glance at Peggy before returning to his chair.

"I won't attempt to refute Mrs. Taxman's allegation," said Amelia, looking from one villager to the next, "because it's true: I haven't been entirely forthright with any of you. I can only apologize most sincerely and hope that the reason for my dishonesty will make sense to you, once you've heard it."

Amelia then displayed an uncanny understanding of Finch's power structure by surrendering to Peggy's demands. She told the truth and she made it snappy by presenting a remarkably succinct account of who she was and why she'd moved to Finch, complete with props — the memoir's pages — and affirming nods from her backup band — Willis, Sr., and me. When she finished, she lowered her eyes and meekly awaited the villagers' verdicts. Surprisingly, given the fact that Peggy Taxman was in the room, Mr. Barlow was the first to speak.

"Well, I'm blowed," he said, pushing his tweed cap back and scratching his head. "A world-famous artist, here in Finch, with zealots chasing after her while she chases after a rector's secret scribbles about a witch." He gave a short bark of laughter. "If you hadn't shown us those old bits of parchment and if I hadn't met those lunkheads with the van, I'd say you were making it all up, Mrs. Thistle."

"I'm not," said Amelia. "Have any of you found a similar piece of parchment hidden in your homes?"

Heads were shaken and noes were muttered with an unmistakable air of regret. No one, it seemed, liked to be left out of a treasure hunt.

"It must be unpleasant to be pursued by such persistent admirers," George Wetherhead observed thoughtfully.

"Unpleasant?" Sally Pyne scoffed. "If a pack of pea-wits was pestering me, I'd plaster them with cream pies, straight to the noggin."

"You'd be wasting good pies," said Henry Cook.

"You'd be arrested for assault," said George Wetherhead.

"Maybe," Sally retorted, "but I'd make my point."

"Seems to me they're the ones should be arrested," Dick Peacock grumbled. "Breaking in on your husband's funeral, and you with a handicapped brother to tend? It's outrageous!" He stuck his thumbs in his massive waistcoat and jutted his bearded jaw pugnaciously. "If I'd been there, I'd've taught 'em a thing or two about respecting a woman's privacy."

"I'm with Dick," said Henry. "They may call it devotion, but it's stalking, plain and simple."

"You're amazing, all of you," Amelia marveled. "I inform you that your quiet village may be disrupted at any moment by a band of pseudo-holy hooligans and you respond by worrying about *me*."

"Oh, we enjoy a bit of disruption now and again," Dick assured her. "Keeps the blood circulating, doesn't it?"

"I'd like another chance to educate that self-righteous little blonde," Sally said with relish.

"Don't you fret, Mrs. Thistle," said Mr. Barlow, bending to scratch Buster's ears. "If they come back again, we'll send 'em packing. You're one of us now, and we look after our own."

"Mae Bowen," Peggy murmured, sinking onto the love seat. Since Peggy rarely murmured, her words silenced the ongoing chatter more effectively than a cannon's blast. "My mother and I went to a Mae Bowen exhibition in London once. I'd never seen such loveliness. The sunflowers were like old men on a bench by the seaside, basking in the warmth. The poppies were like children laughing. The damask rose was an old, old woman remembering her first dance."

The rest of the villagers exchanged bewildered glances, but I understood what had softened Peggy's voice and touched her soul. Mae Bowen's paintings, I thought, could turn a tyrant into a poet.

"I'm sorry I was short with you, Mrs. Thistle," Peggy said, eliciting sharp intakes of breath from those who'd heard her apologize about as often as they'd heard her murmur. "I don't blame you for deceiving us," she went on. "You lied to protect yourself from people who'd destroy what they pretend to worship. And you weren't just trying to protect yourself. You were trying to protect the gift God gave you." Peggy nodded solemnly. "Like Mr. Barlow said, we'll do what we can to keep the bloodsuckers at bay, but *you're not making it easy for us!*"

Peggy's bellow made Amelia jump, but the villagers relaxed, as if they welcomed a return to normalcy.

"I . . . I'm n-not very adept at c-clandestine operations," Amelia stammered. "Using my married name was a stupid thing to —"

"Your name isn't the problem," Peggy

interrupted. "Your choice of guests *is*."

"My choice of guests?" Amelia repeated uncomprehendingly.

"I've seen William pop in and out of your house like a jack-in-the-box," said Peggy, eyeing her shrewdly, "and if I've seen him, others have, too."

"What others?" asked Amelia.

"Four others," Sally announced, her blue eyes glinting with mischief.

Willis, Sr., stood abruptly. His cheeks were flushed and he looked at no one but Amelia.

"Forgive me, Mrs. Thistle," he said stiffly. "I should have foreseen the difficulties my presence might create for you. Had I been thinking clearly, I would have been more circumspect. As it is, I have been unpardonably myopic." He winced and put a hand to his brow, as if his head ached. "My neighbors will, I am certain, elucidate the situation. If you will excuse me . . ." He made a crisp half bow and left the cottage without uttering another word.

"Will someone please tell me what's going on?" Amelia cried, staring after him in dismay. "Everyone in Finch must know that Mr. Willis is a perfect gentleman. Why should his presence in my home create difficulties for me?"

Sally Pyne scampered around the love

seat, plopped herself onto Willis, Sr.'s vacant chair, and leaned eagerly toward Amelia, looking as though Christmas had come early.

"It's those four cats who helped you to unpack," she said. "You remember? Millicent, Elspeth, Selena, and Opal?"

"Of course I remember them," said Amelia. "They were extremely kind to me."

"They were taking your measure," Mr. Barlow observed, sitting on the arm of the love seat. "Sizing up the competition."

"The competition?" Amelia said faintly.

"William's never once paid any of them a visit," said Sally, "but he's beaten a path to your door nearly every day since you arrived. He may give them a nod in passing, but he's given you a book and one of his pet orchids and who knows what else? Don't you see, Mrs. Thistle? They're full up to the brim with jealousy!"

"Jealousy?" Amelia exclaimed, looking appalled.

"They're green-eyed cats," said Mr. Barlow, "with delusions of grandeur."

"Each one of 'em wants to get her feet under William's table," said Dick, "and crown herself queen of Fairworth House."

"Rich widowers are thin on the ground in

Finch," Henry explained. "William's quite a catch."

"He's also out of reach," Sally stated flatly, "but nothing will persuade their ladyships to lower their sights."

"Hope springs eternal," said George Wetherhead.

"It did," Sally allowed sardonically, "until Mrs. Thistle came to town and swept William off his feet."

"I've done no such thing," Amelia protested.

"Whether you've done it or not is beside the point," roared Peggy, seizing control of the conversation. "It's what folk believe that counts. Millicent, Elspeth, Selena, and Opal believe you're a threat, Mrs. Thistle. If they can get rid of you, they will. You can't depend on them to keep their flapping mouths shut when the cult nuts come back. They'll shop you to the petal pushers quick as blinking. They'll see it as a heaven-sent opportunity to drive you out of Finch and away from William."

Looking stricken, Amelia rose to her feet and crossed to the mantel, where she stood with her back to the room, twisting her hands together and gazing at the silver-framed photograph of her late husband. I couldn't imagine what was going through her mind. My neighbors had dropped an awful lot into her lap all at once. If I'd been in her shoes, my brain would have been reeling.

"I can speak with Millicent and the others," Peggy offered, "but I doubt they'll listen, even to me. It's like the Good Book says, Mrs. Thistle. Jealousy is as cruel as the grave."

Amelia's hands fell to her sides. She drew herself up to her full and inconsiderable height and turned to face Peggy, Sally, Henry, Dick, George, Mr. Barlow, Buster, and me. She seemed composed and oddly determined, as if she'd made a momentous decision and would act upon it, regardless of the consequences.

"No, thank you, Mrs. Taxman," she said calmly. "I'll speak with the ladies myself. I'll go to each of them this afternoon, as soon as they return from their art class, and I will explain to them that I do not intend ever to remarry. Once they realize that I have no . . ." Her brow wrinkled briefly as she searched for the right words, then smoothed as she found them. ". . . no *matrimonial ambitions* with regards to Mr. Willis, I'm sure they'll continue to be as helpful to me as they were when I first arrived in Finch."

"Elspeth Binney isn't here," said Dick Peacock. "She's staying in London with her niece. She won't be back until tomorrow."

"Don't you worry about Elspeth," Sally said sagely. "Millicent, Opal, and Selena have her number in London. They'll fight for the chance to break the good news to her. If I know them, they'll be on the phone to her before Mrs. Thistle is halfway home."

"Will you tell them the rest of it?" Mr. Barlow asked Amelia. "About you being Mae Bowen and the witch's tale and the parchment pages and all?"

"Of course." Amelia smiled ruefully. "I expect they'll be relieved to know that I came to Finch to find something other than a husband."

SIXTEEN

I left Pussywillows with the others, but I didn't stick around to hear them review the morning's revelations. Instead, I hopped into the Range Rover and drove to Fairworth House.

I was worried about Willis, Sr. I didn't know whether he'd be upset with me for failing to tell him about Mae Bowen or with himself for making her the object of lurid local speculation or with the villagers for treating his private life like a public spectacle, but I knew he'd be upset about something and I didn't want him to be alone.

Deirdre Donovan answered the door, dressed as always in a pristine white shirtdress to which she had added a fitted black blazer, presumably to ward off the autumn chill.

"Where's William?" I asked.

"He's catching up on some paperwork in

the study," she replied. "He asked not to be disturbed."

"I thought he might," I said uneasily.

"Why?" Deirdre bent closer to me and lowered her voice. "Has something happened that I should know about?"

"Affairs of the heart," I told her. "*His* heart."

Deirdre's eyes opened wide with surprise, but a delighted smile curved her lips as she said, "How wonderful!"

"I hope so," I said anxiously and headed for the study.

I found Willis, Sr., seated behind his walnut desk in the window-lined room, fountain pen in hand, poring over the papers in a slim file folder. He acknowledged my entrance with a faint smile that vanished instantly as he returned his attention to his work.

"I can see that my request for privacy has been ignored," he observed, without looking up.

I shrugged. "Privacy is overrated."

"Mrs. Thistle," he murmured, "would disagree with you."

"William?" I said, approaching the desk cautiously. "Are you okay?"

"I have been a consummate fool and I have made an utter mess of things," he replied, putting a line through one sentence and circling another, "but I will survive." He gestured for me to take a seat in a chair facing the desk, but continued to annotate the papers as he observed, "The group discussion that followed my departure from Mrs. Thistle's residence was, I have no doubt, both lively and informative."

I gulped, cleared my throat, and chose my next words so carefully that I ended up sounding like a pompous college professor.

"It gave Amelia a better understanding of the, uh, social dynamics in the village," I said, "and it opened her eyes to the, um, absurd fantasies entertained by certain members of the community."

"In other words, Mrs. Thistle knows that the Handmaidens have declared war on her," said Willis, Sr., "because of me."

"Well . . . yes," I admitted reluctantly. I'd never heard my father-in-law refer to his admirers as "the Handmaidens." Only the deepest kind of distress could have induced him to use a phrase he considered discourteous and demeaning.

"I should have known that I would be under constant observation in the village," he said, still gazing down at the papers. "I should have known what effect my behavior would have on the Handmaidens. Finally, I should have known the extent to which their disapproval of my behavior would jeopardize Mrs. Thistle's safety and security." His lips tightened as he closed his eyes. "I find it hard to forgive myself for forgetting the many things I should have known."

"William," I said imploringly, but he shook his head and I fell silent.

A moment passed, during which my heart bled for him, then he sat erect, gathered the papers together, and tapped them on the desk to straighten them.

"I will rectify my errors, Lori," he said brusquely, inserting the papers into the file folder. "I shall see to it that Mrs. Thistle will not have to pay for my mistakes."

"Will you come to Dove Cottage tomorrow?" I asked.

"I think not," he replied, still fiddling with the file. "Mrs. Thistle will be ably assisted by you, Mrs. Bunting, and the others. She will not require my help to find or to translate the third page of the Reverend Gowland's memoir." He laid the file folder aside and met my gaze with one so penetrating that I jerked back in my chair. "How long have you known that Mrs. Thistle is Mae Bowen?"

"Since Tuesday," I mumbled miserably. "I promised Grant and Charles I wouldn't tell anyone but my husband."

"One must keep one's promises." He opened the file folder. "Forgive me, Lori, but I must attend to some rather pressing business."

I accepted my dismissal and slipped quietly out of the study, feeling as though I'd slapped a wounded man.

I returned to the cottage, trudged forlornly into the study, took Reginald from his special niche on the bookshelves, and hugged him. I was in dire need of comfort.

"Everything's gone wrong, Reg," I whispered into his pink flannel ear. "Everything!"

As I put him back in his niche, the gleam in his black button eyes seemed to hint that I might be overstating the case, but I wasn't so sure. The trouble with falling in love, I reflected, is that you quite often fall on your face. Willis, Sr., was as bruised and battered as I'd ever seen him.

I carried the blue journal to one of the tall armchairs before the hearth and curled up with it in my lap. I heaved a dolorous sigh as I opened it, but before I could speak, Aunt Dimity's handwriting raced across the page.

I've devised a scheme for scuppering Myron

Brocklehurst! How many times have we seen self-annointed spiritual leaders brought to book for financial malfeasance? How many times have they asked for tithes or gifts or donations from their flock, then pocketed the income? I can think of a dozen instances off the top of my head and I'm sure you can think of many more.

"Dimity?" I sensed where she was going and tried to head her off, but the handwriting did not stop.

It will not surprise me one iota to learn that our prophet, like so many before him, is making a profit. Imagine how rapidly the faithful will fall away when they find out that their high priest is nothing more than a money-grubbing charlatan who's been fattening his own calf at their expense! I know you're hopeless with computers, Lori, but if you ask Bill nicely, I'm sure he'll be willing to look into Mr. Brocklehurst's finances. If history repeats itself, which it does rather more often than most people think, Bill's bound to find something that will give us the leverage we need to eject Mr. Brocklehurst and his deluded disciples from Amelia's life forever.

The handwriting stopped.

"Are you finished?" I asked.

For the moment. It's a good idea, isn't it?

"I'd like to think so," I said, "because I

came up with the exact same idea last night."

Did you mention it to Bill?

"Yes, but I didn't have to," I said, "because he thought of it yesterday." I managed a weak smile. "You can relax, Dimity. An inquiry into the source of Myron's megabucks is well under way."

I see. Then let us move on.

"We'd better," I said, "because I have a lot to tell you. It's been a very strange day, Dimity."

I thought you intended to do housework.

"I did," I said, "but things don't always work out as planned."

I thought wistfully of Willis, Sr.'s, dashed hopes, then gave myself a mental shake and brought Aunt Dimity up to date on what had happened since I'd received Amelia's telephone call in the master bedroom. I told her about the villagers' rout of the Bowenist incursion, the leaflets that led Peggy Taxman and the others to Pussywillows, and the show of support that followed Amelia's confession.

"Everything was going along nicely," I said, "until Peggy took it upon herself to point out four huge, gaping holes in Amelia's armor."

The Handmaidens?

236

"The Handmaidens," I confirmed. "When Peggy broached the subject, it was as if a lightbulb went off in William's head. He suddenly realized that everyone in Finch had been paying attention to him paying attention to Amelia and he immediately understood the damage a quartet of jealous, chatty neighbors could inflict on her. He left it to Peggy and company to explain the situation in greater detail — which they did, gladly — and went home to Fairworth to beat himself up for being stupid, selfish, and blind. I went to see him after I left Pussywillows, Dimity, and believe me, the poor guy is awash in a sea of self-loathing."

Oh, dear.

"It gets worse," I said. "William didn't stick around long enough to hear Amelia's foolproof solution to the Handmaiden problem."

Which is?

"She'll calm the Handmaidens' fears by informing them that she has no intention of ever getting married again," I said. "She means it, Dimity. She'll never marry William. And you know William. He won't consider any arrangement other than marriage."

Did you tell William?

"I couldn't bring myself to break such awful news to him," I said, "but someone else will. Most likely someone named Elspeth, Millicent, Opal, or Selena." I spat out the names, then groaned despondently. "I know what'll happen next, Dimity. William will sacrifice himself for Amelia's sake. He'll deny his feelings and walk away from her, but he'll never get over her. He'll go into a decline. He'll stop eating, become a recluse, and dump his orchids on the mulch pile because they remind him of her. He'll sell Fairworth and go back to the family mansion in Boston to die because he won't be able to stand the pain of living near a woman who's cast him aside, crushed his hopes, and demolished his dreams." I wiped a tear from my eye and sniffed.

Are you finished?

"What more is there to say?" I asked brokenly.

Quite a bit more, apparently. For example: Have you lost your mind? For pity's sake, Lori, William isn't a soppy heroine from a romance novel! He's a mature, well-balanced adult, a man who's as sensible as he is sensitive. If Amelia disappoints him, he may experience a brief period of melancholy, but he won't go to pieces because he knows that romantic love is but one of the many kinds of love that make life worth living. His love of Fairworth, his love of nature, his love of books and maps, and above all his love of family will sustain him, as will his deep and abiding love of Deirdre's excellent cooking. Apart from that, I'm not at all convinced that Amelia will disappoint him.

"I don't think she was bluffing, Dimity," I said. "Amelia said flat out that she'll never remarry."

So did William, after Jane died. People have been known to change their minds.

"It took William nearly thirty years to change his," I reminded her. "He may not have thirty years left to wait for Amelia to change hers."

Are you certain Amelia is attracted to him? The last time we spoke, you seemed to think she was indifferent.

"She's not indifferent anymore," I said heavily. "She served brown bread to him, Dimity, the brown bread her mother used to make, her most special recipe. A woman doesn't serve her mother's special brown bread to a man unless she's attracted to him."

Very true. Perhaps . . . The handwriting paused, as if Aunt Dimity had been struck by a novel idea and needed time to consider it. Perhaps Amelia's renunciation of remarriage has less to do with William than with her unusually strong devotion to her brother.

"Sorry, Dimity," I said, mystified. "You've lost me."

It's quite simple, really. Amelia came to Finch to complete Alfred's quest, a feat she will be unable to accomplish if the Bowenists lay siege to Pussywillows. To reduce the Bowenist threat, she must appease the Handmaidens. To appease the Handmaidens, she must detach herself from William. To detach herself from William, she must take a stand against romantic entanglements in all their myriad forms, including marriage.

I stared down at the journal indignantly. "So she's told a lie — a lie that will hurt William when he hears of it — because telling the truth might complicate her search for the memoir?"

If I'm right, Amelia hasn't lied. She has instead made the difficult decision to place Alfred before William. Please try to remember, Lori, that the memoir is laden with meaning for Amelia. It's a last link to a brother she loved dearly. Searching for it may be her way of keeping faith with him. Finding it may help her move beyond the grief of losing him. Once she's achieved Alfred's goal, she may at last feel free to set a new one for herself.

"And the new goal may be to marry William?" I guessed.

Quite possibly.

"I have to go," I said abruptly.

This minute?

"This second," I said, standing. "I have to put my house in order before I attack Dove Cottage tomorrow. And I intend to attack Dove Cottage with a vengeance."

You sound militant.

"I feel militant," I said fiercely. "William's heart has just begun to beat again. I won't allow it to be broken."

Assuredly not.

"If finding the rest of the memoir is the key to getting William and Amelia back together," I continued, "then I'll devote myself, body and soul, to rooting out those pesky bits of parchment. Which means I have to finish my housework today," I finished somewhat lamely.

Have at it, my dear! I expect to hear great things from you tomorrow.

I smiled, returned the blue journal to its shelf, touched a finger to Reginald's pink snout, and marched upstairs to conquer the laundry.

SEVENTEEN

The sun shone in a cloudless sky on Saturday morning, bathing the cottage in a golden light and giving the sodden fields a chance to dry out. I welcomed the return of fine weather because it meant that Will and Rob would have fewer opportunities to cover themselves and their ponies in mud during their weekly riding lesson.

Bill, on the other hand, felt distinctly shortchanged. After the boys ran upstairs to don their riding gear, he refilled his teacup and announced somewhat gloomily that he would be trapped in his office all day.

"Monsieur Delacroix?" I guessed.

"Naturellement," he replied, rolling his *r* beautifully despite his disappointment. "I had an urgent text message from him twenty minutes ago. He's decided to disinherit his niece."

"Why?" I asked.

"He doesn't like her anymore," Bill answered simply. "According to him, the charming child has become an appalling adult who doesn't deserve one *centime* of his hard-earned cash. Her portion of the estate will now go to a shelter for homeless cats. Stanley approves, of course," he went on, slipping a sliver of fried egg to his cat, "but it means that I'll have to rewrite several sections of Monsieur Delacroix's ever-changing will."

"There should be a law against disinheriting relatives on weekends," I said sympathetically. "But as long as we're on the subject of hard-earned cash . . . Have you found out how Myron Brocklehurst earned his?"

"Not yet," said Bill, brightening. "He's hidden his assets very cleverly."

Most people, including me, would have been frustrated by Myron's cleverness, but Bill shared his father's passion for solving puzzles.

"Why would he hide his assets?" I asked.

"I don't know," said Bill, "but I'll find out. Myron may think he's created an impenetrable maze, but I'll get to the center of it." He nodded confidently, took a final swig of tea, and carried his dishes to the sink. "When does Operation Dove Cottage commence?"

"If all goes well, sometime after midday," I said, getting up from the kitchen table to help him load the dishwasher. "Charles and Grant are lying in wait for Elspeth. When she gets back from London, they'll dart over to Dove Cottage and ask for permission to board ship. When she grants it, Charles will telephone Amelia, Lilian, Bree, and me to give us the go-ahead."

"What happens if Elspeth doesn't comply with your grand plan?" Bill asked.

"She will," I said. "Charles and Grant are still under the impression that William will be joining us. If they play their trump card properly — which they will — Elspeth won't refuse us anything."

"And the boys will spend the day at Anscombe Manor, as per usual?" said Bill.

"Mais oui!" I said with panache. "I won't win Mother of the Year if I deprive them of their ponies."

Bill dried his hands with a dish towel, wrapped his arms around me, and gave me a kiss.

"I hope you find what you're looking for at Dove Cottage," he said.

"Me, too," I said, peering up at him earnestly. "Your father's future happiness depends on it."

"I doubt it," he said, kissing the tip of my

nose, "but I hope you find it anyway."

Bill left the kitchen and I remained behind to rinse dishes in pensive silence. My husband was more sanguine than I was about Willis, Sr.'s, emotional crisis. Like Dimity, Bill believed that his father would continue to savor life, with or without Amelia. I understood their point, but I disagreed with it. Willis, Sr., might have his home, his health, his family, and his flowers, but a blind man could see that he longed for something more. My mission was to make sure he got it.

If Amelia wouldn't budge until the rest of the memoir was found, then I would find the rest of the memoir without delay. To that end, I'd spent the previous evening assembling a tool kit that would enable me to poke, probe, pry, hack, and slash whatever barriers I might encounter during my search. I couldn't count on Bree to always have one of Mr. Barlow's screwdrivers in her pocket, so I'd included one of Bill's along with a needle-nose pliers, a pair of long tweezers, a pocketknife, and a small but powerful flashlight.

The kit was already in the Rover. When the call came from Charles, I'd be ready to take Dove Cottage to pieces, if necessary, to find the memoir's third page. Bill, who'd watched my preparations with ill-concealed amusement, had advised me to keep my intentions to myself, pointing out that Elspeth Binney might object to having her house dismantled, no matter how worthy the cause. A very dark look had shut him up.

"He may be laughing now," I muttered as I finished loading the dishwasher, "but he'll thank me later."

My booted boys came thundering down the stairs to grab their helmets, gloves, and quilted vests from the box beneath the coat rack in the hallway. After subjecting them to a routine inspection — to make sure nothing essential would be left behind — I slipped into a light jacket and herded them into the Range Rover's backseat for the short drive to Anscombe Manor.

"Mummy," Rob said as I backed into the lane. "Is Mrs. Thistle a good witch or a bad witch?"

"She's not any kind of witch," I replied, eyeing him in the rearview mirror. "What made you think she was?"

"We heard you and Daddy talking," Will said.

"You should have listened harder," I told him. "If you had, you'd know that Mrs. Thistle is looking for the pages of a story someone wrote about a witch."

"How did she lose the pages?" Rob asked.

"Someone hid them," I replied. "A long, long time ago, a man named Gamaliel Gowland tucked the pages into secret hiding places all over Finch. We found one in St. George's bell tower on Wednesday."

"How many pages are there?" Will asked.

"Nobody knows," I said.

"We could help you look for them," Rob offered.

"Thanks," I said, "but you wouldn't want to keep Thunder and Storm waiting while you hunted for secret hiding places, would you?"

"No," the boys chorused instantly.

"Don't worry," I said. "Mrs. Thistle has lots of helpers. I'm sure we'll find the missing pages before too long."

"When you do," said Will, "you can read the story to us."

"We'll see," I said, but whether I would read Gamaliel's memoir aloud to my sons or not depended very much upon its ending.

Anscombe Manor had the mongrel appearance of a building that had been altered by succeeding generations of owners over the course of several centuries. The crenelated tower gave it a medieval air, the stables were pure Georgian, and everything in between was . . . in between.

The property had been more or less derelict when Emma and Derek Harris had purchased it, but they'd labored long and hard to turn it into a wonderfully eccentric and eminently comfortable home. Once they'd finished their work on the house, Emma had opened a riding school. She wasn't the sort of woman who liked having time on her hands.

Derek was away from home, restoring a hammerbeam roof in Shropshire, when I dropped the boys off in the stable yard, but Emma was there to greet us. She was dressed in her everyday work clothes — turtleneck, quilted vest, breeches, and boots — and bits of straw clung to her graying, dishwater blond hair. She gave Rob and Will each a friendly pat on the back, then sent them inside to groom and to tack up their ponies. Emma didn't accept students who relied on stablehands to do their chores for them. She believed in teaching responsibility as well as riding.

She was usually too busy with her own responsibilities to keep up with local gossip, so I parked the Rover in front of the house and sauntered back to the stable yard to deliver her weekly quota of village news. I expected to dazzle her with an extravagant array of bulletins, but Emma, as it turned out, had already read the headlines.

"Is Amelia Thistle really Mae Bowen?" she asked avidly. "And is William in love with her?"

I did a double take, then stared hard at her. "When did you hook into the village grapevine?"

"Word gets around," she said with a shrug. "I can't help it if I hear things. Is it true, then? All of it?"

"I'll tell you in a minute," I said, looking over her shoulder. I'd spotted Kit Smith, Emma's stable master and son-in-law, walking toward us with Nell, his young wife, by his side. "Otherwise, I'll have to repeat myself."

Kit and Nell Smith were the most beautiful couple I'd ever seen, not because they dressed well — they had no use for high fashion — but because they were wholly unconscious of their extraordinary natural beauty. Kit was long and lean, with a short crop of prematurely gray hair and delicately chiseled features. His exquisite violet eyes, which had for many years been shadowed by suffering, now shone with the soft glow of complete contentment.

Nell's midnight-blue eyes were as dark

and deep as a moonlit well, and her flawless oval face was framed by a tumble of golden curls. Tall and willowy, she crossed the cobbled yard as gracefully as a swan gliding on a still pond. A few eyebrows had been raised when she'd married a man twice her age, but those of us who knew Kit and Nell best knew that they'd been born to love each other.

Nell smiled tranquilly as she approached, but I could detect a flicker of curiosity in Kit's eyes.

"Is it true?" he asked. "Has William fallen in love with Mae Bowen?"

"Of course it's true," Nell said serenely. "He wasn't looking for her and that's why he found her. She doesn't know it yet, but he's her knight in shining armor." She gave a satisfied sigh as she entwined her fingers with Kit's. "Together, they'll defeat dragons."

Nell often gave the impression that she was from another planet, but her fey manner cloaked a penetrating mind. I believed she possessed a highly refined sense of intuition that allowed her to predict human behavior with eerie accuracy, while Bill maintained that she *was* from another planet. Whatever the case, there was no denying that Nell understood people better than I did.

"William and Amelia had better sharpen their swords, then," I warned, "because dragons are thick on the ground." I went on to describe the Handmaiden threat, the Bowenist menace, the far-from-finished search for the memoir, and Amelia's adamant refusal to consider a second marriage. "It's not a fairy tale, Nell," I concluded. "It's a lot more complicated."

"Fairy tales are always complicated," Nell said imperturbably, "yet they always have happy endings. William and Amelia will, too. You'll see."

"As for the memoir," said Emma, bringing the conversation back down to earth, "Derek and I didn't find any parchment pages while we were working on the manor, and we scoured every nook and cranny."

"Too bad," I said. "I was hoping you'd have a page taped to your refrigerator door."

"No such luck," said Emma with a wry smile.

"Mistress Meg rings a bell, though," said Kit, running a hand through his gray hair. "My stepfather used to tell me grisly stories about a witch named Mad Maggie who would creep through our woods and chop up unsuspecting children with her axe. I thought his nanny had invented her, but I suppose she could have been based on Mistress Meg."

"And your stepfather grew up here, at Anscombe Manor," I said, gazing up at him excitedly.

"So did Kit," Emma reminded me. "The Anscombes owned the manor for a few hundred years before Derek and I bought it."

"Was your stepfather's nanny a local, too?" I asked Kit.

"I believe so," he replied. "Why? Is it important?"

"Mad Maggie is an extremely local legend," I told him. "The only people who know about her are people who were born and raised within the bounds of St. George's parish."

"You were born and raised in Chicago, Lori," Emma pointed out. "How did you learn about Mad Maggie?"

"Aunt Dimity," I replied without the slightest hesitation, because I was speaking with three of the scant handful of people who knew about the blue journal.

"Dimity was certainly a local," Kit acknowledged.

"She still is," said Nell.

"So we have two witches," said Emma, returning to the subject at hand, "one fictional, one real, both inhabiting nearby woods."

"Mad Maggie *must* be a distorted version of Mistress Meg," I said, adding pensively, "At least, I hope she's distorted. I'll be severely disappointed if the memoir's next page tells how Mistress Meg went berserk with an axe one day and made mincemeat of the village children." I turned to Kit. "Can you remember anything else your stepfather told you about Mad Maggie?"

"If I remember correctly, she had goat's horns growing out of her head," he replied. "To tell you the truth, I've done my best to forget those stories. They gave me nightmares!"

The sound of horses and ponies clip-clopping across the cobbles recalled Emma, Kit, and Nell to their duties. The Anscombe Riding Center was a family affair and the trio had students to teach, so they went their separate ways, leaving me to lean on a fence and watch while Will and Rob put Thunder and Storm through their paces.

Though my sons' prowess in the riding ring delighted me, I couldn't keep myself from gazing past them and into the woods that bordered the estate's pastures. Mistress Meg might have built her house in those woods, I mused. She might have raised her goats there. I hoped she'd been allowed to die in peace there, but I feared she'd been dragged from her home to die a ghastly death in a hangman's noose.

Thankfully, my cell phone put an end to my increasingly morbid thoughts. I scurried away from the riding ring to answer it, fully expecting to hear Charles Bellingham's voice informing me that Elspeth Binney had caught an early train back from London. Instead, I heard Elspeth Binney herself.

"Lori?" she said.

"Elspeth?" I said, astonished. "How did you get my cell phone number?"

"William gave it to me," she replied, magnifying my confusion. "He explained *everything* to me, Lori, and I'm *thrilled.* I wish he could join us — as does he, of course — but I promised him we'd soldier on without him. Honestly, Lori, I never dreamt that my humble abode might play a vital role in village history. I wish I were there right now."

"W-where are you?" I stammered.

"I'm at Paddington Station," she replied, "but William wanted me to let you know that I'll be home by ten o'clock at the very latest. I'll need a few minutes to unpack and to freshen up, but I'll expect you and dear Amelia and the rest of the gang by, shall we say, half past ten?"

"Half past ten is perfect," I responded automatically.

"Wonderful," gushed Elspeth, and rang off.

I stood with the phone to my ear and my mouth agape, unable to believe what I'd just heard. Had my father-in-law really telephoned a Handmaiden? Had he actually given her my cell phone number? Had she said *dear Amelia?* None of it made any kind of sense to me until I remembered Willis, Sr.'s, words, spoken brusquely but with great determination as he fiddled with the file on his desk: *I will rectify my errors, Lori. I shall see to it that Mrs. Thistle will not have to pay for my mistakes.*

"He's rectifying his errors," I murmured. "He's made sure that Elspeth will cooperate with us, despite his absence. He's cleared a path for Amelia." I glanced at Nell, who sat astride her chestnut mare as regally as a fairy queen. "The knight has slain his first dragon. . . ."

I paused to wipe away a sentimental tear, then telephoned Charles.

Eighteen

Dove Cottage was the northernmost of three cottages that sat in a row at the very edge of the village, facing St. George's Church. The three cottages were virtually identical. Each was a small, rectangular, one-and-a-half-story stone house, with a pair of dormer windows above, a pair of large diamond-paned windows below, a chimney at either end of the steeply pitched roof, and a front door shielded by a shallow porch.

Since I didn't play bridge or paint pictures or qualify as one of Elspeth Binney's bosom chums, I'd never set foot inside Dove Cottage. The image I had of its interior was entirely imaginary, but crystal clear nonetheless. I envisioned it crammed to the rafters with gaudy knickknacks, spindly furniture, and sloshy watercolors signed: *E. B.*

I felt slightly abashed, therefore, when

Elspeth ushered me into a small but sunny parlor furnished with a carefully edited selection of simple, well-made antiques and decorated with a superb collection of black-and-white landscape photographs. Clearly, the woman had better taste than I'd given her credit for.

The parlor was overcrowded when I arrived, because Charles, Grant, Amelia, Lilian, and Bree had gotten there before me. Amelia sat in a Windsor armchair near the hearth, with her carpet bag at her feet, but the others were milling around restlessly, as if they were already sizing up possible hidey-holes.

"Did you take the photos, Elspeth?" I asked, peering closely at a spare, expansive study of moor and sky.

"Oh, no," she replied. "They were taken by my niece, the one in Yorkshire. She's an amateur photographer, of course, but I think she's rather good."

"She's very good," Amelia stated firmly. "Your niece is an artist, Elspeth. If she ever decides to sell her work to the public, please feel free to tell her to get in touch with me. I'm fairly well connected in the art world."

The understatement won sycophantic chuckles from Charles and Grant, but Elspeth blushed with pleasure and thanked

Amelia effusively. Elspeth's warm and welcoming demeanor seemed to indicate that she no longer regarded Amelia as a rival. The combined effects of Willis, Sr.'s, mysterious telephone call and Amelia's public renunciation of marriage had evidently put the Handmaiden's suspicious mind at rest.

"We should be expressing our gratitude to you," Amelia told her. "Thank you for allowing us to invade your home."

"Not at all," said Elspeth, beaming. "When I was a schoolteacher, history was my favorite subject. I confess I felt a twinge of envy when William told me that the first page of the memoir had been found in Opal Taylor's chimney all those many years ago, but it vanished the moment he explained that the third page might be concealed in *my* house." She turned to me. "Dearest Amelia has shown me what you're looking for, but I'm afraid you won't find any pieces of parchment in my chimneys. I have them swept twice a year, you see. Anything that might have been hidden in them would have fallen out long ago."

The moment Elspeth stopped speaking, everyone else began offering their own ideas as to where the third page might be be found. I endured the cacophony for less than half a second, then stepped forward and raised my hands for silence. Amazingly, it worked.

"Thank you," I said, doing my best to imitate Lilian Bunting at her most authoritative. "Before we start running in circles and duplicating each other's work, let's ask ourselves a few questions, shall we? Gamaliel Gowland hid the pages of his memoir sometime between 1649, when he became the rector of St. George's, and 1653, when he left St. George's for a post at Exeter Cathedral."

"Correct," said Lilian.

"First question," I said. "What parts of Dove Cottage existed before 1653? There's no point in searching later additions, is there?"

"None," said Lilian, with an approving nod.

"Elspeth?" I said. "Can you enlighten us?"

"As it happens, I can," she said. "Dove Cottage was built in 1587. Its various owners have made numerous cosmetic changes since then, but the house's basic structure has remained the same."

"It's expensive to alter a stone building," Lilian observed.

"It is," Elspeth agreed. "Only three features have been added to Dove Cottage since the early seventeenth century: the porch, the scullery, and the little sunroom Mr. Barlow built for me five years ago."

"Did you hear Elspeth, everyone?" I said. "We don't have to search the porch, the scullery, or the sunroom. Since they didn't exist in Gamaliel's time, he couldn't have used them as hiding places." I sensed impatience in my troops, but I was determined to impose method on their madness, so I hurried on. "Similarly, if he didn't enter a room, he couldn't have hidden anything in it, which brings me to my next question: Would a visiting clergyman have access to the entire house or would some rooms be off-limits to him?"

"It depends on the purpose of the visit," Lilian answered knowledgeably. "If it were a casual call, I imagine the Reverend Gowland would be entertained in the parlor."

"Lilian and Amelia," I said, "you search the parlor."

"If he came for a meal," Lilian went on, "he would be invited into the dining room."

"Grant and Charles, take the dining room," I said.

"If his purpose was to visit a sick family member or to administer the last rites," said Lilian, "he would most likely be taken to the ailing person's bedside."

"How many bedrooms are there?" I asked Elspeth.

"Two," she replied. "Both upstairs."

"I'll take one bedroom and Bree will take the other," I said. "So far, we've covered the parlor, the dining room, and the two bedrooms . . . What about the kitchen, Lilian?

"I doubt he'd be welcome in the kitchen," said Lilian. "The family might spend most of their time there, but it wouldn't be considered a suitable place to entertain a man of rank. The same would hold true for the attic and the cellar. It would be almost impossible for a clergyman to enter the less public areas of a parishioner's house without arousing comment."

"Okay," I said. "We'll set aside the kitchen, the attic, and the cellar for now, but if we come up empty everywhere else, we'll return to them."

"There's the upstairs lavatory," Elspeth suggested. "It wouldn't have been there in the Reverend Gowland's time, but it was inserted into a space that had been a part of a bedchamber."

"You search the upstairs lavatory, Elspeth," I said decisively. I held up the old book bag containing my tool kit. "If any of you have trouble reaching into a narrow crevice or seeing into a dark corner, come

261

to me. I may have an implement that will help you."

Bree shouted "Bravo!" and began to applaud, but I wasn't finished yet. For my grand finale, I opened the book bag and removed from it seven scrolls I'd made by rolling up pieces of notepaper. I kept one dummy scroll for myself and handed one to each member of the search team.

"Put yourselves in Gamaliel's cassock," I advised them. "You enter a room with a scroll of parchment and you leave without it. Ask yourself where you would — and could — hide it."

"I say, Lori," said Charles, examining his scroll appreciatively. "You've thought of everything."

"I seriously doubt it," I said with a modest smile, "but we won't know what I've forgotten until we need it, so let's get started. Good luck, everyone."

Bree snapped to attention, saluted, and ran upstairs, laughing uproariously, but the others wished me good luck in turn before moving to their designated search areas.

Elspeth and I were about to follow Bree up the steep, narrow staircase when the doorbell rang. Elspeth bustled over to answer it and found Opal Taylor standing on her doorstep.

"Good morning, Elspeth," said Opal. "Amelia told me last night that she'd be here today to hunt for the rector's memoir, so I thought I'd come along and volunteer my services."

"Thank you, Opal," Elspeth said sweetly, "but your services aren't required. Lori has everything under control."

"Another pair of eyes won't hurt, surely," Opal protested. "As you know, the first page came from my cottage. It could be said that I have a personal interest in finding the rest of the pages."

"It could also be said that too many cooks spoil the broth," countered Elspeth, folding her arms. "We have all the volunteers we need, thank you, Opal."

"But Elspeth . . ."

I sensed that Opal's attempt to horn in on the search would be quashed by Elspeth, who had no intention of sharing the spotlight Willis, Sr., had shone on her. Experience had taught me that Opal wouldn't give up easily, however, so I left the two ladies to fight it out on the doorstep and went upstairs.

Since Bree had already claimed the larger of the two bedrooms, I settled for the one that had lost nearly a third of its floor space to the latter-day lavatory. It was a snug little guest room, simply furnished with an iron bedstead, a small chest of drawers, a tidy bookcase filled with books about the Cotswolds, and a modern but unobtrusive wardrobe that had in all likelihood been assembled after traveling up the staircase in a flat pack.

The room was full of character. Chunky rafters crossed the low ceiling, a chimney breast protruded from the wall opposite the door, and the oval rag rug glowed in a splash of sunlight coming through the gap between the checked curtains hanging in the dormer window.

I placed my tool kit on the floor and opened the curtains all the way, then faced the room and held my fake scroll at arm's length. I gazed at it unblinkingly, hoping for inspiration, but my attempt to concentrate was foiled by a new set of noises coming from the ground floor.

I heard the front door close and the sound of Elspeth's step upon the stairs, but before she'd reached the halfway point, the doorbell rang again. Elspeth gave an irritable sigh and a moment later Millicent Scroggins's voice drifted up to me.

"Good morning, Elspeth. Amelia told me all about the goings-on here today. May I be of assistance?"

"Thank you, Millicent," Elspeth replied in exasperated tones, "but —"

"Elspeth!" Selena Buxton sounded out of breath, as if she'd rushed to catch up with Millicent. "Have you started without us? No matter. I'm sure you'll find something for us to do."

"As a matter of fact," Elspeth said forcefully, "there's *nothing* for you to do. I appreciate your willingness to help, but —"

" 'Morning, Elspeth." Dick Peacock's voice was unmistakable. "We heard you might need a hand today."

"Always happy to chip in," said Henry Cook.

"Have you found anything yet?" asked George Wetherhead.

"Have I found anything?" Elspeth expostulated. "I haven't been given the chance to look! If you'd *please* go about your business . . ."

I suspected that Elspeth would spend the rest of the morning fending off a host of helpful friends and neighbors, so I closed the guest room door and resumed my meditations.

I had no idea how the guest room would have been furnished in Gamaliel's time, but if Lilian was right, it would have been occupied by someone in dire need of prayer

— a feverish child, a fading grandparent, a mother worn out from giving birth too often. I wondered if Mistress Meg had administered her potions near the spot where I stood, and whether the man of God had given her his blessing or cursed her as an unholy hag.

Though the visiting rector might have been left alone in the parlor or the dining room, it seemed to me that a sickroom wouldn't have afforded him much privacy. A sleeping child, grandparent, or mother might wake at any moment, so Gamaliel would have been compelled to use a hiding place he could reach quickly. It would have to be a place that wouldn't be dusted or used for storage or altered easily, I reasoned, a place that wouldn't be discovered until long after Gamaliel's death.

My gaze traveled up to the rafters. Though I was relatively short, I could lay my palm against them. A man of average height could have curled his hand over them to feel for spaces that might exist between the ancient beams and the plastered ceiling. I peered upward for some moments, lost in thought, then took two thick volumes from the bookcase, stacked them one atop the other on the floor, and, after conscientiously removing my shoes, stood on them to examine the rafter nearest the chimney breast.

The wood was as hard as iron and beautifully textured, with the grain running in frozen wavelets along the length of the beam. I saw no holes or cracks large enough to conceal my faux scroll, but when I looked several feet to my left, a slight bend in the otherwise straight timber caught my attention. Since it was beyond my reach, I stepped down from the books, glanced guiltily over my shoulder, and stood on the bed.

I slid my hand into the space created by the rafter's curve, felt along the top of the beam, and gasped as my questing fingers encountered a hollow no deeper than a shallow bowl. The carpenter who'd constructed the cottage's framework had concealed the minor flaw by turning it upward and away from discerning eyes, but the rector seeking the perfect hiding place had spotted it.

My fingers trembled as they touched parchment that had not been touched for more than three hundred years.

Nineteen

"I've found it," I whispered. I stuffed the faux scroll carelessly in my pocket and lifted the real one from the bowl-shaped hollow as if it were made of glass. Like the scroll we'd found in the bell tower, it was tied with a black ribbon, but it was thicker and more tightly rolled, as if the third part of Gamaliel's story were longer and more involved than the previous parts. For a moment I could do nothing but stare at the scroll in awed silence. Then I threw back my head and hollered, "I've found it! I've found the third page!"

Bree burst into the room as I hopped down from the bed.

"Where was it?" she asked.

"In the rafter," I said, pointing to the ceiling.

Before I could conceal the liberties I'd taken with Elspeth's guest room, Elspeth herself appeared in the doorway. She looked from my stockinged feet to the stacked books to the rumpled bedclothes and appeared to draw the obvious conclusions, but instead of scolding me for behaving like a hooligan, she smiled.

"Thank you for removing your shoes, Lori," she said graciously. "Did your gymnastics produce the desired result?"

"Yes," I said and handed the scroll to her. "You should be the one to present it to Amelia. Without you, I never would have found it."

"Lori?" Grant called up the stairs. "Did I hear you correctly? Have you found the third page?"

"Yes," I called back. "Wait for me in the parlor. I'll be down in two ticks."

I smoothed the bedclothes, returned the books to the bookcase, stepped into my shoes, picked up my completely pointless tool kit, and followed Bree and Elspeth down the stairs.

Charles, Grant, Lilian, and Amelia had assembled in the parlor, but they weren't the only ones awaiting developments. The rejected volunteers — Opal Taylor, Millicent Scroggins, Selena Buxton, Dick Peacock, Henry Cook, and George Wetherhead — were standing just outside the large front window, looking in.

Elspeth scowled when she caught sight of the onlookers, as if she resented the hoi polloi witnessing an event she'd hoped to savor with a select few.

"Well, really . . . ," she said through tightened lips. "Of all the nerve . . ."

"It's their village's history, too," Amelia said gently. "It's only natural that they should take an interest."

"Half the fun of making a discovery is sharing it with others," said Lilian.

"They'll hear about it anyway," Charles muttered.

"Why don't we give Lilian a chance to translate the scroll," I proposed, "then read it aloud to anyone who cares to hear it?"

"It would be a generous, inclusive gesture," Grant observed.

"Educational, too," Bree put in craftily.

The word "educational" must have resonated with Elspeth, because she took a deep breath and swallowed her disappointment.

"My parlor is too small to accommodate such a large number of people," she said. "The schoolhouse would be a better venue. We won't even have to set up the chairs. Mr. Barlow neglected to put them away after the Guy Fawkes Day committee meeting."

"Mr. Barlow is the church sexton," Lilian

reminded her. "He is not responsible for stacking chairs after committee meetings."

"Be that as it may," Amelia interceded smoothly, "the schoolhouse seems an ideal place for our purposes. Shall we reconvene there in an hour? Two hours?" She looked inquiringly at Lilian.

"Give me an hour," said Lilian. "I've been boning up on my Latin."

"Elspeth?" I said. "If you would do the honors?"

Elspeth lifted her chin, held the tightly rolled sheet of parchment out for everyone to see, and took three stately steps toward Amelia. I'd never suspected Elspeth of having a theatrical streak, but she was certainly putting on a show for her uninvited audience.

"William guessed that the glyph was an olive branch," she said in a voice that had once paralyzed wrongdoers in the far corners of crowded classrooms, "Charles linked the olive branch to Dove Cottage, and Lori discovered the scroll in my guest room. It is my privilege, Mrs. Thistle, to present the third page of the Reverend Gamaliel Gowland's secret memoir to you."

Amelia, as if sensing Elspeth's need to milk the moment for all it was worth, took the proffered scroll, kissed Elspeth on both

271

cheeks, and thanked her formally on Alfred's behalf as well as her own. She then presented the scroll to Lilian.

"Good luck with the translation," she said. "We'll meet you at the schoolhouse in one hour."

Bree and I spent the hour with Grant and Charles, who'd invited us to lunch at Crabtree Cottage. While Charles whipped up a cheese soufflé and Grant showed Bree the proper way to clean an oil painting, I telephoned Willis, Sr.

I wanted to tell my father-in-law that I'd found the third page and ask him what he'd said when he'd telephoned Elspeth Binney in London, but he'd given Deirdre strict orders to hold his calls.

"He really means it this time," she told me. "He's been locked in his study since four o'clock this morning. I'm allowed to bring him meals on trays, but other than that, he refuses to see or to speak with anyone."

"Has he eaten the meals you've brought him?" I asked apprehensively.

"I think he's licked the plates," she replied. "There's nothing wrong with William's appetite, Lori. He's just very, *very* focused on his work."

272

"Good," I said, relieved. "Work will take his mind off . . . other things. Keep an eye on him, Deirdre."

"I will," she said. "I, too, am very focused on my work."

After a pleasant meal, my lunch mates and I strolled across the green to the schoolhouse. We arrived ten minutes early, but the joint was already jumping. The rejected volunteers had evidently forgiven Elspeth for spurning them because she sat among them, chatting animatedly about the weather, the rising cost of petrol, and the impact a seventeenth-century memoir might have on Finch.

Bree, with her customary foresight, had posted herself in the doorway to act as a lookout, in case Daffodil Deeproots or others of her ilk reappeared in the village. Charles and Grant chose seats in the back row, but I sat up front with Amelia in the chair she'd saved for me. As the automated bells in the church tower struck half past twelve, Lilian entered the schoolhouse, carrying the scroll I'd found in Dove Cottage and a notepad similar to the one she'd used to record the second page's translation.

The villagers quieted as she made her way to the dais at the front of the schoolroom.

She placed the scroll and the notebook on the long table that had last seen action during the Guy Fawkes Day committee meeting, then faced the assembly and gave a succinct summary of the memoir's origins as well as the contents of its first and second pages.

"Sounds as if the rector admired Mistress Meg," Dick Peacock opined when Lilian had finished her introduction. "Says she cured folk without asking for payment. What's *fearsome* about that? Wish I could find a doctor today who put his patients before his bank account."

A murmur of agreement rippled through the room. Lilian waited for it to pass, then picked up the scroll.

"The third page of the Reverend Gowland's memoir is considerably longer than the first two," she said. "I have translated it from Latin into English to the best of my ability in the short space of time I requested." She exchanged the scroll for the notepad. "I will now read my translation to you. Please hold your comments until I've finished."

I could tell by Lilian's somber expression that something was troubling her, but she read the translation in a deliberately neutral tone of voice, as if she were reading the minutes of a duller-than-average committee meeting.

"The summer of 1652 was fraught with misfortune," she began. "The rains failed, crops withered, livestock struggled, and my people knew hardship and hunger. To console my flock, I read to them from the Book of Job and preached that God in His wisdom sends trials to test and to strengthen our faith in Him. I reminded them of Christ's suffering and bade them endure their afflictions as He did, humbly and with their minds turned always to the kingdom of heaven."

Lilian flipped to the next page and continued, "But Jenna Penner twice stood up in church to contradict me. In the first instance, she testified that God had sent the drought to punish us for harboring a pagan. She railed against the woman in the woods who came not to church to sing God's praises, but sang to her goats on the Sabbath, in mockery of God's law. She said the woman who used black magic to heal would one day use it to do great harm. She warned that God would turn his face from us until we cast the wicked woman into darkness."

Lilian flipped to the third page in her notebook.

"In the second instance, Jenna Penner

stood in church to accuse the woman in the woods of killing her pig. Jenna said: 'I saw the witch behind my house, bathed in the full moon's light, calling upon the Adversary to help her to take revenge on the one who spoke against her. She chanted strange words and made queer signs in the air with a forked branch. When she pointed the branch at my pig, it fell down dead.' "

Lilian's rapt listeners shuffled their feet and shifted uncomfortably in their chairs. She forestalled any mutterings with a sharp look, then bent her head over her notepad and resumed reading.

"A visiting cleric heard Jenna Penner's testimony and brought word of Mistress Meg's offenses to the witch finder in Cheltenham. The witch finder and his men came to subject Mistress Meg to the required ordeals. When they came, I led the faithful to the house in the woods, for I wanted them to see justice done."

Lilian looked up from her notepad. "So ends the text. It's followed by another small drawing, or glyph. I've made an enlarged sketch of the glyph. If it means something to you, please speak up."

She handed a sheet of white paper to Amelia, who held it out for me to see. On it, Lilian had drawn three arrows bound in the middle like a bunch of flowers. I studied it briefly, then shook my head.

"Doesn't ring the faintest bell," I said.

Amelia passed the sketch to Elspeth and it quickly made the rounds, drawing blank looks from everyone who examined it.

"Questions?" Lilian asked.

"Yes," said Henry Cook. "What does the rector mean when he talks about Mistress Meg's ordeals? Does he mean they tortured her?"

"It depends on your definition of torture." Lilian's manner changed from neutral to scholarly as she continued, "By the mid-seventeenth century, most educated Englishmen regarded extreme forms of torture as an unreliable means of extracting the truth from a suspected criminal. Techniques such as flaying, branding, the gouging out of eyes, and the breaking of bones on the rack were, therefore, no longer used to coerce confessions from alleged witches."

"Well, that's good, isn't it?" Henry said uncertainly.

"It was progress of a sort, I suppose," Lilian allowed. "Unfortunately, witch-hunters resorted to less flagrant forms of torture. The three principle forms were known as swimming, pricking, and watching and walking."

"What's wrong with swimming?" asked Millicent.

"The swimming test was meant to prove that a woman had rejected the water of baptism and was therefore both a heretic and a witch," said Lilian. "It involved tying a woman's limbs together or tying her to a chair, and tossing her into a pond or a river. If the woman sank, she was released from custody. If she 'rejected' the water and floated, she was found guilty as charged. As you can imagine, the swimming test resulted in many drownings. On the other hand, buoyant women were sent to the gallows, so they weren't much better off than their more leaden sisters."

"They did that to Mistress Meg?" said Millicent, aghast. "After all the good she'd done?"

"I don't know," said Lilian. "The Reverend Gowland doesn't specify the types of ordeal Mistress Meg faced."

"What about the other thing?" said Opal. "The pricking?"

"Pricking was a way of finding a witch's mark," said Lilian. "It was believed that all witches had a place on their bodies that wouldn't flinch or bleed if pricked with a needle. Sometimes a dagger like needle — a bodkin — was used for the pricking. A woman could be stabbed hundreds of times by a witch finder intent on finding a witch's mark."

"They stuck Mistress Meg with needles?" Opal said, her face pale. "Hundreds of times?"

"Again, I don't know," said Lilian. "Gamaliel doesn't say."

"What was the third one you mentioned?" asked Selena Buxton, almost fearfully. "The watching and walking?"

"It was, perhaps, the most wicked torture of all," said Lilian. "I regret to say that some elements of it are still practiced in so-called civilized countries. Watching and walking combines acute sleep deprivation with starvation. A suspected witch's clothing would be taken from her. She would be dressed in a simple shift and made to sit in a cell for hours, sometimes for many days and nights, without sleep or food, while the witch hunters watched her."

"What did they expect to see?" asked Selena.

"They hoped the witch's familiar — a demonic cat or dog or, in Mistress Meg's case, a demonic goat — would turn up to feed her," said Lilian.

"They thought a *goat* would appear in the cell, carrying a plate of *food?*" Henry said incredulously.

"You have the general idea," said Lilian. "When no familiar appeared, they ordered the suspect to walk barefoot around her cell for hour after endless hour, while they pelted her with questions. I doubt that many women survived watching and walking without giving the witch hunters precisely the answers they sought."

Selena bowed her head, Opal shook hers, Millicent clucked her tongue in disgust, and Elspeth shuddered. Charles and Grant looked uncharacteristically grim. Dick and Henry were clearly revolted, Amelia bit her lip, and gentle George Wetherhead looked as if he might faint. I wrapped my arms around myself, as if an icy breeze had blown through the room. I'd foreseen Mistress Meg's tragic end, but hearing my hunch confirmed gave me no pleasure.

"Makes you sick to think of it," Dick muttered.

"What's sick," snapped Lilian, in a voice that was far from neutral and no longer scholarly, "is the willingness of one human being to brutally torment another in the name of God or country or anything else. I'd hoped for something better from Reverend Gowland, but he was, after all, a man of his times. He, and others like him, stood by and did nothing while an innocent woman was taken away to be tortured and hanged. If and when we recover the memoir's fourth page, I shall find it distasteful in the extreme to translate his description of Mistress Meg's miserable death."

She stepped off the dais, passed the scroll and the notepad to Amelia, and left the schoolhouse, her eyes blazing with fury. A hushed silence ensued, followed by the rustling noises of people collecting their belongings and getting quietly to their feet.

"We'd best be in church tomorrow morning," Henry said wisely. "We don't want Mrs. Bunting any more upset than she already is."

"You needn't remind me to go to church, Henry Cook," said Millicent. "I'm sure I've never missed a Sunday service."

"You missed four Sunday services in a row last March," Selena reminded her.

"I had pneumonia," Millicent retorted. "Missing a service doesn't count if you're sick."

"I don't recall reading anything in the Bible about sick leave," said Opal.

"I never said it was in the Bible," Millicent barked.

The familiar strains of Handmaidens bickering came as a welcome relief after Lilian's harrowing lecture. I glanced at the scroll in Amelia's hand and felt strangely guilty for finding it.

"Will you be in church tomorrow?" I asked.

"Yes," she said, gazing fixedly at the scroll. "Mrs. Bunting invited me to sit up front with her."

"New parishioners usually do." I hesitated, then asked, "Are you all right, Amelia?"

"Mmm-hmm," she replied absently, turning the scroll to look at it from different angles. "It's a terrible thing, isn't it? The way the past can haunt the present?"

"You don't have to go on with the search, you know," I said. "If it's too disturbing for you, we can stop it right here, right now."

"The search?" she said, as if coming out of a trance. "Must we go on with the search? Of course we must. Alfie would have seen it through to the end, regardless of the outcome, and so will I." She stowed the scroll and the notepad in her carpet bag, stood, and walked up the center aisle, saying, "Thank you for finding page three, Lori. I'll see you at church tomorrow."

I watched my new friend leave the schoolhouse, feeling as though I'd missed something important.

TWENTY

The three-arrow glyph stumped Aunt Dimity, but she thought she knew what I'd missed in my unsettling exchange with Amelia.

Night had fallen. Will and Rob were upstairs, asleep, and dreaming, no doubt, of winning the Grand National on Thunder and Storm. Bill was stretched out on the couch in the living room, reading the newspaper he'd abandoned to work on Monsieur Delacroix's will, Stanley was sleeping on Bill's chest, and I was in the study, curled comfortably in a leather armchair before a crackling fire, with the blue journal open in my lap.

"Enlighten me," I said. "Tell me what Amelia meant when she said that the past haunted the present."

I stretched my feet toward the fire as the familiar copperplate scrolled confidently across the page.

You've evidently forgotten that Amelia is related by blood to Gamaliel Gowland. If she feels a personal connection to him, his words are bound to affect her more strongly than they would someone whose interest in Gamaliel is purely academic.

"She's depressed because her distant ancestor was a rat?" I shook my head. "I don't buy it, Dimity. If I looked hard enough, I'm sure I could find a rat or two dangling from my family tree, but it wouldn't send me into a tailspin. Amelia didn't even know Gamaliel was her multi-great-granduncle until she read Alfred's papers. Why would she care so much about him now?"

Because the memoir has brought Gamaliel Gowland to life, made him real to her, in a way a family tree never could.

"The memoir's made him real for all of us," I said. "And in that sense, I agree with you. I felt pretty haunted by the past after Lilian's talk about witch hunts. It made me think of how tempting it is, even today, to look the other way while terrible things are done to innocent people. I'd like to believe I'd rush to their defense, but maybe I'm not so different from Gamaliel."

You? Look the other way? With your sharp tongue and quick temper? Ha! You would have chased the witch-hunters off with a pitch-fork.

I chuckled ruefully. "Thanks, Dimity. I think."

At any rate, I'm not convinced that the rector was a rat. His sermons weren't aimed at finding scapegoats for the drought. They were stories of endurance in the face of catastrophe. Furthermore, he seems to have ignored Jenna Penner's initial rant about Mistress Meg, and it was a visiting cleric, not Gamaliel, who used Jenna's second tirade as an excuse to bring the witch finder to Finch. Perhaps Gamaliel was in love with Meg after all.

"If he loved her," I said flatly, "he would have protected her."

How? Remember the times, Lori. Superstition was rife, witch-hunting was legal, and rectors who refused to toe the line could be accused of advocating witchcraft. If Gamaliel had spoken out —

" 'He could have lost his livelihood and quite possibly his life,' " I said quickly. "I'm quoting you, by the way."

I know you are and I stand by my words. It's a lot to ask of a man, even a man in love. Speaking of which, is William pining away?

"No," I said. "He's coping with the situation by throwing himself into his work."

Bully for him. I told you he was a sensible

sort of chap. Was Bill of any help with the latest glyph?

"None at all," I replied. "He doesn't know what it means."

Don't lose sleep over it. Something will turn up.

"Something did turn up this morning," I said. "Not about the glyph, but about Mad Maggie. Kit heard about her from his stepfather. In his version, Mad Maggie roamed the woods on the Anscombe Manor estate. She also had goat's horns growing out of her head."

Goat's horns and an affinity for the woods? How interesting. It seems that Mistress Meg and Mad Maggie have more in common than the name Margaret.

"I knew you'd make the connection," I said. "I suppose, if I were a little kid playing in the woods, the sight of a strange woman cutting firewood might scare the wits out of me."

I believe you've put your finger on the origins of Mistress Meg's transformation from a healer into the hideous hag of my childhood.

"I'd like to put my finger on where she lived," I said. "Wouldn't it be wonderful to discover the remains of her house?"

There wouldn't be much left of it after three hundred years.

"Even so," I said, "I'd love to find it."

You've grown fond of Mistress Meg, haven't you?

"Yes, I have," I said.

I can understand why. She was independent, bullheaded, energetic . . . Hmmm . . . Who does she remind me of?

"Good night, Dimity," I said with a wry smile.

Good night, my dear.

The fine weather was still with us when we left for church the following morning. As usual, we were running late. Bill had forgotten his handkerchief, the boys had tried to sneak out of the house in their riding boots, and I'd had to run back into the cottage for my purse. By the time we reached St. George's, Elspeth was playing the last chords of the voluntary and Mr. Barlow, whose many roles included that of church usher, was standing at his post to the left of the chancel, armed with the collection plate. We slid into the very last pew on the center aisle, trying but failing spectacularly to be inconspicuous.

Henry Cook's advice to attend the service had apparently been heeded because the church was packed. Amelia gave me a friendly wave from her place of honor next to Lilian in the front pew and Mr. Barlow favored me with a wink, but the Handmaidens sniffed disapprovingly while I tried to settle the boys, and Peggy Taxman emitted a loud, disparaging grunt. Thankfully, the rest of the congregation was too intent on private meditation to pay much attention to us.

The vicar began to pray and I bowed my head reverently, but my mind was on other matters. Deirdre had telephoned the cottage at half past seven to inform us that Willis, Sr., was too wrapped up in his work to attend church or to host our regular Sunday brunch at Fairworth House. While I shared Aunt Dimity's belief that Willis, Sr., was better off working than pining, there was a limit to everything. What kind of work, I asked myself, would require him to cancel a visit from his grandsons?

Aunt Dimity had once told me that retired attorneys never really retired, so I had to assume that an elderly client — perhaps one on his deathbed — had, like Monsieur Delacroix, changed his mind about his will and asked Willis, Sr., to rewrite it before the grim reaper's arrival. As the vicar mounted the pulpit to give his sermon, I found myself wondering if more homeless cats were about to benefit from a niece's disinheritance.

I could tell that Lilian had influenced the vicar's choice of subjects because the crux of his sermon seemed to be that we each had a responsibility to protect the weak from the strong, the individual from the mob. Sadly, I was too preoccupied with my own thoughts to listen closely to his wise and heartfelt words. I was so self-absorbed that I didn't even bother to look around when the west door opened and a group of latecomers shuffled furtively into the church.

"Mummy?" Will asked, craning his neck to look behind us. "Who are those people?"

I turned to follow his gaze and felt a thrill of shock and horror when I saw Daffodil Deeproots and at least twenty-five of her colorfully dressed cronies filing in to range themselves across the entire west end of the church. The smell of patchouli hit me like a pie in the face.

The vicar shocked me further when he stopped preaching in mid-sentence and bellowed, "All rise! Hymn 294, Mrs. Binney! Let us sing!"

As Elspeth leaned on the opening chords of "Jerusalem" and the parishioners bounced to their feet to belt out the lyrics, I tried frantically to locate Amelia. I leaned sideways to peer past the broad back of the farmer in front of me, but the singing, swaying congregation had created a human wall that blocked my view as effectively as an old-growth forest. I caught a brief glimpse of Mr. Barlow's elbow as he disappeared into the sacristy before the song came to an end and the vicar asked us all to be seated.

I remained on my feet to scan the front pew, but Amelia wasn't there. Instead, Bree was sitting in the place of honor beside Lilian, her face turned attentively toward the vicar.

"Sit," Bill hissed, tugging on my trench coat.

I sank onto the pew, bewildered.

"Is it a circus, Mummy?" Rob asked, squirming around to gaze curiously at Daffodil and her motley companions.

"Something like that," I said. "Eyes forward, please. It's impolite to stare."

In the meantime, the vicar had begun preaching an entirely different sermon. It was one of his classics, a dry, drawn-out, desperately dull analysis of an Aramaic word, the derivations of which were crucial to the understanding of an obscure commentary on a passage in Leviticus. Knowing what was to come, mothers with infants or toddlers immediately carried or led their progeny out of church.

After the first ten minutes of the vicar's sermon, I gave the boys crayons and paper to keep them from fidgeting. After forty, Bill took them home. By the time the vicar had spoken for a solid hour, nearly every head in the church had drooped, and when he hit the ninety-minute mark, the snores of the sleeping could be heard in our land.

I was two blinks away from a coma when the west door opened again and I regained consciousness. The Bowenists wanted out. I suspected that some of them had finally realized that their prey had flown the coop while others had simply had their fill of Aramaic derivations, because their departure was accompanied by mingled mutterings of "Mother Mae isn't here" and "I think my brain's gone numb." Wherever Amelia was, I hoped she would have the sense to lie low until her followers left the village. With most of her neighbors napping in church, she was well and truly on her own.

The vicar droned on, as did the snoring, but Bree was alert and watching the retreat intently over her shoulder. When the last Bowenist closed the west door with a thud that roused the sleepers, Bree dashed into the south porch. She returned ten minutes later, grinning broadly and making a slashing movement across her throat.

The vicar stopped talking, leaned on his pulpit, and beamed at his flock.

"Thank you," he said. "You were marvelous. I will, of course, administer the Eucharist to any who desire it. May I see a show of hands?"

Not a single hand was raised.

"I understand," said the vicar. "We shall attempt a full service next Sunday — with a much shorter sermon, I promise you."

He descended the pulpit to a chorus of polite chuckles and gave the benediction, but instead of processing down the center aisle while Elspeth played the recessional, he walked only as far as the front pew and stayed there to speak with Bree. I avoided the main torrent of departing parishioners by darting up the north aisle to the front of the church, where a few others had lingered to chat with Bree and the Buntings.

"I sense a plot," I said, when I reached them. "Did you revamp the liturgy to confound the Bowenists?"

"It was Bree's idea," said Charles Bellingham. "She thought it was awfully quiet on the Bowenist front yesterday, so she predicted that they would make a push today."

"Since the church would be a likely target," said Lilian, "we put together a reaction plan. Teddy explained it before the service and the entire congregation agreed to play along, if necessary."

"If the Bowenists showed up," Bree went on, "Mr. Bunting would call for a hymn and we'd stand to sing it. That way, we could mask the sight and the sound of Mr. Barlow smuggling Amelia into the crypt."

"Amelia's in the *crypt?*" I said. "*I've* never been in the crypt. I didn't know we *had* a crypt."

"It's dark and damp and musty," said Millicent Scroggins, with a delicate shudder.

"Mr. Barlow's the only one who ever goes down there," said Elspeth Binney, "and he does so only to make sure the sump pump is still working."

"The entrance is in the sacristy," said Henry, pointing at the door to the left of the chancel. "Barlow reckoned it would take him no more than a couple of minutes to get Mrs. Thistle from the front pew, through the sacristy, and down into the crypt. By then the hymn would be finished and we could be seated."

"Next came the question of how to get rid of the Bowenists," said Charles.

"For reasons beyond my comprehension," said the vicar, "Bree gave me the job of boring them into submission." He smiled at her. "I hope I lived down to your expectations."

"You outdid yourself," said Bree. "No offense, Mr. Bunting, but your second sermon made me want to tear my own ears off. I'm surprised the Bowenists lasted as long as they did."

"I'm surprised any of us lasted as long as we did," said Lilian. "You were brilliant, Teddy."

"Mr. Bunting had to keep talking until I gave him the signal to stop," said Bree, making the throat-slashing motion again. "Which I did, after I sneaked outside and watched the Bowenists drive away."

"I am impressed," I acknowledged, making a deep bow to the triumphant conspirators. "I am bowled over. I am in awe of your devious minds as well as your capacity to organize and motivate a crowd."

"They didn't need us to motivate them," said the vicar. "My parishioners don't approve of persecution and they don't care to see a woman bullied. Once I described Mrs. Thistle's dilemma, they were quite willing to help her. Besides, they thought it would be rather good fun. There's nothing quite so satisfying as raising the roof with a rousing rendition of 'Jerusalem.' "

"It's a pity William missed the service,"

Millicent said, giving Amelia a sly, sidelong look. "He has a wonderful singing voice."

"As I told you before, Millicent," said Elspeth, with an air of all-knowing superiority, "William is engaged in an important project at the moment. I'm sure he'll be back in church next Sunday."

"Let's hope the Bowenists won't be," said the vicar.

"Let them come," Lilian said defiantly. "With Bree on our side, we cannot fail."

"Before my head gets any bigger," said Bree, "I'll pop down to the crypt and let the fugitives know it's safe to come up."

"There's no need," I said. "They're here."

Mr. Barlow and Amelia had emerged from the sacristy with cobwebs in their hair, mud on their shoes, and looks of barely suppressed excitement on their faces.

"You'll never guess what happened in the crypt," Amelia said breathlessly. "Never in a million years. It simply defies belief."

"You'd better tell us, then," I said, half expecting her to announce her engagement to Mr. Barlow.

Instead, Amelia thrust out her clenched fist and cried, "We found the fourth page!"

Twenty-One

Protruding from either side of Amelia's fist were the ends of yet another scroll of parchment.

"Good grief," I said, stunned.

"I haven't opened it yet," said Amelia. "The crypt was rather dirty."

"Millicent," Elspeth said bossily, "fetch Selena and Opal. They won't want to miss this."

"Why must I fetch them?" Millicent protested. "Your legs appear to be working."

"A bit of hush, if you please, ladies," Lilian scolded. "Mrs. Thistle is about to reveal how she and Mr. Barlow made their miraculous discovery."

"Shall we be seated?" the vicar suggested.

He promptly took his own advice and lowered himself onto the front pew. The rest of us followed his example, but Amelia blocked Mr. Barlow's bid to join us and tugged him over to stand with her before the altar rail.

"*You* must be the one to explain," she told him. "It was your stroke of genius, not mine." She gave him a gentle shove, then stepped back, to give him center stage.

"Not much to explain," he said gruffly, thrusting his hands into his pockets and hanging his head, like a schoolboy forced to perform a recitation. "Everything went according to plan. Got Mrs. Thistle down to the crypt, lit the lantern, parked ourselves on the camp chairs I'd set up, and that was that." He raised his head and cocked it to one side. "Thing is, we had a lot of time to kill down there, thanks to Mr. Bunting."

The vicar bowed good-naturedly in response to a short round of applause.

"We didn't have to sit there like a pair of scared rabbits, though," Mr. Barlow continued. "The crypt's near enough soundproof as makes no difference, so we got to talking. Mrs. Thistle told me about Lori finding the third page and Mrs. Bunting translating it." Mr. Barlow pursed his lips, as if the translation's disturbing contents had crossed his mind, but he forbore to comment. "Then she told me about the little drawing the rector had made, the one with the three arrows."

Amelia came forward, as though she could

contain herself no longer.

"Then Mr. Barlow said, 'Must be the coat of arms' and I said, 'What coat of arms?' and he said, 'The old knight's coat of arms' and I said, 'Which old knight?' and he said, 'Sir Guillaume —' "

"— des Flèches!" Lilian interrupted, sitting bolt upright on the pew. "Sir Guillaume des Flèches, the Norman nobleman who built St. George's. Good gracious, how stupid I've been." She shook her head, looking chagrined.

"How stupid have you been?" asked Charles.

"Extremely stupid," Lilian replied. "I've been so busy studying Latin that I've forgotten my French."

"Nonsense," said Amelia. "I speak French fluently, but I missed the clue as well. It's not a word that comes up often in everyday conversation."

"Which word would that be?" Henry inquired.

"*Flèches,* of course," said Lilian. "It's the French word for *arrows.* Sir Guillaume des Flèches, in English, is Sir William of the Arrows."

There was a general murmur of pleased comprehension and much nodding of heads.

"And he had a coat of arms, did he, this

knight of the arrows?" Henry asked.

"He most certainly did," said Amelia, resuming the thread of her story. "And Mr. Barlow knew just where it was."

"Goodness knows I've bumped my head against it often enough," grumbled Mr. Barlow, rubbing his abused pate.

"Sir Guillaume had it carved into the crypt's ceiling as a bas relief," Amelia explained. "All we had to do was to look up — and there it was!" She raised her arm dramatically and tilted her head back, as if she could see the coat of arms hovering above her. "A shield surmounted by a plumed helm and emblazoned with three arrows bound together by a slender banner bearing the motto: *Toujours honnête.*" She lowered her arm and explained more matter-of-factly, "The motto means *always honest* as well as *always straight.* It's a pun, you see."

"Our knight was a straight arrow, was he?" said Henry. "Good on him."

"I scratched around the coat of arms with my pocketknife to see if I could find a hole behind it," said Mr. Barlow, "but I didn't have any luck there."

Amelia motioned toward the wall painting in the north aisle. "Then I remembered how Sir George's cross pointed us in different directions in the church."

"And sure enough," said Mr. Barlow, "the center arrow pointed us to a fake stone, like the one Bree found in the bell tower. I used my pocketknife to dig it out and —"

"— he found page four!" Amelia concluded, holding the scroll aloft.

I stood with the others to congratulate her and to marvel at the strange chain of events that had led her to the scroll's hiding place.

"If Mr. Barlow had been in the schoolhouse yesterday," she said, "he would have recognized the arrows and taken us to the crypt without delay. As it is, I suppose I must feel some sense of gratitude toward Mr. Brocklehurst's herd of damp cows."

"Damp cows?" said Millicent.

"My unwanted acolytes," Amelia clarified. "They're distressingly bovine, but without them I would have had no reason to enter the crypt today."

"If I might have the scroll, Mrs. Thistle?" Lilian requested. "I'd like to get started on it."

Amelia's joy in finding the fourth page seemed to drain away as she remembered what it might contain. I felt the same way and my neighbors' faces indicated that they, too, understood the difficult nature of the task Lilian was about to undertake.

"I suggest that you return to your homes for a midday meal," Lilian said, as Amelia passed the scroll to her. "I'll bring my translation to the schoolhouse in one hour." She hesitated, then said, "On second thought, make it two hours. It may take me a little longer to translate page four."

Since Fairworth House was out of bounds, Bill decided to take our sons to the Cotswold Farm Park after lunch. Will and Rob were enthralled by the prospect of a boys-only adventure and Bill claimed that he'd rather pet a polka-dotted pig than listen to Gamaliel's account of Mistress Meg's demise. I sympathized with him, but felt an overriding need to follow the story through to its end.

I waved them off as they sped away in the Rover, then backed my ancient Morris Mini out of the garage and drove slowly to Finch. There was no other way to drive the Mini, but its sluggish pace suited my mood. I felt as if I were on my way to an execution.

I parked the Mini in front of Bill's office and joined the steady stream of people entering the schoolhouse. It looked as though the only locals who weren't there were those who had livestock to feed or businesses to manage. When I commented on the large turnout, Selena Buxton informed me that the vicar had mentioned Amelia's scroll hunt in passing when he'd spoken to his parishioners before the morning service.

"They've come to find out what it's all about," she said. "No one wants to be the last to know."

Especially not in Finch, I thought, but I kept the thought to myself.

Amelia had again saved a seat for me in the front row, but hers was empty when I arrived because she was on the dais, asking for quiet. When she had the crowd's attention, she repeated the general introduction Lilian had made the previous day, presumably to save Lilian the trouble of repeating it.

Amelia had just finished adding the chapter about the crypt when Lilian entered the schoolroom, carrying the scroll Mr. Barlow had found and a notepad. Amelia exchanged a few quiet words with Lilian, then stepped down from the dais and sat beside me, looking at once expectant and resigned.

I couldn't tell what was going on in Lilian's mind. Her face, which had seemed troubled prior to her reading of the third page, was now an inscrutable mask. I wondered if she was holding her emotions in check to avoid being overwhelmed by them.

"Since Mrs. Thistle has brought you up to date on the memoir's history," she said, "I'll read my translation without preamble. I would ask you again to hold your comments until I've finished." She cleared her throat, gazed down at the notepad, and began to read.

"When the witch finder arrived at the house in the woods, thirty of us stood waiting for him, with Mistress Meg seated before us on a large, flat stone. He ordered her to confess her crimes. She said she would not, for she had committed no crimes. He repeated Jenna Penner's accusations and called for more witnesses to come forward.

"Mistress Brown came forward. She said: 'There is no harm in talking to goats. I am no witch, but I talk to my cow and sing to her, too. The biggest simpleton in the parish knows that singing calms a fussing creature and helps the milk flow.'

"Mistress Tolliver came forward. She said: 'There is no black magic in Mistress Meg's potions. She makes them from the herbs God grows in the woods and in the fields and along the riverbanks. The biggest fool in Finch knows how to use herbs to soothe a sore throat or to reduce a fever.'

"Master Hooper came forward. He said: 'Jenna Penner's pig died because Jenna would not go to the well to fetch water for it. Jenna has always been too lazy to look after her animals.'

"Mistress Cobb came forward. She said: 'Jenna as a young girl would always blame others for her troubles, and she would tell lies to make herself appear blameless. She has not changed.'

"Master Malvern came forward: He said: 'Jenna covets Mistress Meg's goats. To have them, she would let Mistress Meg hang.'

"Others came forward to give further instances of Jenna Penner's guile and greed. Jenna said they were all witches in a coven meant to ruin her, but the witch finder told her to be silent. He asked me if Mistress Meg attended church. I answered that I had seen Mistress Meg attend church on many occasions. Jenna Penner called me a liar, but again the witch finder told her to be silent.

"The witch finder weighed the testimony of the one against the testimony of the many. He weighed Jenna's bitter, resentful words against Mistress Meg's dignified silence. After much deliberation, he declared Mistress Meg's innocence.

"He ordered Jenna Penner to be placed in

the stocks for three days. But for her children, he said, he would have placed her in the stocks for thirty. If she dared ever again to bear false witness against anyone, he warned, he would not be so lenient.

"The witch finder and his men departed. My flock and I departed. Master Tolliver and Master Cobb took Jenna Penner to the stocks."

Lilian looked up from her notepad. "There the text ends."

For a moment nobody moved or said anything. Then whispers ran through the room like a summer breeze.

"Innocent?"

"Not hanged?"

"Not tortured?"

"They spoke up for her."

"He lied."

"He was a priest and he lied."

"Jenna lied, too."

"Doesn't make it right."

"Innocent?"

Lilian coughed peremtorily and the whispering ceased.

"I'm as surprised as you are by the verdict," she said, smiling, "and I'm ashamed to say that I was stunned by the villagers' testimony. I expected them to jeer at Mistress Meg as she was taken away. Instead,

305

they defended her and discredited her attacker. I wish I could apologize to them for underestimating their intelligence, their courage, and their loyalty."

"What about the rector?" Millicent said primly. "He fibbed, didn't he? In page two, he said Mistress Meg never went to church, but he told the witch finder she did. It can't be right for a man of God to be telling lies."

"It's not right," Lilian acknowledged. "The rector should have told the truth and trusted in God's grace. It's possible that the witch finder would have been open-minded enough to overlook Mistress Meg's repeated violations of church law. It's also possible that he would have condemned her as a witch for those violations alone. Before we judge the rector too harshly, I suppose we all must ask ourselves: Would I tell a lie to save a cherished member of my community from incarceration, torture, and execution?"

I knew what I'd do, but many of my neighbors appeared ready to debate the issue loudly and enthusiastically until nightfall. Before they could work up a full head of steam, however, Amelia spoke.

"Is it finished, then?" she asked, peering anxiously at Lilian. "Is the memoir complete? Have we found the last page?"

"I'm afraid not," said Lilian.

Silence returned as the villagers absorbed Lilian's weighty words.

"There's more?" called Mr. Barlow from the back of the room. "How can there be more, Mrs. Bunting? Jenna Penner got her comeuppance and Mistress Meg lived happily ever after. The story should end there."

"Perhaps it should, Mr. Barlow," said Lilian, "but it doesn't. There's another small drawing at the end of the text. There must, therefore, be another page hidden somewhere within the bounds of St. George's parish."

Inspired, no doubt, by a desire to earn Willis, Sr.'s, undying gratitude, Selena instantly volunteered her home, Wren Cottage, for the search, while Millicent all but insisted that we tear Larch Cottage apart to find page five, but both offers were politely refused.

"I'm sorry, ladies," said Lilian, "but the new glyph bears no resemblance to a bird or a tree. I'm not quite sure what it is. I tried to replicate it, but my sketches were rather pathetic." She looked at Amelia. "Mrs. Thistle? Do you think you might have a go at it?"

Amelia returned to the dais to study the parchment while Lilian held it flat for her on the long committee table. She then took a pencil from her carpet bag and a blank page from Lilian's notebook and with swift, sure strokes made an enlarged copy of the glyph. Lilian promptly handed it down to George Wetherhead to pass around.

I was the last to see the sketch, but though I held it right side up, upside down, and sideways, it conveyed nothing to me. The new glyph seemed to depict the face of a yawning monkey, but I couldn't connect the bizarre image with any reference point. To my knowledge, there was no Yawning Monkey Cottage in Finch.

The glyph left everyone else at the meeting equally baffled, but the idea of a "next page" struck sparks in more than one imagination. As my neighbors filed out of the schoolhouse, they began a lively discussion of what the fifth page might contain. "Jenna's Revenge" was a popular theme, along with "The Rector's Confession" and "The Witch Finder's Return."

"I don't know why we should bother to find the fifth page," I murmured after Amelia and Lilian had descended from the dais to join me. "They're entertaining themselves perfectly well without it."

"With tragedy outrunning comedy by a mile," Amelia observed.

"They can't help it," said Lilian. "Melodrama is in their blood."

"Amelia," I said, "would you make another sketch of the new glyph for me to show to Bill? I'd do it myself, but I find even stick figures challenging."

Amelia obligingly produced a second sketch and I tucked it into my purse. I felt no need to inform her that I intended to share it with one other person before I showed it to my husband.

I was about to press Willis, Sr., master glyph guesser, into service.

TWENTY-TWO

Or not.

Though I went to Fairworth House with high hopes, I left in high dudgeon after Deirdre stopped me at the front door, saying that she'd been absolutely forbidden to interrupt Willis, Sr., for any reason short of a major house fire or a nuclear emergency. As I didn't qualify in either category, I drove home, but I had no success there, either. The monkey-face glyph meant nothing to Aunt Dimity or to Bill.

In the morning, I brought the sketch with me into the kitchen, hoping it would inspire a flash of insight. The strategy didn't work for me, but produced a result nonetheless, from a wholly unexpected quarter. Will and Rob took one look at the drawing and burst into fits of suspiciously merry giggles.

"What's up?" I asked.

"It's Howling Hal," Will managed between gurgles of laughter.

I stared at him. "Who's Howling Hal?"

"He's one of the funny faces at Anscombe Manor," Will told me.

"Whit Kerby tried to wee in him once," Rob explained happily, "but he couldn't wee high enough."

"And he hit the door instead," Will continued with a mighty guffaw.

"No one uses the door, Mummy," Rob said hastily, seeing my appalled expression.

"It's all bricked up," Will added.

I made a mental note to speak with Emma about Whit Kerby's notion of fun, gave the boys a short lecture on the importance of personal hygiene, and interrogated them about Howling Hal on the way to school. Hal was, according to them, one of a dozen or so stone carvings sprinkled across the rear wall of the manor's medieval tower.

The tower's rear wall met my criteria for a potential hiding place — it was very old, it was easily accessible, and it stood within the bounds of St. George's parish — so I took the lead and ran with it. On the way back from Upper Deeping, I used my cell phone to call Amelia and Lilian. Both agreed to meet me at Anscombe Manor within the hour. Lastly, I telephoned Emma to warn her of our imminent arrival. I also asked her to hose down the bricked-in door beneath Howling Hal.

Lilian and Amelia beat me to Anscombe Manor by ten minutes. By the time I arrived, Lilian had introduced Amelia to Emma, Nell, and Kit, who had no lessons scheduled until late in the afternoon and were eager to help with the search. Lilian had also shown them Amelia's original sketch of the monkey-face glyph. They'd recognized it immediately as Howling Hal.

"Derek named the grotesques when we moved in," Emma explained, leading the way around the east end of the sprawling house to the back of the tower. "There's Howling Hal, Whining Wally, Grimacing Gert, Mourning Millie —"

"Excuse me," I interrupted. "What are grotesques?"

"They're little stone sculptures attached to a building," said Emma.

"Like gargoyles?" I said.

"They're often mistaken for gargoyles," Emma acknowledged, "but grotesques, unlike gargoyles, serve no practical purpose. Gargoyles are downspouts. Rain funnels into an opening in a gargoyle's back and flows out through its mouth. Grotesques, on the other hand, are purely decorative sculptures. Ours portray human faces, but they can depict imaginary creatures as well."

"Grotesques could be quite satiric," Amelia chimed in. "Stonemasons sometimes gave them distorted but recognizable features, to ridicule people they disliked."

"Imagine having an unflattering portrait of yourself set in stone," I said, shaking my head. "I guess it pays to be polite to masons."

As we rounded the tower's northeast corner, Emma pointed to the "funny faces" Will and Rob had observed. Most of the little sculptures were high up along the crenelated roofline and all had exaggerated expressions, except for Mourning Millie, who would not have looked out of place at a funeral.

We came to a halt halfway along the wall, before an arched doorway that had been sealed from top to bottom with bricks and mortar. The grotesque Derek had dubbed Howling Hal protruded from the wall at the arch's apex, with its little eyes screwed up and its wide mouth agape in a perpetual scream. A bucket of soapy water and a scrub brush lay in the grass near the doorway, indicating that Emma had followed my advice to give the bricks a good dousing.

"Thanks for letting me know about Whit," she said. "I'll have a chat with him when he comes in for his lesson on Thursday. The topic will be: setting a good example for our younger students."

"Don't be too hard on him," I said. "Now that I've seen Howling Hal, I have to admit that he's a pretty inviting target."

"But he's not a good hiding place," Kit pointed out. "Look at him. His mouth is open to the elements. A scroll of parchment exposed to wind, rain, sleet, and snow wouldn't stand a chance of surviving for three months let alone for three centuries."

"I can tell you for certain that there's no concealed pocket behind him," Emma added. "Derek and I didn't want to be concussed by plummeting grotesques while we were renovating the manor, so we made sure they were firmly affixed to the wall. We looked in Hal's mouth, too, and we found nothing there but rainwater."

"I think we can dismiss Hal as a hiding place," said Amelia, "but he could be a marker directing us to the scroll's actual location."

My gaze alighted on the disused doorway.

"What's on the other side of the bricks?" I asked.

"A storage room," Emma replied. "The doorway's invisible from the inside. It was plastered over to look like a solid wall long before Derek and I bought the manor."

"My great-grandfather had the plastering done," said Kit, "but the bricks predate him. Do you see how irregular they are? They were handmade rather than mass-produced."

"Derek thinks they could have been made as far back as the fourteenth century," said Emma. "I can't remember his exact reasoning, but it's something to do with the type of clay, the manufacturing technique, and the weathering."

I'd heard enough to convince me that Gamaliel could have used the sealed doorway as a hiding place. I stepped forward and began pushing on the bricks one by one, to find out if any of them would move.

"Don't be silly, Lori," said Emma. "If one of the bricks was loose, it would have fallen out years ag—" She choked slightly when the center brick in the topmost row yielded to my touch.

"You were saying, Emma?" I asked, glancing back at her.

"Given that it's not a weight-bearing brick and that it's placed beneath the lintel, where it would be more or less protected from the elements," she muttered, frowning, "I suppose it could have stayed put for a few hundred years without a solid base of mortar."

"It not only *could*," I said impatiently, "it *did*." I stepped back from the doorway. "Kit, you're taller than I am and you have stronger hands. See if you can coax it out."

Kit had to use his pocketknife as well as his fingers to finish the job, but before too long the loose brick was in his hand and a beribboned scroll was in Amelia's.

I thanked him, then looked up at the screaming grotesque. "Many thanks to you, too, Howling Hal. I shall instruct my sons to show you due respect in future."

"Tea, anyone?" said Nell.

While the rest of us indulged in tea, scones, and copious amounts of homemade black currant jam at the refectory table in Emma's enormous kitchen, Lilian retired to the library to translate page five. I was reaching for a second scone when Lilian rejoined us, looking as grave as Mourning Millie. I left the scone untouched and glanced at my watch. To my surprise, she'd been gone for less than an hour.

Kit pulled a chair out from the table for her, but she shook her head and remained standing.

"I won't be on my feet for very long," she said. "The fifth page is rather short." She paused, as if to settle herself, then peered down at her notepad and began to read her translation aloud.

"Jenna Penner died in childbed after freely confessing her many sins. She died clinging to Mistress Meg's hand, ten months after she falsely accused Mistress Meg of witchcraft. The child, a girl, came alive into the world, to be raised by her father and sisters. Jenna asked with her last breath that the child be called Margaret.

"A month after Jenna Penner's death, I was awakened at midnight by strange noises in the churchyard. I rose to investigate and found goats grazing among the headstones. Mistress Meg called to me from the shadows cast by the yew tree near the lane.

"She said: 'Do not approach me. I have been nursing the Tollivers but I could not save them. The Black Death took them, mother, father, and all, down to the smallest babe in arms. I cleansed them and their dwelling, but the pestilence followed me home. Its signs are upon me. I will do what must be done. Look after my goats.'

"She then vanished into the night. I never saw Margaret Redfearn alive on this earth again."

"Did you say Margaret Redfearn?" Kit asked.

"Yes," said Lilian. "Didn't Lori tell you?

317

Mistress Meg's full name was Margaret Redfearn."

"No," Kit murmured. "Lori didn't tell me."

A silence as deep as the ocean filled the room. Each of us sat motionless, absorbed in our own thoughts, until Lilian spoke.

"The Tollivers," she reminded us, "were the only members of St. George's parish to die of the plague. Mistress Meg must have isolated herself after she was infected, to avoid infecting the villagers. She must have died alone in her house in the woods, with no one to ease her passing." Lilian bowed her head. "God rest her soul."

"Our neighbors were right after all," Amelia said softly. "Gamaliel's story ends in tragedy."

"Um, sorry," Lilian said. With an apologetic wince, she held up the scroll Kit had liberated from the bricked-in doorway. "It's not over yet, I'm afraid. There's a new glyph."

"We're not going to discuss it or even look at it until you sit down and have a cup of tea," Kit said firmly.

He rose, plucked the scroll and the notebook from her hands, and led her to a seat at the table. Nell had just lifted the big brown teapot to fill Lilian's cup when the doorbell rang.

"I'll get it," said Emma and left the room.

She returned a moment later with Willis, Sr. He was a bit pink in the face and his white hair was slightly ruffled, but his black three-piece suit was as flawless as his gray silk tie.

"I apologize for the interruption," he said, "but I am here on a matter of some urgency. I must inform you that Mr. Myron Brockle-hurst is at this moment on his way to Anscombe Manor, accompanied by approximately fifty of Mrs. Thistle's most ardent admirers."

Amelia gasped and the color drained from her face.

"How did they find me?" she whispered.

"They did not find you, Mrs. Thistle," said Willis, Sr. "I invited them."

"You *invited* them?" I said, thunderstruck.

"I invited them," he confirmed. He walked past me to stand over Amelia. "Do you intend to flee from your oppressors for the rest of your life, Mrs. Thistle? Shall you continue to cower in the shadows while others protect you? Will you remove yourself from the village, purchase another walled compound, and sequester yourself from the world once again?" He shook his head sternly. "You are too brave, too self-reliant,

319

and too sociable to live happily with any of the choices I have presented to you. There will be no more hiding, Mrs. Thistle. The time for confrontation has arrived." He cocked an ear toward the front door. "And so, too, have our guests. I shall now put an end to a state of affairs that has troubled you for far too long."

My father-in-law was a slightly built man, but he looked ten feet tall and broad shouldered as he turned to face the foe, head held high and eyes flashing. In his reflection in the teapot, I thought I caught the glint of shining armor.

TWENTY-THREE

Five jaws dropped simultaneously as Willis, Sr., strode out of the kitchen. Nell, the only one among us who didn't look as though she'd received an electric shock, brought us to our senses by calmly offering Lilian a scone. Suddenly, we were on our feet and chattering like magpies.

"I'll get the stablehands," said Kit. "We may need them for crowd control."

"Where are we going to put fifty cars?" Emma asked.

"I can't face them," Amelia groaned. "I just can't."

"Come to the library," said Lilian. "We'll bar the door."

"They won't storm the house," I scoffed.

"Who knows what they'll do?" said Emma. "Fanatics are unpredictable."

"Then why are we standing around?" I demanded. "We can't let William face those nutters alone."

I sprinted to the front door, prepared to throw myself bodily between my father-in-law and the savage hoard, but when I dashed onto the flagstone terrace I saw that Willis, Sr., wasn't alone. To the contrary, it looked as though he had a small army at his disposal, but what he was doing with it was anyone's guess.

Mr. Barlow and Henry Cook were perched atop a pair of extension ladders, attaching a king-sized white bedsheet to the manor's facade. Bree Pym sat on a camp chair at a folding table in the graveled parking circle at the bottom of the broad stone staircase, bending over Bill's laptop and what appeared to be a slide projector. My father-in-law stood on the terrace next to a long-haired man in a flannel shirt, jeans, and a denim jacket, and my husband stood at the bottom of the stairs, surrounded by stable-hands who were armed not with pitchforks, spades, and other traditional crowd-control implements, but with handfuls of sky-blue leaflets.

At a word from Bill, the stablehands disbursed. Two went to open the south pasture's gate and the rest stood shoulder-to-shoulder at the foot of the stairs, facing the drive. Mr. Barlow and Henry climbed down from the ladders to join the line and

Bree left her folding table to check the connections between a series of extension cords that snaked past me and into the house. She nearly collided with Kit, Emma, and Lilian as they came through the front door, looking bewildered.

"What on earth . . . ?" said Emma, taking in the bustling scene.

"Don't ask me," I said. "Where's Amelia?"

"In the kitchen with Nell," Lilian replied. "We weren't providing her with the tranquil atmosphere she needed."

"What are the stablehands doing?" asked Kit.

"Following Bill's orders," I replied.

"What orders?" said Kit.

"No idea," I said.

Kit ran down to confer with Bill, accepted a handful of leaflets, and positioned himself next to Mr. Barlow. Bill, catching sight of me, came bounding up the stairs to the terrace.

"What's going on?" I asked.

"A little scheme Father and I have cooked up," he said. "I think you'll find it to your liking." He peered into the distance and nodded. "They're here."

A ragtag fleet of vehicles led by Myron's red Ferrari came into view between the azaleas lining Anscombe Manor's curving drive. One of the two stablehands manning the south pasture's gate directed the cars, camper vans, and pickup trucks through it to park. The second stablehand instructed the alighting drivers and passengers to gather on the graveled circle before the stairs. I spotted Daffodil Deeproots among them.

Myron emerged from his sports car and sauntered casually through the crowd, flashing peace signs and murmuring words of support in his soft, soothing voice. He looked exactly as Bree had described him, as if he were posing for pictures at a hippie museum. Everything about him seemed false. I suspected that a couple of firm tugs would remove his blond pony tail as well as his mustache, and his spotless jeans looked as though they'd been starched and pressed.

He was too old to be a flower child — in his late forties, at least — and though his thin, ascetic face was mildly attractive, his eyes were almost frightening in their intensity. Bree had called his laser-beam gaze creepy, but I found it predatory as well, as if he believed he exercised a form of mind control over his minions. For all I knew, he did.

The line of stablehands parted to allow Myron to approach the stairs. He placed a sandaled foot on the bottom step, but when his piercing blue eyes met Willis, Sr.'s, mild gaze, he stopped short. After a moment's hesitation, he withdrew his foot.

"We have come at Mother Mae's beckoning," he said. "Do you mean to stand in our way?"

"Not at all," Willis, Sr., said pleasantly. "I am the good lady's humble servant. I am here merely to entertain the masses while you are given a private audience."

"Naturally," said Myron, with a cocksure smirk that made me want to smack him.

"I'm on," Bill whispered. He motioned for Myron to ascend the stairs and precede him into the manor. Bill followed him inside, almost bumping into Bree, who was scurrying back to her folding table.

"William's not really foisting Myron on Amelia, is he?" Lilian asked in a worried undertone. "She'll go to pieces."

"Don't worry about Amelia," Emma said confidently. "Nell's more than a match for Myron."

"So is Bill," I murmured.

Willis, Sr., waited for Bill to close the door behind Myron, then lifted his head to address the gathering. He spoke in a calm, clear voice that penetrated, then silenced the murmurs that had risen in Myron's absence.

"Let us speak of the beauties of nature," he began.

"Right on," said a rosy-cheeked woman in a bobble cap.

"Dig it," said the brunette standing next to her.

"Let us speak of the beauties of nature," Willis, Sr., repeated, "and your part in their destruction."

It took a moment for his words to register with the Bowenists, but eventually they stirred. Some muttered and shook their heads.

"Not cool, man."

"What's he on about?"

"Man's talking rubbish."

"Who is this clown?"

Daffodil Deeproots came forward and the muttering died away.

"We love Mother Earth," she proclaimed. "We would never harm her."

"Not knowingly, perhaps," said Willis, Sr. "How many of you have donated money to the Bowenist movement?"

"All of us," said Daffodil, adding in a singsong voice, "There's no better use of pounds and pence than to fill the world with enlightenments."

" 'Enlightenments'?" Lilian murmured,

rolling her eyes.

"You are not alone in your beliefs, Miss Deeproots," said Willis, Sr. "Over the past ten years, the Bowenist website has raised more than ten million pounds through donations and through the sale of private papers extracted from Mae Bowen's trash."

"Ten . . . million . . . pounds?" Daffodil said faintly, her eyes widening.

"If you would like to know how your donations have been spent, I can tell you," said Willis, Sr. "Are you familiar with mountaintop removal mining?"

"It's a crime!" shouted a bearded man.

"A crime against nature!" shouted another.

"What's mountaintop removal . . . thingy?" asked a third.

"Thank you for asking, sir. Please turn your attention to the screen." Willis, Sr., swept his arm in a wide arc to indicate the bedsheet, onto which Bree had projected an aerial image of a heavily forested mountain peak. "Instead of boring into the side of a mountain to work a coal seam, the mining company decapitates the mountain."

A second slide appeared, showing a barren moonscape where the forest had been.

"Trees, ferns, flowers, grasses, mosses — every living thing is scraped away," said Willis, Sr., "along with the topsoil. The underlying rock layers are pulverized by explosives and the coal is removed."

The third slide showed bulldozers pushing enormous piles of rubble over the edge of the flattened, deeply scarred mountaintop.

"What remains is dumped into streams," said Willis, Sr. "The streams are poisoned and choked by debris. Fish die, birds die, insects and amphibians die. With so many streams obliterated, the few that are left tend to flood catastrophically. People die."

The slides were coming without pause now, showing scene after scene of breathtaking devastation.

"They have to restore it, don't they?" called a woman at the back of the group. "After they're done, I mean. They have to restore it."

"How does one restore a mountaintop?" asked Willis, Sr. "How does one replace the abundance of plant and animal life that once flourished there? When the miners are finished with one mountain, they spray grass seed on sterile rock and move on to the next."

A young blonde in a crocheted poncho cried, "Stop! Stop! I don't want to see any more pictures!" Then she burst into tears.

Rumbles of rage, horror, grief, and disbelief rolled through the group as Willis, Sr., signaled to Bree to terminate the slide show.

"It's a crime," the bearded man repeated vehemently. "A crime against nature."

"It is a crime that is being carried out with your help," said Willis, Sr.

"You're mad!" shouted Daffodil.

"I am angry, yes, Miss Deeproots, but I am not insane," said Willis, Sr. "I have procured literature that confirms my claims. It takes a form you and your friends will find familiar."

He gestured to the stablehands and the others in the half circle and they passed among the Bowenists, handing out the sky-blue leaflets.

"As you can see, the leaflets were produced by the Clear Sky Mining Corporation," said Willis, Sr. "Clear Sky is the foremost practitioner of mountaintop removal mining. If you turn to the back of your leaflet, you will find a list of investors. The name at the top of the list is —"

"— Myron Brocklehurst!" Daffodil exclaimed.

"Myron Brocklehurst is Clear Sky's principal investor," said Willis, Sr. "He has used your pounds and pence, Miss Deeproots, to spread death and destruction, not enlightenment. I need hardly mention that the profits from his illegal investments have been deposited in his personal bank accounts."

"No," said Daffodil, almost pleadingly." He gave our donations to conservation groups. I have it in writing!"

"You were misled," said Willis, Sr. "I am sorry, Miss Deeproots. You put your faith in the wrong man."

"It's impossible," she whispered, shaking her head.

"If you do not believe me," said Willis, Sr., "please feel free to speak with a gentleman who has witnessed firsthand the desolation caused by mountaintop removal mining." He indicated the longhaired man in the flannel shirt. "Lester Turek has worked tirelessly, though so far unsuccessfully, to close down Clear Sky's mining operations. He flew in from America last night to answer your questions about the company's practices as well as its corporate structure. If you please, Mr. Turek?"

As Lester Turek waded into the crowd, fielding questions, Lilian, Emma, and I clustered around Willis, Sr.

"Your demonstration was a bit brutal," Lilian commented gently.

"It could have been more so," said Willis, Sr. "I did not mention Mr. Brocklehurst's investments in genetic engineering, arctic oil, the fur trade, and the deforestation of Borneo. It is unlikely to occur to any of his acolytes that he could not have acquired his wealth through coal mining alone. I therefore felt no need to distress them further."

"Why did Myron embezzle money from the faithful?" I asked. "He was already rich when he invented Bowenism."

"Not as rich as he is now," said Willis, Sr. "He inherited his initial fortune and apparently decided to acquire additional funds with a similar lack of effort. He seems to have but a passing acquaintance with the work ethic, or with any honorable ethic at all."

"You're no stranger to hard work, though," I said. "I couldn't figure out what could keep you occupied for three straight days — and nights, if I know you — including a Sunday you were supposed to spend with your grandsons, but now I know what you were doing behind the locked door in your study. You were building a case against Myron."

"I did not construct the case on my own," said Willis, Sr. "Bill had already gathered a large amount of vital data and he was instrumental in acquiring more. I could not have concluded my research in such a short period of time without my son's invaluable assistance."

"Did he find Lester Turek?" asked Lilian.

"Yes," said Willis, Sr. "I invited Mr. Turek to join us because he is an honest man and an expert in his field. I was also favorably impressed by his appearance."

"He looks pretty scruffy to me," Emma said, craning her neck to survey Lester's attire.

"I felt that Mr. Turek's scruffiness, as you put it, would add credibility to my claims," Willis, Sr., explained. "Those who dress informally are more apt to trust a man in a flannel shirt than a man in a bespoke suit."

I had to laugh. My father-in-law had arranged his presentation as meticulously as he'd arranged his tie.

"What have you done with Myron?" I asked. "Bill didn't really take him to see Amelia, did he?"

"I did not say that Mr. Brocklehurst would have a private audience with Mrs. Thistle," Willis, Sr., pointed out. "I said only that he would have a private audience, which was a statement of fact. Bill had the pleasure of introducing him to a number of people who were eager to make his acquaintance. Ah!" A gleam of quiet satisfaction lit Willis, Sr.'s eyes as he spied a black sedan pulling out of the stable yard and onto the curving drive.

"Who's leaving?" I asked, as the sedan disappeared among the azaleas.

"I don't know," said Emma. "I don't recognize the car."

"The automobile belongs to Scotland Yard's fraud squad," Willis, Sr., informed us. "They have taken an interest in Mr. Brocklehurst's financial affairs, as have a number of other agencies. When I expressed concern over the possibility of Mr. Brocklehurst fleeing the country to escape prosecution, they were kind enough to send a car for him."

"It was a two-pronged attack," I marveled. "While you ripped Myron's saintly image to shreds out here, Bill took him inside to be grilled by the fraud squad." I gave a low whistle. "Talk about having a bad day."

"Do I get to keep the Ferrari?" Emma asked brightly.

"I fear not," said Willis, Sr., smiling. "The Ferrari will be impounded by the authorities this afternoon."

"It wouldn't have done me much good anyway," said Emma. "No room for hay bales." She frowned questioningly at Willis, Sr. "I don't recall giving you my permission to use the manor for your . . . event."

"I apologize most sincerely for the liberties I have taken with your property as well as your personnel," Willis, Sr., said, regarding her contritely. "I would have used my own home, but I required help to distribute the leaflets and there are, alas, no stablehands at Fairworth."

A commotion in the crowd interrupted our conversation. At first I thought the Bowenists were coming after Willis, Sr., but as they surged forward I realized that their faces were exultant rather than hostile and their collective gaze was focused on a point beyond my father-in-law. I wheeled around just in time to see Amelia march through the doorway and onto the terrace, with Bill at her side and Nell gliding serenely in their wake.

Cries of "Mother Mae!" rent the air, but Amelia silenced them with disparaging "Tut!"

"It's lucky for you I'm not your mother," she said, "because if I were, I'd box your ears. You gave your money to a slippery hypocrite who used it to defile God's green earth. Shame on you!"

"It's Myron's fault!" shouted the rosy-cheeked woman.

"Don't you dare blame Mr. Brocklehurst," scolded Amelia. "If you abdicate responsibility for your lives, you have only yourselves to blame for the consequences. Mr. Brocklehurst couldn't have taken advantage of you if you hadn't allowed him to lead you around by the nose."

"We're sorry, Moth—"

"I beg your pardon?" Amelia interrupted ferociously.

"We're sorry, Ms. Bowen."

"That's better," Amelia snapped. "Now, stand up straight and listen with both ears. You don't need a guru to tell you what to think. If you must find meaning in my work, find your own meaning. Better yet, stop seeing the world through my eyes and start using your own. While you're at it, you might start using your brains as well. Heaven knows they've lain dormant long enough."

"Can we volunteer to help Lester?" Daffodil asked.

"Why are you asking *me?*" Amelia thundered. "Haven't I just told you to make your own decisions?"

"Oh, right," said Daffodil, nodding.

"I'm not your mother or your best friend or your guide to spiritual awakening," Amelia said severely. "I'm a painter and I need peace and quiet to get on with my work. I don't want to hear you chanting at my exhibitions ever again, and if I catch you anywhere near my cottage, I *shall* box your ears. Have I made myself clear?"

She was answered by a ragged chorus of affirmatives.

"If you're very good and do as you're told," Amelia continued, "I *may* allow you to attend a special sale of my work, for old time's sake. The sale will be held at my London gallery in December and one hundred per cent of the proceeds will go to Lester Turek's campaign to bring an end to mountaintop removal mining."

A cheer went up and many hands reached out to pat a grinning Lester Turek on the back. Amelia flashed a brief smile, then raised her arms for silence.

"It's time for you to leave," she said, pointing to their vehicles. "Go forth and spread the good news: Bowenism — detestable word! — is dead!"

The ex-Bowenists still resembled a herd of damp cows as they shuffled obediently to their vehicles and drove away, but a handful, including Daffodil, accepted Lester's invitation to discuss his campaign over drinks at the pub. I hoped Dick Peacock wouldn't throw them out of his establishment. I wanted Daffodil to discover what it was like to be involved in a truly worthwhile cause.

Willis, Sr., thanked everyone who'd contributed to the production, and the stable-hands returned to their chores. The bed-sheet, ladders, folding table, camp chair, extension cords, laptop, and slide projector were collected and stowed in their respective owners' vehicles. Mr. Barlow, Henry, and Bree congratulated Amelia and Willis, Sr., then headed for home. The two men left without further ado, but Bree cruised down the curving drive with her clenched fist thrust out of the window at arm's length, honking her horn in triumph.

"We pulled it off, Father," said Bill. "Myron's spinning a pretty tale about identity theft, but he's not dealing with gullible airheads anymore. By the time Scotland Yard, the Inland Revenue, the Charity Commission, and the rest are finished with him, his tale-spinning days will be over. He'll spend the next ten years of his life trying to zap his cell mates with his laser-beam eyes. Something tells me he won't have much success."

While Bill was talking, Amelia was hugging. She embraced Lilian, Emma, Kit, Nell, and me twice over before she gave Bill a kiss on each cheek as well as a hug. Then she turned to face Willis, Sr.

"I don't know how to thank you, William,"

she said. "You've set me free."

I noted with immense interest her use of his first name, but Willis, Sr., didn't bat an eye.

"It was my civic duty to report Mr. Brocklehurst's illicit activities to the appropriate authorities," he said. "If you will excuse me . . ."

"Must you go?" Amelia gazed at him imploringly, then ducked her head and stammered, "W-we've found the fifth page. I-I was rather hoping you might stay to help us with the new glyph."

Willis, Sr., must have been ready to drop after his marathon effort to nail Myron Brocklehurst. He must have been yearning for a hot bath, a warm bed, and hours of deep, dreamless sleep. He must have known that the rest of us had enough brain power to decipher the glyph without him, but none of it seemed to matter.

His chest rose and fell in a slow, silent sigh as he gazed at Amelia's bowed head and said, "Of course I shall stay, Mrs. Thistle."

TWENTY-FOUR

"I'm glad you're staying, William," said Kit, "but we may not need your help to decipher the glyph. I glanced at it before I left the kitchen and I think I know what it means."

He drew from his shirt pocket the scroll he'd taken from Lilian and unfurled it to reveal the drawing at the end of the Latin text.

"Is it a feather?" I guessed.

"I think not," said Willis, Sr., eyeing the drawing judiciously. "I believe it represents a fern."

"So do I," said Kit, "which makes perfect sense when you think about it."

"Does it?" I said.

"Yes," he said. He gave the scroll to Amelia, then stood back to survey Willis, Sr.'s, elegantly shod feet. "You'll need to borrow a pair of my Wellies, William. Your leather shoes won't serve you well where we're going."

"Where are we going?" I asked.

"Into the woods," Kit replied.

Since the woods were still dripping wet from the recent rains, Emma decided to outfit us all in Wellington boots and the long, brown slickers she kept on hand for rainy-day riding lessons. By the time we set out, we looked like a posse of gardeners, and baffled gardeners at that, because the only person who knew where Kit was leading us was Kit.

We followed him down a muddy two-rut track that skirted the north pasture and ended at the edge of the forest that stretched from the fence line all the way to the Fairworth estate.

"There's no trail, I'm afraid," said Kit. "We'll have to bushwhack from here."

"Kit," I said patiently, "why are you taking us on a jungle safari?"

"Didn't I say?" He scanned our blank faces, then smiled sheepishly. "Sorry. It's so clear to me that I stupidly thought it would be clear to you, too. I've been turning it over in the back of my mind ever since Lilian read her translation to us in the kitchen. Until then I didn't know Mistress Meg was called Margaret Redfearn, so it took me a while to fit the pieces together."

"And now that you have . . . ?" Lilian coaxed.

"Once I saw the fern glyph, it became even more glaringly obvious," he said. "It's another pun, you see, like the three arrows and Guillaume des Flèches. The fern refers to Margaret Redfearn, of course, but I suspect it also refers to a place known as Redfern Meadow."

"Redfern Meadow?" said Emma. "I've never heard of it."

"You wouldn't have heard of it unless you'd grown up playing in these woods," Kit explained. "It's not on any map. It's a local name for a local spot and there's really not much to it. But I think . . ." He bit his lower lip, then shook his head. "No, I *know* it's the right place. Come. You'll see."

Nell had an elvish ability to move through the woods without apparent effort, but we mere mortals slipped, tripped, and stumbled our way through vegetation that seemed bent on our destruction. Bill uttered a number of ripe words before he remembered that ladies were present and I uttered a few more before I remembered that I was a lady. I couldn't imagine how Willis, Sr., managed to stay upright after three sleep-deprived days, but he was second only to Kit in his bushwhacking prowess. Amelia was surprisingly sure-footed as well, but no one, of course, could compare with Nell, who seemed to float over the slippery roots, muddy holes, and snapping branches that made me wish I'd spent the day in bed.

We came at last to an opening in the trees, a glade filled with chest-high bracken that had turned from summer green to autumn red. Glittering raindrops bejeweled each flaming frond and velvety mosses glowed in the lacy shadows. The sight was so beautiful and so unexpected that I almost forgot what I'd gone through to see it.

"Redfern Meadow," said Kit.

"It's not really a meadow," Emma pointed out.

"Not anymore," said Kit. "But it used to be a lot bigger. We're surrounded by some of the youngest trees in the wood. If you poke around, you'll see that a swathe of forest was cleared away at one time to enlarge the glade."

Amelia, who'd been busy restoring order to her disheveled hair, dropped her hands and asked in a startled voice, "Could Mistress Meg have enlarged the glade?"

"It's possible," said Kit. "There's evidence that a small house once stood here. I found the post holes when I was a child. I think I can find them again." He waded into the bracken, gave a short cry, and plunged headfirst into the sea of crimson fronds.

"Kit?" I called. "Are you okay?"

"I'm fine," he said, grinning ruefully as he pushed himself to his feet. "I forgot about the rock."

"The rock?" Amelia said faintly.

"Yes," said Kit. "There's a big, flat rock here. When I was little, I used to stand on it and pretend I was a giant looking out over trees. It tripped me up."

"Mistress Meg sat on a large, flat stone when the witch finder came to arrest her," said Amelia. She gazed about the glade wonderingly. "Could we be standing where she once stood?"

"Let's have a look at the rock," said Bill, and waded in after Kit.

Both men disappeared in the bracken. The fronds above them rustled and swayed as they crouched to examine the stone. I heard Kit say "Let's use my knife," followed by a series of grunts and scraping noises. After several suspense-filled minutes, the two stood up in the bracken, red faced and wet haired but smiling.

"We found it," Bill said. He held up an old glass bottle stoppered with a thick plug of beeswax. "Gamaliel buried it under the rock. He placed the scroll in a bottle, to keep it from disintegrating, and he marked the rock with a miniscule fern to show where the bottle was hidden."

"Even if I'd seen the fern when I was little," said Kit, "I couldn't have found the bottle. I wasn't strong enough to shift the rock."

He and Bill pushed their way through the bracken to rejoin the rest of us.

"Shall we open it here or back at the manor?" Bill asked.

"Here, please," said Amelia.

Kit used his knife to dig though the beeswax. Amelia extracted the scroll, removed its limp black ribbon, and unrolled three sheets of parchment with trembling hands.

"Three pages?" said Lilian, raising her eyebrows. "The rector must have been in a chatty mood."

Amelia looked at the third page.

"No glyph," she said. "We've reached the end of Gamaliel's memoir." She turned to pass the scroll to Lilian. "I may be asking too much of you, Mrs. Bunting, but could you possibly translate it here and now? I'd like to hear Gamaliel's last words here, in this place."

"An extemporaneous translation of three full pages of Latin text?" Lilian looked doubtful. "I wouldn't attempt it on my own, but perhaps, with William's help . . . ?"

"I am at your service, madam," said Willis, Sr., but he swayed slightly as he spoke.

Amelia glanced at him anxiously and said, "I need to sit down. Scolding those young idiots, tramping through the woods — it's all been a bit much for me. Are there any logs nearby?"

"Over here," said Kit, and led us a short distance away from the glade to a fallen tree that had made its own clearing.

"Nature provides," said Amelia. She lowered herself onto the log and beckoned to Willis, Sr., and Lilian to join her. "The scholars shall share my bench. Come, have a seat, you two. Save your energy for your work."

It was a kind and clever way to give my tired father-in-law a chance to rest. I smiled at Amelia gratefully as "the scholars" accepted her invitation and sat side by side with their heads bent over the curling sheets of parchment in Lilian's hands. Kit, Nell, Bill, and I ranged ourselves before them while they pored over the Latin text, but it took less time than I'd expected for them to complete their daunting task. Apart from a few brief pauses to consult with Willis, Sr., Lilian translated the text on the spot with remarkable fluency.

"I was sent as a youth to live and study with my uncle, a vicar in Oxford," she began. "I seldom returned home because the journey was costly and my father's income was modest. After my ordination, I was appointed to several parochial parishes before I became the rector of St. George's parish church.

"Within days of my arrival in Finch, I learned of a heathen called Margaret Redfearn who lived without male protection in the forest to the south of the village. I made my way to her dwelling place, determined to save her immortal soul from damnation.

"I found her grazing her goats in a pasture not far from her house in the woods and I called to her, asking her if she had some quarrel with God.

" 'Not with God,' she replied, 'but with men I have quarreled mightily.' She smiled at me and said, 'Do you not know me, my brother?'

"I studied her face more closely and saw my sister's eyes gazing at me."

Amelia gasped. "Mistress Meg was Gamaliel Gowland's *sister?*"

"Please let me finish," said Lilian, and continued her flowing translation.

"I knew Margaret's eyes, though everything else about her had changed beyond recognition. My eldest sister had been a lithe and beautiful girl when I'd last seen her, but she was now a thick-waisted woman, with arms as muscular as a man's and a face as brown and creased as a walnut's shell. Her blue eyes, though, were the same eyes that had watched over me and my younger siblings through many a childhood illness.

" 'Father wrote to me years ago,' I said when I could speak. 'He told me you had entered a convent.'

"Margaret laughed and said, 'Sit, my brother Gamaliel, and I will tell you the truth.'

"We sat at the edge of the meadow, with the goats grazing peacefully before us, and she told me a marvelous tale.

"She said: 'Our father wished me to marry. When I refused, the priest advised him to send me forthwith to a convent. They would have caged me in marriage or within the walls of a nunnery, but I took to the woods in the night and set out to live a life of my own choosing.

" 'A kindly cook at a manor house gave me a meal one day and told the lord of the manor I was skilled in the healing arts. He asked me to tend to his mother, who had lost all faith in surgeons. I eased the old woman's chest pains and the lord was grateful. He gave me a place in his wood for my house as well as a pair of goats and grazing rights in his pasture. My goats and I have lived here ever since. The villagers do nothing to hinder me and I do my best for them when they are ill. I have no desire to go elsewhere.'

"I asked why our father had lied to me. She laughed again and ruffled my hair, as she had done when I was a child, and told me I would die as innocent as the day I was born.

" 'Father had to save face," she explained. 'He could not admit that his daughter was beyond his control.'

"I asked why she was called Margaret Redfearn rather than Margaret Gowland.

" 'I left our father's name behind when I left his house,' she said. 'The villagers rechristened me, naming me after the glade that is my true home.'

"I asked why she came not to church, as she had attended services faithfully when we were children.

" 'I am not fond of stone walls built by men,' she replied. 'I speak to God in the church He created. I hear His voice in the wind and the birdsong and the silence. I serve Him by using the gift He gave me to heal. I have no need of your church.'

"She then made me promise to tell no one of our close kinship. She knew the perils of the life she had chosen. She foresaw a time when she would be accused of witchcraft. She did not want me to be tainted by her misfortune should the witch finder knock on her door. I kept my promise.

"On the night Margaret came to me in the churchyard, fire lit the sky above the Tolliver farmstead. My sister had cleansed their lifeless bodies and their dwelling place by setting them alight. After she left me, fire lit the sky above Redfearn Meadow. I ran to the glade still clad in my nightshirt, but I was too late. The wooden house she had built with her own hands was ablaze and" — Lilian's voice quavered — "Margaret was inside it.

"I do not believe Margaret's death was an accident. The signs of the Black Death were upon her. I believe she cleansed herself and her home with fire to keep her affliction from spreading to the village. In the eyes of the Church, suicide is a mortal sin. In my eyes, Margaret committed a virtuous act to save those who had saved her from the gallows. God alone knows the truth, but in my heart I know that she is with Him.

"I have told no one of my close kinship with Margaret Redfearn. I acknowledge it now, in secret, because I do not want her story to die with me. May you who read these words remember my congregation and my sister in your prayers. Take from my tale what lessons you will. I leave for Exeter in a fortnight. May God give me the strength to live a life of tolerance, service, and self-sacrifice in Margaret's honor. In the name of the Father, the Son, and the Holy Spirit, Amen."

Lilian slowly rolled the three pages of parchment into a scroll and inserted it into the bottle. She placed the bottle on the ground and leaned forward, with her elbows resting on her knees.

"It's true that the persecution of witches slowed to a standstill in the late seventeenth century," she said. "Perhaps Gamaliel used his influence as an archdeacon to teach the lessons in tolerance he'd learned from the villagers. When enough people raise their voices to speak out against superstition and prejudice, change can happen."

"He was telling the truth when he told the witch finder he'd seen Mistress Meg in church on many occasions," I said. "According to him, she'd attended services faithfully when they were children."

"I've always wondered why the post holes I found were black inside," said Kit. "Now I know why. The house posts must have been charred by the fire."

I turned to look at the glade and saw in my mind's eye a small wooden house engulfed in flames redder than the bracken. I shivered and turned away.

"What a horrible way to die," I said.

"To die of bubonic plague would have been worse," said Lilian. "Margaret Redfearn spared the village unspeakable suffering. She may even have saved Finch. Many small villages simply ceased to exist after the Black Death took its toll, but Finch flourishes to this day. Was Margaret right to stop the contagion by taking her own life?" Lilian shook her head. "I'll leave it to God to decide whether she committed a mortal sin or a virtuous act of self-sacrifice."

"Mrs. Thistle," Willis, Sr., said suddenly, "what is wrong?"

I looked at Amelia and realized with a start that she was crying. Nell was already standing behind her, stroking her back, but I hadn't even noticed her tears. Nor had Lilian, Kit, or Bill, to judge by their startled expressions. Willis, Sr., pulled a pristine linen handkerchief from his pocket and presented it to Amelia, who buried her face in it.

"Forgive me, Mrs. Thistle," said Lilian, looking mortified. "I've been chuntering on about witch hunts and bubonic plague when the story is much more personal for you. As the Reverend Gowland's sister, Margaret Redfearn would have been your ancestor. It must have been dreadfully upsetting to hear about the manner of her passing."

"Margaret died three hundred years ago," Amelia managed between sobs. "I'm not crying for her. I'm crying for my poor brother Alfred."

"Why are you crying for Alfred?" I asked.

"Because he killed himself," she blurted, her face crumpling. "Suicide runs in the family."

There was a fleeting moment of shocked silence before we converged on Amelia, each of us murmuring whatever words of consolation came to mind. Her sobs slowly abated, though her face remained a mask of inconsolable grief.

"Amelia," Kit said gently. "I have some idea of what you're going through. My stepfather killed himself. If you ever want to talk, I'm only a phone call away."

"Thank you, my dear," she said, wiping her eyes, "but I may as well talk now. I don't think I can stop myself."

"Don't even try," said Kit.

"Alfie was such a good brother to me," she said softly. "We didn't know he was ill until the first time he tried to kill himself. The paramedics saved him, but he was never the same. He would be fine for months, then he would plunge into an abyss of despair."

Raindrops pattered to the ground as a breeze shook the branches overhead. It was as though the trees, too, were shedding tears for Alfred.

"After his second suicide attempt, he was placed in a special care facility," she went on. "The doctors diagnosed him as schizo-phrenic, bipolar, manic-depressive, obsessive-compulsive — whatever term was fashionable at the time. He was given all sorts of drugs and sometimes they'd work for a while, but even when they did, the side effects were unbearable."

Amelia swallowed hard and twisted her hands in her lap.

"Sometimes I couldn't bring myself to visit him," she said. "Sometimes I ignored his calls. It gets tiring, you see, year after year, always bracing yourself for the worst, never knowing what will happen next, and after our parents died, Alfie was wholly dependent on me. I had no energy to spare for a husband or children, so I didn't think I'd ever marry. Then I met Walter."

"Walter Thistle," I said. "Your late husband."

"Walter was unfazed by Alfie's illness," she said, a ghost of a smile touching her lips. "He found new doctors, better treatments, and suggested that we bring Alfie to live with us at Highburn. I was doubtful at first, but Walter knew best. The tranquil atmosphere helped Alfie to stay on an even keel. My brother spent the last ten years of his life at Highburn and the only symptom of his disease to manifest itself in all that time was a reluctance to leave the estate. As long as he was at Highburn, working busily on his projects, he was content and happy."

I put a hand to my forehead as the light of understanding dawned. Alfred hadn't been physically disabled, as Aunt Dimity and I had assumed. It had been a mental disorder that had prevented him from coming to Finch to search for the remaining pages of Gamaliel's memoir.

"Gradually, Alfred's world became smaller and smaller," Amelia was saying. "After Walter died, he couldn't bear to leave his room. I found him there almost a year ago, sprawled on the floor beside his overturned desk chair."

"There is no doubt that he committed suicide?" asked Willis, Sr.

"A paramedic found the empty tablet bottles," she said dully. "They had rolled under Alfie's desk. And the postmortem extinguished any faint hope I might have had that the overdose could have been accidental."

Amelia blew her nose in the tear-soaked handkerchief and sat up straighter.

"You can have no idea how happy I was to find the biscuit tin," she told us. "I couldn't go on living at Highburn after what had happened and I needed to do something to . . . to commemorate my brother's life. I sold the estate, bought Pussywillows, and came to Finch to finish a project that was dear to his heart." She looked down at the scroll in the old bottle. "I'm almost sorry we found the final pages. I thought finding them would free me to move on, but I feel . . . paralyzed. Now that I've done what I set out to do, I don't know what to do next."

Nell continued to stroke her back and Kit put a comforting hand on her shoulder.

"It's the waste I can't stand," she said, through a fresh trickle of tears. "Alfie was a genius. A mind like his comes along once in a century, but it was all for nothing. Margaret Redfearn died to save a village, but my brother died because a disease would not let him live. Alfie wasn't a hero. He was a poor, pathetic victim."

Willis, Sr., coughed almost inaudibly, but Amelia heard and turned to him. With her puffy eyes, pink nose, and escaping tendrils of hair, she looked as vulnerable as a woebegone child.

"May I ask how old Alfred was when he died?" Willis, Sr., inquired.

"He was sixty-six," she replied.

"And how old was he at the time of his first suicide attempt?" Willis, Sr., went on.

"Twenty," Amelia answered, her voice breaking.

"Your brother lived for nearly half a century, fighting demons most of us can scarcely imagine," said Willis, Sr. "There are many kinds of heroism, Mrs. Thistle. Living with mental illness is one of them. Allowing life to fill the emptiness death leaves behind is another. You may at this moment feel paralyzed, but soon you will be making a new backdrop for the Nativity play, selling chipped Coronation mugs at the jumble sale, and nurturing a nasturtium for the flower show." His gaze shifted to the blazing red bracken. "You will also return to the glade time and again, to capture its soul with your paintbrush."

"How can you be certain?" Amelia asked.

"Because heroism runs in your family." Willis, Sr., stood. "Shall we return to the manor? I believe a nice cup of tea would do all of us a world of good."

Willis, Sr., took a step forward, wavered, and nearly fell, but Amelia jumped to her feet to steady him.

"Lean on me, William," she said, putting an arm around his waist.

"Perhaps, Amelia," he said, wrapping his arm around her shoulders, "we can lean on each other."

EPILOGUE

Fairy tales, as Nell had said, are always complicated.

Although there is not one micron of doubt in anyone's mind that Willis, Sr., is deeply in love with Amelia, and she with him, he hasn't pressed an engagement ring on her or urged her to marry him by Christmas. He continues to court her delicately and deliberately, as if he wants her to catch her breath before plunging heart-first into the life they will build together.

I knew that, with his help, Amelia would emerge from her grief like a spring crocus bursting through the snow. But it would take time.

"It's a terrible thing, isn't it?" I said. "The way the past can haunt the present?"

It is indeed.

It was a blustery night in mid-November. A hard freeze and a biting wind had set the stage for winter. It felt wonderful to be indoors, curled in the tall leather armchair in the study, with a fire in the hearth, Reginald in the crook of my arm, and the blue journal open in my lap.

Thankfully, Amelia's past won't haunt her forever. Life insists that we go on. As does Finch.

I smiled. "Peggy Taxman's already roped Amelia into baking brown bread for the bake sale and Millicent Scroggins invited her, somewhat frostily, to serve as a judge at next year's art show."

Millicent, I take it, has not yet forgiven Amelia for revising her position on remarriage.

"No," I said, "but Elspeth Binney seems reconciled to the new reality. She asked Amelia to tea the other day."

A sensible woman. Now that William is out of the running, perhaps she'll turn her sights on more a likely prospect.

"The pickings are pretty slim in Finch," I said.

One of Elspeth's delightful nieces may introduce her to an appropriate suitor. Or a stranger may come to the village and sweep her off her feet.

"I hope so," I said. "I like Elspeth. A few strangers came to Finch today, as a matter of fact," I went on, "but they were too strange for Elspeth. Some of Myron's minions missed the message about the death of Bowenism. They tried to stage a sit-in, in front of Pussywillows, but Amelia ruined their plans."

How?

"She couldn't sweep them off their feet because they were sitting down," I said, "so she swept them off the pavement — with a broom. I'd say they didn't know what hit them, but I'm pretty sure they did."

Mr. Brocklehurst has a lot to answer for.

"Oh, he'll answer for it, all right," I said cheerfully. "According to Bill, the prosecution has a mile-long list of people eager to testify against Myron. Bill also found out that Bree and I were right to trust our instincts about Ol' Laser Eyes. Myron's mustache and ponytail were fake and his hippie wardrobe was tailor-made."

Inauthenticity is a common malady among self-appointed spiritual leaders.

"Myron was a New Age version of a plastic preacher," I said, nodding, "and behind every plastic preacher, there's a con."

The phrase "a goat leading sheep" comes to mind, but I don't wish to be unkind to goats. Speaking of which, have Rob and Will persuaded William to go along with their latest scheme?

I laughed. Bill and I had decided that Will and Rob were too young to hear the story of Margaret Redfearn, but word of her goat herd had somehow reached our little pitchers' big ears. They'd immediately dug out of their toy chest a pair of cuddly toy goats Bill had bought for them at the Cotswold Farm Park and used them as a starting point in a discussion aimed at persuading their grandfather to raise goats at Fairworth. Willis, Sr., had promised them solemnly that he would give their proposal careful consideration.

"I don't know what William will decide," I admitted. "He tends to be putty in his grandsons' hands, though, and he might like the idea of having a few goats about the place, as a tribute to Mistress Meg. I suspect he'll leave the final decision to Amelia."

I'm glad the boys like her.

"They'll like her better if she gets them their goats," I said, "but they like her well enough as it is. A woman who bakes their favorite cookies *and* paints portraits of their ponies can do no wrong in their eyes."

I'm surprised that Amelia has enough time to bake cookies. It seems as though she hasn't put her paintbrushes down since she walked out of the woods with William.

"She's been busy," I agreed.

In addition to painting pony portraits for my sons, Amelia was painting house portraits for each of her neighbors, as a way of thanking them for coming to her aid when she needed them.

When she wasn't painting portraits, she was reacquainting herself with her first love: botanical art. I often spotted her with her gear in a pack on her back, tramping across a field to study the berries or grasses or mushrooms that had caught her eye. Almost as often, I spotted Willis, Sr., tramping with her.

As he had predicted, she'd returned to the glade several times, but she hadn't yet recorded it with her paintbrush. She'd have to get to know the place very well, I reflected, before she could capture its complex soul.

Lilian, too, had been busy. In response to popular demand, she'd read all six parts of Gamaliel's secret memoir aloud to a standing-room-only audience at the schoolhouse at the end of October. Her reading had generated so much interest among the villagers that she'd produced a printed booklet of her translation. She'd then buckled down to write a full-length book about the memoir, which she intended to dedicate to Alfred Bowen.

I hoped Lilian's book would be success-ful, but not *too* successful. Hoards of black-clad Mistress Meg fans demanding access to Plover Cottage, the bell tower, Dove Cottage, the crypt, Anscombe Manor, and Redfern Meadow would be no more welcome in Finch than the Bowenists had been.

My copy of Lilian's slim booklet was lying on the old wooden desk beneath the diamond-paned windows in the study. I glanced at it and wrinkled my brow.

"What puzzles me," I said, looking down at the blue journal, "is the memoir's first page. Why did Gamaliel call Mistress Meg a 'fearsome and most potent witch'? Why did he talk about calamity and retribution? He must have known when he started writing that Margaret Redfearn wasn't a witch."

Wasn't she? She rejected the church, she was fearsome in her determination to live her own life, and she brewed potent potions in a house in the woods. In most English villages, she would have been identified as a witch and the retribution for consorting with her, or worse, being related to her, would have been calamitous. The villagers were incredibly brave to stand up for her as they did, but even here, her image was distorted. As the years passed, she became Mad Meg, the horned, axe-wielding crone who maimed helpless children. I'm proud of Gamaliel for setting the record straight. Margaret Redfearn was a heroine, not a hag. If I had my way, a statue of her would be erected on the village green.

When I thought of Gamaliel's flock testifying before the witch finder, I couldn't help picturing my neighbors defending Amelia. Finch, it seemed, had a long tradition of protecting gifted women.

In my mind's eye I saw the animated faces of the women who'd gathered around the bonfire on Guy Fawkes Night — Amelia, Lilian, Bree, Emma, Nell, Peggy Taxman, Sally Pyne, Christine Peacock, Elspeth, Millicent, Opal, and Selena. Married or not, they were all strong and independent. Some might even call them fearsome and they were nothing if not potent. If Margaret Redfearn had returned to Finch that night, I thought, she would have recognized many kindred spirits.

If there ever was a statue of Mistress Meg on the village green, I hoped its plaque would read:

In Finch, we cherish witches.

AMELIA THISTLE'S
BROWN BREAD

Makes three loaves

Ingredients
5 1/2 cups whole wheat flour
1 1/2 cups unprocessed bran
2 1/2 cups white flour
1/2 cup Crisco shortening
2 packets dry yeast
1 teaspoon sugar
1 1/2 tablespoons salt
4 cups water (adjust for humidity)

Please note: The recipe calls for three 6 × 9 × 3-inch bread loaf pans.

Mix together brown flour, white flour, bran, and salt in a very large mixing bowl. Rub in shortening. Warm 3 3/4 cups water to 110 degrees. Reserve 1/4 cup heated water. Mix together the yeast, the sugar, and the reserved 1/4 cup of water. Add the yeast mixture to the rest of the warmed water. Make a well in the center of the flour. Pour the yeast/ water mixture into the well. Mix together to make a soft, slightly sticky dough. Knead for 10 minutes.

Return the dough to the mixing bowl. Cut a large cross in the center of the dough. Spray the surface of the dough with cooking spray to keep it moist. Cover the bowl with a damp towel, and place it in a warm place to rise to twice its size, about 1 hour.

Knead the dough again, then divide it into three balls. Shape each ball into a large sausage and put each sausage into a greased and floured 6 × 9 × 3-inch loaf pan. Preheat oven to 450 degrees.

Allow the dough to rise again for 20–30 minutes, until the loaves reach the tops of the pans. Place the pans on the center shelf of the oven, and bake at 450 degrees for 15 minutes. Reduce heat to 350 degrees and bake for another 45 minutes. Allow to cool on rack.

Serve well-buttered slices with cups of your favorite tea, preferably before a roaring fire, during a thunderstorm. Although a snowstorm will work well, too.

ABOUT THE AUTHOR

Nancy Atherton is the author of eighteen Aunt Dimity novels. She lives in Colorado Springs.